LIES
I Told

LIES
I Told

MICHELLE ZINK

HARPER TEEN
An Imprint of HarperCollinsPublishers

Lies I Told
Copyright © 2015 by Michelle Zink
All rights reserved. Printed in the United States of America.
No part of this book may be used or reproduced in any manner whatsoever without written permission except in the case of brief quotations embodied in critical articles and reviews. For information address HarperCollins Children's Books, a division of HarperCollins Publishers, 195 Broadway, New York, NY 10007.
www.epicreads.com

Library of Congress Cataloging-in-Publication Data
Zink, Michelle.
Lies I told / Michelle Zink. — First edition.
    pages   cm
Summary: Since Grace was adopted by the Fontaines, she has been carefully taught the art of the scam and has an uncanny ability to create a personality to help her "parents," but their latest job has her questioning everything she has been taught and the family she has grown to love.
ISBN 978-0-06-232712-3 (hardcover)
[1. Conduct of life—Fiction.   2. Interpersonal relations—Fiction.   3. Moving, Household—Fiction.   4. Family life—California—Fiction.   5. Adoption—Fiction.   6. California, Southern—Fiction.]   I. Title.
PZ7.Z652Lie 2015   2014005870
[Fic]—dc23   CIP
                                                    AC

Typography by Torborg Davern
15 16 17 18 19 CG/RRDH 10 9 8 7 6 5 4 3 2 1
❖
First Edition

For Jennifer Klonsky,
who gave me a second chance

Wild honey smells of freedom
The dust—of sunlight
The mouth of a young girl, like a violet
But gold—smells of nothing.

—ANNA AKHMATOVA

Prologue

Looking back, I should have known Playa Hermosa was the beginning of the end. We'd had a good run, and if things were sometimes tense between Mom, Dad, and Parker, it was nothing a new job couldn't fix. Just when they'd be at each other's throats, we'd move on to another town.

And there was nothing like a new town to remind us which team we were on.

But Playa Hermosa was different. It was like another world. One where the old rules didn't apply. Like the exotic birds on the peninsula, we were suddenly all on our own.

Except it didn't feel like that right away. In the beginning, it was business as usual. Plot the con, get into character, work our way in, stick together.

I don't know if it was my relationship with Logan that tipped everything over the edge or if the signs had been there long before. Either way, I tell myself it was for the best. The universe seems to have its own mysterious plan. I guess we're just along for the ride. I can live with that. The harder part, the impossible part, is living with what I did to Logan and his family.

We knew what we were doing. Knew the risks. But Logan and his family were *good*. Maybe the first really good people I'd ever met. They loved one another, sacrificed for one another. Not because they didn't have anyone else, but because that's what love is.

What happened to them is my fault. And I'm still trying to figure out how to live with that.

Then there's Parker. Deep down, I know the choice was his. But I can't help wondering if he stuck around because of me. If he hadn't, everything would be different, and he'd probably be drinking beer in Barcelona or coffee in Paris or something.

I can't think about the other stuff. Thinking about it forces me back to the question: Why didn't I see it? Had the end of our family been one sudden, impulsive decision setting into motion a string of events that changed everything? Or had it all been a long time coming? I think that would be worse, because if it was true, it meant that I was hopelessly, unforgivably naive.

And there's no crime as unforgivable as naivety when you're on the grift.

One

I swam my way up from sleep, trying to remember where I was against a mechanical roar outside the window. The room didn't help. Filled with the standard furniture and a few unpacked boxes, it could have been any bedroom in any house in any city in America.

I ran down the list of possibilities: Chicago, New York, Maryland, and then Phoenix, because that was where we'd worked last. But it only took a few seconds to realize that none of them were right. We'd arrived the day before in Playa Hermosa, a peninsula that jutted out over the Pacific Ocean somewhere between Los Angeles and San Diego.

It was like a different world, the slickness of Los Angeles falling away as we entered an almost tropical paradise, shady with low-hanging trees and dominated by Spanish architecture. I caught glimpses of the Pacific, a sheet of shimmering blue silk in the distance, as my dad navigated the Audi up the winding roads and my mom pointed things out along the way. Parker sat silently beside me in the backseat, brooding and sullen like he always was when we started a new job. We'd passed fields, overgrown with dry brush, that led to turnouts where people could stop and take pictures. We didn't take any, because that was one of the most important rules: leave no proof.

And there were more rules where that one came from, rules that allowed us to run cons in affluent communities all over the country, worming our way into the lives of wealthy neighbors and trust-fund babies with more money than sense. Rules that allowed us to make off with tens of thousands of dollars, staying in place just long enough after every theft to insure that we weren't under the cloud of suspicion. That was one of the worst parts: staying put, pretending to be as shocked and innocent as everyone else.

Only after the dust settled would we move on, citing a job transfer or start-up opportunity for my dad and changing our identification through one of his underground sources. If anyone ever suspected us of committing a crime, we were too long gone to know about it.

A portion of each take was split between us, the rest of it used to set up the next con. From the looks of things, it hadn't been cheap this time around.

The roar of the leaf blower outside grew louder as it moved under the window, and I put my pillow over my head, trying to block out the noise. We'd spent the last few weeks in a hotel in Palm Springs, preparing for the Playa Hermosa job, but I still wasn't ready to face my first day in a new school. There had been too many of them. Right now, in this unfamiliar room, I was in a pleasant kind of limbo, the last town far enough away to be a memory, the new one still a figment of my imagination.

But it was no use. The down in my pillow was no match for the rumble outside, and I finally tossed it aside and got out of bed, digging around in a still-packed box until I found a hair tie. My gaze was drawn to the reflection in the mirror over the dresser. The brown hair was a surprise. I hadn't been a brunette since Seattle, and I still approached every mirror half expecting to see my face framed by a sheet of straight, shiny blond hair. My eyes—a dark blue—were the only thing I could count on to be the same when we moved from city to city. But they were a little different now, too. Older, shadowed with something weary that echoed the way I'd felt ever since our near miss in Maryland the year before.

Lately, it had begun to feel like too much. Too much lying. Too much risk. Too much *work*. I had been eleven when I was adopted by my mom and dad. I'd spent a year thinking my life would be normal, then Parker joined the family and we were quickly initiated into life on the grift. It had been nonstop ever since. I hadn't been this tired since my fifth foster home, back when survival meant dodging a woman who was a little too quick with the back of her hand, her son a little too generous with the creepy glances.

I leaned away from the mirror and took a deep breath, forcing the past back into the dark corners of my mind where it belonged. Then I reached into the unpacked box, feeling past my books, the little makeup I owned, the one framed photograph I had of our family. When my hand brushed against a smooth wooden container, I pulled it from the box.

It was a simple unfinished rectangle, the kind you could buy in any craft store for five bucks. It was meant to be a jewelry or treasure box, but I'd never gotten around to decorating or staining it. I probably never would. Its contents were against the rules. I'd never be able to keep it out long enough to make it look nice.

Anyway, that wasn't the point. It was the stuff inside that mattered, and I reached for the flimsy gold clasp and lifted the lid, pushing aside the carousel ticket from Chicago, the postcard from DC, the cheap plastic taxicab I'd bought from a street vendor in New York City. Finally, I found what I was looking for, and I brought the plastic ID card—*Chandler High School* emblazoned across the top—close to my face for a better look.

My teeth were white and straight in the picture, my blond hair shining even in the crappy fluorescent lighting. The picture belied none of the fear and anxiety I'd felt in Phoenix. I could have been any popular high school student. A cheerleader. Class president. Lead in the school play.

The ID was dangerous, against the rules. All my mementos were. But they were the only things that made me feel real, that made real all the places I'd been, all the people I'd met. Sometimes I thought my forbidden trinkets were the only proof I existed at all.

I closed the wooden container and placed it back in the still-packed box. Then I slipped the ID card into the pocket of my boxers, pulled my hair into a loose ponytail, and stepped out into the hallway.

Two

The house wasn't huge, but already it was one of my favorites. I ran my hand along the walls as I headed for the stairs, enjoying the rough feel of plaster under my fingertips. The house was authentic in a way the McMansion outside Chicago hadn't been, its walls and windows more solid than in the flimsy house we'd rented in Phoenix. That one had looked fancy on the outside, but the walls were thin, the windows so poorly sealed that a steady stream of hot air blew on my face when I lay in bed during the 115-degree summer.

This one was nice, even if I didn't recognize any of the furniture, which we'd bought brand-new like we did at the start of every new job. At first it had been hard, leaving everything behind at the end of each con. But like a lot of things, I'd gotten used to it. Now I could pack my clothes and books in less than fifteen minutes.

I took the staircase to the main floor, the giant ceiling fan whirring softly in the tall-ceilinged foyer, and headed for the kitchen at the back of the house.

Parker was already there, sitting at a table under a bank of open windows and spooning cereal into his mouth while he read the business section. I hardly thought about my share of the money we earned, but Parker was obsessive, determined to invest his piece of each take so he wouldn't have to rely on Cormac and Renee—or anyone like them— ever again. Articles and books about stocks, bonds, and IPOs were his reading material of choice, something that stood in contrast to his new appearance. It was always a little weird watching everyone in the family transform, and I stood in the doorway, trying to get used to this new version of my brother.

He'd ditched the preppy young Republican he'd played in Phoenix in favor of a Southern California surfer boy. The longer hair worked on him. Dark blond and a little messy, it made him look like he'd just climbed out of the water. He was my brother in everything but blood, yet I could understand why girls fell all over themselves for his attention. With his perfect white teeth, strong jaw, and boyish dimples, he was every girl's type. Add in the bad-boy brood, and he was basically irresistible.

I glanced at the lines of leather cord marching up his arm, strategically placed to hide his scars. I'd asked him about the bracelets once, wondering why he wore them in any kind of weather, even when long sleeves covered his arms all the way to his wrists. He'd just shrugged and said, "They remind me who I really am."

I didn't understand it. I wanted nothing more than to forget the past, riddled with unfamiliar beds and unfamiliar faces. But Parker didn't want to forget. The past was what drove him, and I had a sudden flash of him at thirteen, the day he'd been adopted into the family, eyes hooded, his forearm wrapped in gauze. In a foster care system that had seen everything, Parker's record had rendered him unplaceable in another home.

Even good-hearted people didn't want to come home to a bathroom covered in blood.

It made my heart hurt to remember Parker that way, alone and unwanted. I shut the memory down and sat across from him at the table.

"Hey," I said quietly, not wanting to startle him.

He looked up, his eyes a little glazed. "Hey."

He lowered his eyes back to the paper, and I looked around the room, surprised by the lack of moving boxes on the counters and floor.

"Wow . . . Mom must have really gone to town unpacking last night."

"You know how she is," Parker said, not looking up.

As if on cue, the sound of heels clicking on tile sounded from the hall. A couple of seconds later my mom walked into the room, trim and lithe in white slacks and a halter top that managed to look both classy and subtly sexy. It was one of her many gifts: the ability to fit into any town in a matter of hours. She nailed New York, donning designer clothes that cost a fortune but looked effortless. In DC she was all about crisp, menswear-inspired slacks and tailored button-downs that hugged her still-youthful body. And I would never forget Arizona, where she'd spent thousands of dollars on linen trousers, perfectly cut sleeveless dresses, and expensive golf ensembles. I'd laughed out loud the first time I'd seen her in one of the Phoenix getups. Golf skirts and polo shirts were the antithesis of the tight jeans and slinky tops she favored when we were between jobs.

Still, I envied her. It always took me a while to figure out the wardrobe code of a new high school, and I usually had to enlist the help of a new friend under the guise of a joint shopping spree to get it right. In the meantime I fell back on a style I thought of as "neutral trendy." I never hit the sweet spot right away, but I managed to not be cast as a misfit, either. I cut a glance at Parker, looking just right for anywhere in fitted jeans and a tailored Euro tee. Guys had it so much easier.

"Good morning." My mom's green eyes were bright, her blond hair perfectly styled as she crossed the kitchen to the coffeepot. No one would have guessed she'd been up half the night unpacking.

"Morning, Mom."

Maybe it was because I remembered so little about my biological parents, but from the start, having someone to call Mom and Dad had felt like a gift. Parker was different. He called our parents by their first names unless we were working. Sometimes it seemed like he did it on principle. Like he was trying to prove that while he lived and worked with them, they couldn't make him love them. Deep down I thought he did, though. It was just hard for him to show it.

My mom poured coffee into two mugs and sat down at the table, pushing one toward me. Parker didn't drink coffee.

"Everybody sleep okay?" Mom asked, taking a sip from her steaming cup.

I nodded and followed her lead, the coffee dark and bitter in my mouth, as a fresh round of noise started up outside.

I tipped my head at the window. "They're already doing yard work?"

She nodded. "It was a little overgrown."

I laughed. "We've only been here a day."

"First impressions are important, Gracie. You know how it is."

"I guess." I tried not to sound like a brat, but the truth is, I was tired. We'd lived in three different states in the last year alone. I'd started sophomore year in Maryland and hadn't even been able to finish it in Arizona. I was a good student, but I'd still have to retake some of the classes this year to get credit, something that was made harder by the fact that I'd missed the start of the school year in California. I was only sixteen, and I was house-lagged, worn out from all the packing and moving, the changing of hair colors and names, the running. It wasn't the life I'd imagined the day my mom and dad adopted me out of the Illinois foster system.

My mom reached over and took my hand, her eyes full of

concern. "I know it's hard sometimes, honey," she said gently. "But we'll be able to take a break soon, maybe even go on that girls' trip to Paris: shop, visit the Louvre, wear berets."

I forced a smile. Ours wasn't an easy life, but I loved my parents, and I knew they loved Parker and me.

She squeezed my hand. "You just have first-day jitters, Gracie. It's natural, but everything will be okay, you'll see."

I nodded, turning toward my dad as he walked into the room.

"Morning." He stalked across the kitchen, staring out the windows that overlooked the backyard. "What is that racket?"

"The landscapers." My mom took a last drink of her coffee before walking to the sink and dumping the rest of it. "I told you they were coming, remember?"

My dad turned away from the window. "Tell me again why we need landscapers?"

"You have to spend money to make money," the rest of us said in unison. Parker didn't bother to look up from the newspaper.

It was true, but I knew my mom enjoyed it. In her eyes, buying clothes to fit the part or furnishing a new house every six months wasn't work—it was a perk of life on the grift. My dad didn't get it. For him, the con was all about the con. It was the challenge he loved. The danger.

He leaned against the counter, looking like a middle-aged but still good-looking actor, his dark hair dusted silver at the temples.

"What's on tap for you today?" my mom asked him.

"I'm touring Allied Security," he said. "I might buy a system for the house. I also need to check out the club and ask about membership. How about you?"

"I have a hair appointment in town. Figured I'd get the lay of the land."

I wasn't surprised by the vague dance of questions and answers. No one said anything specific about a job outside of the War Room. Ever. It was one of the rules.

"Good. We'll have a family meeting tonight." He tossed a set of keys to Parker. "Saab's out front and ready to go." He turned to me. "You ready, Gracie?"

I nodded, remembering the dark-haired boy with deep brown eyes from the subject files. It was time to go to work.

Three

A balmy breeze lifted my hair as I followed Parker down the stone path at the side of the house. Foliage grew thick overhead, blocking out the sun as the strange green pods of the paloverde trees crunched under our feet.

We were almost to the driveway when a chill iced the back of my neck. It was that universal feeling of being watched, and I looked up at the house next door just in time to see a curtain drop over one of the second-story windows. I kept walking. Some things were different city to city, but nosy neighbors were everywhere. I made a mental note to be extra vigilant.

The black Saab was like a jungle cat, sleek and gleaming in the morning sun. My dad had arranged it—in addition to the Volvo he'd purchased for my mom—just like he did everything. Parker didn't even pause to admire it. He just climbed into the driver's side, waiting for me to buckle my seat belt before backing out of the driveway.

We didn't talk on the way to school, which wasn't unusual. We spent a lot of our time together in silence. It was one of the things I loved most about being with Parker: we didn't have to pretend. We both had our demons, and we knew from experience that talking about them didn't change anything. I needed to concentrate anyway.

The new school wasn't a big deal. Mom made that easy, insuring that we were pre-enrolled, our fake transcripts and immunization records sent over ahead of time so that all we had to do was show up and get our schedules.

It was the other stuff that was hard. The pretending to be someone else. The being careful not to let slip who we were, where we came from, what we'd done.

More and more, I had to really think about that part. Had to prepare myself for weeks or months of being in character, of losing a little more of myself with each passing day.

Parker turned a corner and the sign for Playa Hermosa High School came into view. His face was impassive as he reached over, cranking the music until the car vibrated. He hated loud music, but it went with the territory. A successful con required careful balance between avoiding the wrong kind of attention and getting the right kind.

And we needed the right kind at Playa Hermosa High.

The parking lot was nearly full when we pulled in. Some of the kids got out of their cars and hurried into the building, while others stood around, talking and goofing off in the warm September sunshine. School had only been in session for a few weeks, but most of Playa Hermosa's student body had probably gone to kindergarten together.

Parker made a show of backing smoothly into a spot next to a sleek BMW. Several kids were leaning against the car and standing around it, the girls subtly tan in the way people are when they spend a lot of time on the beach—complete with SPF 50 as protection against the aging effects of the sun—the boys all sporting versions of a familiar haircut, a little bit long, slightly sloppy, totally surfer.

Parker knew his stuff.

The parking spot was no accident, either. I recognized a couple of the kids, including the dark-haired boy, from the subject files we'd read while preparing for the job.

This was the group Parker and I were assigned to infiltrate. They were all seniors, like Parker, but I wasn't worried about doing my share. Parker and I were only eighteen months apart, and I spent most of my time with him. Besides, I hadn't had the luxury of acting my age since, well, ever.

He cut the engine and surveyed the crowd. Some of the kids glanced over, trying to be sly, because everyone knows there's nothing more pathetic, more desperate, than being too curious about anything.

"There's your mark," Parker said quietly, his eyes drifting to the dark-haired boy.

I nodded. "Yeah."

He glanced at me. "You good?"

Parker was tough. Some would even say hard. But he had

looked out for me since the day he'd joined the family, even when it seemed he needed looking after more than anyone.

I smiled. "Yeah."

It was the only possible answer, because it didn't really matter if I was good or not. This was why we were here.

"Okay, then," he said. "See you on the flip side."

He got out of the car and started across the parking lot without a backward glance. We had to act like other siblings now. We couldn't afford to display our closeness, born of all the times we'd moved, all the cons and near misses we'd weathered together when there was no one else we could trust.

I dug through my tote bag like I was looking for something, trying to stifle a wave of panic. I always got a little anxious before a new job, but I usually rallied at the last minute, remembering the payoff of doing my part, of keeping the family together.

Now I had the feeling that there were things I didn't know. Things I hadn't anticipated. I should have studied the subject files more thoroughly, should have taken a couple of days to get settled before starting school, just to get a feel for the place.

But it was too late. The group—especially the girls—had watched with interest as Parker sauntered toward the school.

Now their focus was on me.

I took a deep breath and opened the door. Walking to the front of the car, I avoided eye contact with the guys. Instead I cast a hesitant smile at the long-legged redhead standing at the center of the crowd. Her name was Rachel Mercer, and I knew from our research that she was the unofficial leader of Logan's social circle.

A bell rang somewhere inside the building, and I walked purposefully toward the entrance, their eyes on me every step of the way.

Four

I picked up my schedule from the main office and headed to Precalc, fingering the Chandler High ID card in the pocket of my capris. It was way out of line, and I knew it. Not just a random memento that could be picked up at any souvenir stand in any big city, but a photo ID with my picture. I wasn't sure why I'd chosen something so incriminating, but I couldn't stand the thought of destroying it. I promised myself I would only keep it for a while, just long enough to let go of the people I'd met in Arizona, the life that had been on loan. Then I'd put it back in the wooden box with all the other stuff I wasn't supposed to have.

And someday I'd have a souvenir of Playa Hermosa, too.

The high school was different than I'd expected. Instead of one building, the school was made up of multiple structures connected by a series of outdoor walkways. I hurried across campus in the dry autumn heat, a fragrant breeze scenting the air with the jasmine that seemed to grow wild all over the peninsula.

I wasn't surprised by the whispering of my new classmates. Playa Hermosa was a public school, but the town was small and exclusive, one of a handful of communities that were home to Southern California's elite. It would be a while before anyone approached me. First they would observe me, like an exotic new animal in their familiar menagerie. This was doubly true for the girls who had been standing around the BMW in the parking lot. They were a pack, and Rachel Mercer was their alpha female. Winning her over was the quickest way into the group. There were others, but they would require more finesse, more time. It would be easier to work with Rachel than around her.

I made mental notes throughout the morning, keeping track of the classes I had with Rachel's posse, the hallways I saw them in the most, the lockers they seemed to congregate around. It was always good to know where to find your players in case you had to stage an "accidental" meeting.

By fourth period, I was feeling better. My first-day jitters had subsided as I became more familiar with the school, and I made my way to AP Euro totally unprepared to see Rachel Mercer occupying a desk near the back of the room. I stood at the front of the class, playing the part of self-conscious new kid while the teacher, Mr. Stein, checked his seating chart. A moment later, he pointed to the desk next to Rachel.

"You can take that seat there."

I made my way to the empty chair, careful to keep an expression of calm boredom on my face. Still, I had to resist the urge to stare as I slid into my seat. Up close, Rachel was stunning, with deep green eyes and skin so pale, so perfect, it was almost translucent. Her hair, a true, natural red, fell in a satin sheet almost to her waist. Confidence emanated from the straightness of her back, the tilt of her chin. This was a girl who had gotten what she wanted for a very long time, and I was willing to bet she wasn't going to let that change anytime soon.

Or ever.

We were halfway through Mr. Stein's lecture when something scratched noisily next to me, slowly at first and then more urgently. I looked over at Rachel, who was making inkless circles on her notebook, trying to get her pen to work, while Mr. Stein droned on, leaving her further behind with every passing second.

She finally gave up, digging around in her bag before letting out a sigh of frustration, looking helplessly at her paper while Mr. Stein babbled about the Weimar Republic. I felt her pain. This was the third AP Euro class I'd been assigned to in the past year, and one thing was true in all of them: without notes, you were screwed for the AP exam.

Reaching into my bag, I pulled out an extra pen and handed it across the aisle, careful to keep my smile a little cool. Seeming desperate for the attention of a girl like Rachel was the kiss of death. In high school, any high school, there was a fine line between friendly and needy.

She took the pen, flashing me a brief but appraising smile. I pretended not to notice her eyes skimming my hair (loose, beachy waves), makeup (a little mascara and tinted lip balm, in keeping with California natural), clothes (silk drawstring capris and a snug white tee), and shoes (gold sandals). Usually, that kind of appraisal didn't bother me, but I had to fight not to squirm under the weight of her stare. I had the sensation of being laid bare. Of being really seen for the first time in ages.

And not in a good way.

I was relieved when class ended and she left without a word. Hopefully, I'd done enough to pique her interest, but only time would tell. It was hard, the waiting, the patience required to let a mark come to me, the deliberate positioning to make it look natural while being careful not to draw the wrong kind of attention.

But I was good at it. Good at drawing people out, getting them to like and trust me. It didn't matter if they were popular kids or misfits. It wasn't difficult to find a common thread with all of them. I tried not to think about the implications. About what kind of person it made me and whether or not it was a gift or a curse. It had to be done, and Parker wasn't exactly a candidate for the job.

I was heading to the cafeteria for lunch when I spotted Logan Fairchild, he of the dark hair and brown eyes, leaning against a bank of lockers, goofing off with some of the guys he'd been with in the parking lot.

I slowed down. Logan was my mark, but only acceptance

by the group would earn me concentrated time with him. And Rachel Mercer could speed up that acceptance by a mile.

According to the subject files, Rachel and Logan had once had a heated relationship, history that made my job a lot trickier. I had to earn Rachel's trust to be included in the group's social scene and then find a way to hit it off with Logan—without bringing out territorial jealousy in Rachel.

Not an easy task, which was why I'd planned to work Rachel first.

Still, I knew a golden opportunity when I saw one, and there was no harm in getting an early start on the Logan angle as long as I was careful.

I took a quick inventory of the situation: Logan, standing near a kid with hair so bleached it was almost white. Next to them was a tall guy with swingy black hair and another one with perfect brown skin that I recognized from the morning BMW hangout.

They got quiet as I passed, but I pretended not to notice as I slipped a hand into my binder, tugging on the class schedule I'd stuffed there. I let it fall to the floor and kept walking.

I was almost to the end of the hall when a voice called out behind me.

"Hey! Wait up!"

I turned around. Logan was jogging toward me with a piece of paper in his hand.

"I think you dropped this, uh . . ." He looked down at the schedule, searching for my name. "Grace."

"I did?" Looking innocent was second nature.

He nodded. "It's your schedule. I thought you might need it."

I took it from him, holding his gaze just a second longer than normal. I'd been wrong about his eyes. To say they were brown didn't do them justice. They carried traces of mossy green, too, like something you'd find in a tropical pool at the bottom of a hundred-foot waterfall. His dark brown hair fell over his forehead, giving him a boyish quality that was surprisingly sexy against his all-American good looks.

"Thank you." I held out my hand. "Grace Fontaine, resident new girl."

He smiled and took my hand. "Logan Fairchild." His skin was warm and dry. "I saw you this morning, in the parking lot."

I nodded. "With my brother, Parker." Best to clear that up right away. "We just moved here from San Francisco."

The lie was an easy one.

Sympathy moved behind his eyes. "Must be tough now that school's already started."

"I'm managing." I held his gaze until he pulled his eyes away.

He shuffled from foot to foot. "Well, nice meeting you, Grace. Maybe I'll see you around."

I smiled. "Maybe."

I turned and headed for the cafeteria, surprised by the possibility that Logan Fairchild might actually be nice.

Five

I threw together a salad, grabbed a bottle of water, and surveyed the lunchroom.

Parker was by himself, but joining him was out. Teenagers were more likely to approach a new kid sitting alone. It changed the psychology of things if they thought you had someone, which was why we would try separately to get in with Rachel and Logan's crowd. Whoever got in first would introduce the other one. Until then, we were on our own.

I looked around the cafeteria, scouting for a spot, wondering which of the kids eating lunch, studying, and messing around I'd get to know. Which of them I would miss when we left. We'd pulled five good-size cons in the last four years. I had lied, cheated, and stolen on behalf of the family. But it only got harder to befriend people I would eventually betray.

I forced the thought away. There was no point thinking about the end of a con before we got there. It only increased the odds of getting distracted, making a mistake.

Right now I needed a place to set up shop until I got in with Rachel and her posse, who were eating and talking at a table near the window. I avoided looking their way as I scanned the room, not wanting to seem interested in them.

My gaze landed on a table occupied by three girls. Two blondes were talking while a curly-haired brunette read a book. The blondes were obviously tight, their postures relaxed as they leaned toward each other, deep in conversation. The short-haired blonde said something to the dark-haired girl. She glanced up and smiled before turning back to her book.

Acquaintances, then. Friends, maybe, but not super close.

I studied her from across the cafeteria, trying to gauge the impact my association with her would have on the con. Pretty enough to be under the radar but not so pretty that someone like Rachel would view her as competition, the girl had pale skin, lush black hair, and the kind of demeanor that suggested she spent a lot of time alone reading books. One of many kids who traveled the back roads of high school unnoticed.

In other words, perfect. It was just a bonus that she was reading.

I crossed the cafeteria and stopped in front of the table. "Hey."

The girl looked up, blinking, a far-off expression in her

eyes. I recognized it, understood the shock of realizing the world inside your book wasn't real. Even worse, you were in another world entirely and no one understood—or even cared—that you preferred the one living on the page.

"Oh . . . hey," the girl said.

I smiled. "Mind if I sit here?"

She glanced at the blondes, who shrugged almost in unison.

She turned back to me. "Sure."

I sat across from her. "I'm Grace."

"Selena Rodriguez," the girl said, closing her book. "This is Ashley." She gestured to the short-haired girl before turning to the other one, her waist-length waves too frizzy to be anything but natural. "And that's Nina."

After a perfunctory round of nice-to-meet-yous, Ashley stood, raking her fingers through her short spiky hair. "I've got to make up a quiz in Mrs. Beamon's class."

Nina stood. "I'm gonna hit it, too." She looked at Selena. "See you after school?"

"Yep."

I waited for the girls to get out of earshot. "Friends of yours?" I asked.

She smiled a little. "More or less."

I nodded, tearing open the packet of salad dressing on my tray. "What are you reading?"

Selena held up the book.

"*White Oleander*?" I don't know why I was surprised. "That's my favorite book in the whole world."

I wasn't lying, but I would never be able tell Selena why it was true. Why I identified so much with Astrid and everything that happened to her in foster care. With the strength it took to keep trudging through life when my legs were so heavy I couldn't even think about how far I still had to go.

Selena blinked. "Seriously?"

I nodded. "Yeah. It's . . . well, it's amazing. I've read it, like, five times."

Selena's gaze got sharper, like she was suddenly really seeing me. "Me too."

We sat in silence for a minute, a strange kind of kinship moving between us, like we'd already shared all our secrets.

"So," Selena finally said, "you're new. Where'd you move from?"

I finished chewing. "San Francisco."

"I've always wanted to go there. Is it nice?"

"It's okay," I said, even though I'd never been. "But I think I'm going to like it more here."

She laughed a little. "Give it time."

I let my eyes skip to Rachel Mercer's table, hoping for some info. Selena followed my gaze.

"You know Rachel?" she asked.

I shook my head. "She sits next to me in AP Euro. Do you?"

"Nah. I mean, I know *of* her. Everybody does. But her crowd's not really my speed."

"How come?" I was careful not to seem eager, but I knew that Selena would have information that wasn't in the files. It was one thing to collect facts and figures on a mark. Understanding the nuances of who they were, what made them tick, that was a lot more difficult. "Are they assholes?"

She thought about it. "Not exactly. But my dad's a dentist who bought our house in PH before home values went crazy. He was older when I was born and is totally old-school."

"What about your mom?" I asked.

A veil seemed to drop over her eyes. "She's not around anymore."

The words took me by surprise, but I tried to recover, not wanting to blow it by seeming nosy. "So your dad won't let you hang with Rachel's crowd?"

"It's not that." She seemed to think about it. "It's just . . . if I want a car, I have to buy it, plus pay for insurance. Rachel and her friends have big money and parents who throw it their way to keep them busy while they travel to Bali or Switzerland."

"So you can't be friends because they're rich?"

"It's not just the money thing . . . ," Selena hedged.

"What? They're a little wild?" I guessed.

"Let's just say when I'm home reading *White Oleander*, they're drinking it up at a bonfire, and while I'm studying for finals, they're smoking at the Cove."

"The Cove?"

"It's a local spot, and super secluded. Unless you walk two miles across the sand, the only way to get there is down a rocky pathway on the peninsula."

"Sounds nice." I let it sit, leaving the door open for Selena to say more.

"It is. I walk there a lot before dinner."

"Alone?" I asked.

She grinned. "I'm not exactly on Rachel's radar, if that's what you mean. And I'm totally fine with that."

A smile rose to my lips. One that had nothing to do with the con. I was used to operating in a kind of haze, my connection to the world buffered by enough distance to survive the severing of contact with everyone we met.

But Selena's clear-eyed gaze touched something inside me. Some forgotten remnant that operated apart from the con. That was still real.

We talked easily through the rest of lunch. She was my age, excited to start scouting colleges at the end of the year, and was saving money to travel Europe on the cheap. She promised to show me around, and we exchanged numbers as the bell rang for seventh period.

I left the cafeteria feeling conflicted. It didn't matter that Selena was nice. I just needed a cover while I waited for an in with Logan's crowd—something to prevent me from seeming like an outcast.

Liking Selena wasn't part of the equation.

Six

"You closed the windows, right, honey?" my mom asked, checking them anyway.

We were in the upstairs den, the designated War Room for the Playa Hermosa con. Every job had some kind of War Room. It was the only place we were allowed to discuss strategy, brainstorm solutions to problems, and give progress reports. Limiting our discussion of the job to one room meant we couldn't make a mistake in deciding if it was safe to talk. Couldn't forget where we were and discuss the con near an open window or out in public where anyone could be listening. It was a rule that had been ingrained in Parker and me since the beginning. I couldn't remember anyone breaking it.

The Playa Hermosa War Room looked like any suburban media room. Overstuffed sofa? Check. Bar? Check?

Massive TV complete with surround sound? Double check. Except it also had a small table for our meetings and a shredder, essential for adherence to our leave-no-proof rule.

My dad sighed. "I said I was going to, didn't I?"

"Sometimes things slip." She bristled, taking a seat on one of the chairs. "I was just asking."

"Security doesn't 'slip.' Not now, not ever," he said tightly.

I shifted nervously on the sofa. It had been happening between them more and more often, little annoyances and irritations, disagreements over seemingly insignificant details. I told myself that it wasn't unusual. Everyone got nervous at the start of a job. We were like an overworked acting troupe, trying to keep our roles straight even as we were given new lines and costumes every few months. It would be stressful for anyone.

But part of me knew it was more than that. Our cracks were starting to show, spreading out like the fault lines that lay under California, the pressure building and building until, one day, the earth moved with it.

"Let's just get started." My mom looked from me to Parker. "How did it go today?"

Parker made no move to answer, so I spoke up. "I sit next to Rachel Mercer in AP Euro."

"That's an unexpected bonus. Any interest?"

"A little. She's a queen bee, though, so I have to play it cool."

She smiled affectionately. "I'm sure you can handle

Rachel Mercer. And if she doesn't let you in, Logan will."

"I actually ran into him in the hallway."

"I thought you weren't working him until we were inside," Parker said from the other end of the couch.

I shrugged, avoiding his eyes. "I had an opportunity, so I took it."

Parker took his job as older brother seriously. He hated it when I ran point, when I was "used" to further a con. But I never saw it that way. We were a family. As much as I sometimes struggled with what we did, I liked doing my part, pulling my own weight.

"What happened?" he asked.

"I pretended to drop something and he picked it up, so I introduced myself."

"Nicely done," my dad said. "Any other interesting contacts?"

"I met a girl I really like," I answered. "Selena Rodriguez. I sat with her at lunch."

"Selena Rodriguez." My mom repeated the name. "Was she in the subject files?"

I shook my head. "I needed a place to sit and ended up at her table. She's nice."

She smiled. "I'm glad you made a friend. Maybe you can use her."

I flashed on Selena's clear brown eyes, her unguarded smile. Something twisted in my stomach, and I immediately regretted mentioning her. "Yeah, maybe."

I was relieved when my dad turned his eyes on Parker.

"What about you?"

"Not much. I have gym with Logan and one of his friends. The coach put us on the same basketball team. It's only the first day, but I think I can work my way in."

"Sounds like a productive first day." He leaned forward. "Now, let's go over some details."

I sat back to listen. The broad strokes of the Playa Hermosa job had been laid out before we arrived, but we were never given all the details of a con until we were in character and on-site.

"As you know, the target is the Fairchild family," my dad began. "More specifically, Warren Fairchild, son of Richard Fairchild the Third, CEO of Fairchild Industries, one of the oldest and richest companies in the world. Fairchild Industries got its start in transportation and now has divisions in technology, pharmaceuticals, communications, even space tourism."

He was selling us the mark, making it seem like Warren Fairchild wouldn't miss what we were stealing. Either that, or Warren didn't deserve what he had in the first place. It was something my dad did to alleviate any guilt we might feel over what we were about to do. Most of the time, I believed him. I tried not to think about the other times.

"Warren wasn't the only Fairchild offspring," he continued. "He had an older brother who died in a boating accident when Warren was sixteen, leaving him the only remaining Fairchild heir. It was unfortunate for Richard, because Warren was unstable from the beginning."

That got my attention. "Unstable how?"

"He had brushes with paranoid delusions from a young age, but Richard managed to keep it quiet with a string of discreet therapists and expensive clinics," he explained. "A few years ago, he finally gave up on Warren ever assuming a role in the business. Now Warren lives quietly on his trust fund, which is just the way Richard likes it."

"So, what? We're going after the trust fund?" Parker asked.

My dad shook his head.

"Then what?"

I recognized the shine in his eyes. He would grift for a nickel if there wasn't a bigger mark around.

"For at least a decade," he began, "Warren has been convinced there's going to be some kind of catastrophic worldwide event. And he's been preparing for it."

"A catastrophic event?" I repeated.

My mom looked at me. "A major earthquake, an asteroid hitting the earth, a—"

"Zombocolypse," Parker finished dryly.

I couldn't help laughing.

"We don't know," my dad said. "And obviously, Warren doesn't know, either. It's something he's been preoccupied with for years, according to my sources. Part of his paranoid delusions."

I didn't bother asking how he knew so much about Warren Fairchild. He just did. He never told us how or where he got his information.

"You said he's been preparing for it," I said, trying to read between the lines. "What do you mean?"

"Word is he's been stockpiling."

Parker narrowed his eyes. "Stockpiling what? Food? Water?"

My dad nodded. "And gold. Lots of it."

Seven

"Gold?" I was trying to get my head around the idea that Warren Fairchild, member of one of the richest families in America, would stockpile anything. "But . . . why?"

"Money would be worthless in a catastrophic event," my mom explained. "A lot of things would be. Warren is covering his bases, hoarding not only food and water, but gold for trade."

"How much?" Parker asked.

"Last time we heard, he had about seven hundred bars weighing one kilo each and worth about thirty-five thousand dollars," my dad said.

"Thirty-five thousand . . . ," I said softly. "That's not very much. Not for everything we'd have to do to get it."

Our last job had gone well, but rent on the house in Playa Hermosa had to be setting us back big-time. Not to mention the new furniture, landscaping, cars, clothes, and everything else we needed to look as rich as everyone else who lived on the peninsula.

"Thirty-five thousand *each*," my dad clarified. "In total, about twenty million dollars at the current price for gold."

Twenty million dollars. The number echoed through my mind. It wasn't the money. It was what it could buy. Freedom. A chance to be a real person. Someone who didn't have to lie and hurt people and leave them behind every time I finished a job. Who could keep one last name for more than four months and could go to college, not to get close to some rich kid but to make friends, to learn and experience things. To build the kind of life I really wanted instead of chasing the big houses and offshore bank accounts that preoccupied our mom, the danger that fueled our dad.

"Twenty million . . . ," Parker finally said. "Are you sure?"

My dad raised his eyebrows. He was always sure.

Parker nodded. "Right. Well, now I know why we're in Playa Hermosa." He looked around the room, the rich plaster walls, the big windows, the plush draperies. "And why you sprang for this place."

"Have to look the part," my dad said. "Especially with this one."

"So what's next?" Parker asked.

My dad leaned forward in his chair. "The Fairchilds have a pretty high-tech security system. The details are under lock and key. We know that the feeds are monitored around the clock by Allied Security, but other than that, we've got nothing."

"Do we know if the feeds are monitored by computers?" I asked. "Or by real people?"

"By people," my dad answered. "I have Parker on that part of the puzzle, but we need to get information about the rest of the system."

I didn't expect him to give me more detail. Parker and I were insulated, given only the information we needed to focus on our part of the con. It was a way to hedge our bets if one of us was picked up by the police. Sometimes I wondered if even my mom knew everything.

"Do we have any idea where he keeps the gold?" Parker asked.

My dad shook his head. "That's why we're here."

"How do we even know it's on the Fairchild property?" I asked.

"We don't. Not really. But it's a safe assumption. If he's as paranoid as my sources tell me, he wouldn't keep something out of reach that he's stockpiled for a crisis. My guess is a panic room or safe hidden in the house."

"And if it is off-site, getting close to the Fairchilds will help us figure out where it is," my mom added.

I thought about it, trying to stem the tide of fear washing through my body. This was different from what we normally did. Bigger. Scarier. But looking around the table, I knew it didn't really matter. This was the only way we knew how to live.

I took a deep breath. "Okay, what's the plan?"

"I'm going to work on the details of the Fairchilds' security system while your mom and I get to know Leslie and Warren Fairchild. In the meantime, you need to get close to Logan. See if you can find out anything off the record. Anything we might not have in the file."

I had a flash of memory: Logan looking back at me in the hall, his eyes clear of the duplicity and guardedness I saw in my own when I looked in the mirror.

I swallowed a wave of guilt. "Okay."

"What about me?" Parker asked.

"Keep working Allied. We need to make sure no one has a visual on the place the night we make our move. Until then, try to get into Logan's group; befriend him and the others if you can."

Parker glanced at me before turning back to our dad. "If I'm going to be buddy-buddy with Logan, why does Grace have to come on to him?"

"Because," he sighed. "People say different things to friends than they do to significant others. Pillow talk and all that."

Parker's face tightened, but he nodded. "How long will the setup on this take?"

"Hard to say." He looked at each of us. "But it'll be worth the wait."

Eight

I was stepping onto the back patio, trash bag in hand, when Parker's voice came from the shadows.

"You don't have to do it."

I peered into the darkness, letting my eyes adjust until I could make out the smudge of his body. He was leaning against the house, a tiny orange light glowing in front of his face. The scent of pot, tangled with night jasmine and salt water, drifted to me on the sea breeze.

"You can't do everything," I said carefully. "I'm part of the family, too, you know."

A bitter laugh escaped his throat. He took a drag on the joint. "Family, huh?"

His words jabbed painfully at my heart. I didn't like it when Parker got like this. Dark and brooding, his sarcasm a shroud for the anger that seethed underneath it. I wasn't stupid. I knew our life wasn't perfect. But we were safe and healthy. We had parents who loved us. It was more than a lot of people had.

"Parker . . ." I put a hand on his arm, choosing my words carefully. The backyard was shielded on either side by bougainvillea-covered fences, but it still wasn't the War Room. "Let's not do this again. There's no point. This is the way it is."

"Well, the way it is sucks." He pushed off the wall of the house and lifted a black backpack from the ground near his feet. Swinging it over his shoulder, he stalked into the dark.

"Where are you going?"

"To do my job."

I stared after him as he faded into the night. Then I picked up the trash bag and headed for the side of the house, looking for the trash can my mom had said was there.

I was halfway down the walkway, so overgrown with trees and vines that the light of the full moon was almost completely obliterated, when I heard humming. I stopped walking and listened, trying to determine the source of the sound. A few seconds later I realized it was coming from the backyard next door, hidden from view by the fence that separated the properties, and was accompanied by a low gurgling that could have been the jets on a hot tub.

A man's voice rose into the night, singing.

> *You always hurt the one you love*
> *The one you shouldn't hurt at all.*

The song sounded old and a little sultry. I wondered if the man singing it was the same person who had watched Parker and me walk to the car that morning. And then I wondered something else: Had he heard me talking to Parker in the dark?

I walked carefully to the fence, peering through one of the gaps, hoping to get a look at him.

At first all I could see was the backyard. It was lush, almost overgrown, with so many flowers and trees I could barely make out the glow of lights on the deck, steam rising into the night air. A hairy arm was flung over the wooden edge of a hot tub, but the rest of the man was obscured by climbing vines on a trellis that acted as a screen for the Jacuzzi. I adjusted my position, trying to get a better look, but all I got was a glimpse of a baseball cap.

Stepping away from the fence, I forced myself to think, to remember what I'd said to Parker. Had I given us away? Broken one of the cardinal rules by talking about the job outside the War Room?

But no. I hadn't said anything incriminating—only that Parker couldn't do everything, that I was part of the family, too.

It could have meant anything.

I shook off my unease and continued to the trash can, dropping the bag inside before heading back down the path. A gust of wind blew through the trees, and a commotion rose in the branches over my head, a cacophony of flapping wings as birds took flight. I looked up, but all I saw was the shadow of leaves and twisted branches.

"Yes, yes!" the man next door called out, his voice magnanimous.

I froze.

"Take flight, my little parrots. Be free," he continued. "As free as you can be in this gilded cage. As free as any of us can be."

I hurried to the back door, rubbing my arms against a sudden chill.

Nine

I was staring out the window the next morning, hoping for a glimpse of the birds, when my mom's heels sounded on the tile in the kitchen.

"Are there really parrots here, Mom?" I asked, still scanning the trees.

"There are. I thought I told you."

I turned to her. "You didn't."

She twisted the cap on a bottle of vitamins and shook a couple into her hand. "The Realtor said it started sometime in the 1980s. A bunch of people had them as pets, and they got out or were let go or something. Now they're naturalized."

"What does that mean?"

She thought about it. "They've been here so long they've gotten used to it. It's like they belong here now."

I turned my eyes back to the window, hit with an unexpected pang of loss.

My mother's voice pulled me from my thoughts. "You okay, Gracie?"

I looked away from the window. "I'm just tired, I guess."

She reached out and smoothed my hair. "It's tough getting used to a new place." She surveyed me with knowing eyes. "Maybe we can do takeout tonight, watch a movie on the sofa if you don't have too much homework."

I smiled. Girls' movie nights were my favorite. "That'd be nice."

I said good-bye and went upstairs to take a shower and get dressed. Luckily, the style in Playa Hermosa wasn't that different from Phoenix. The girls were slightly less tan, and they wore less makeup, but with some minor additions most of my old clothes would work. I wondered if Selena would be up for a shopping trip to pick up a few things and then remembered that it wasn't Selena I needed as a friend.

It was Rachel Mercer.

I chose something simple to wear, slipped the Chandler ID into my pocket, and twisted my hair into waves before meeting Parker downstairs. He was quiet as we made our way outside, but at least he'd ditched the angry edge from last night. I relaxed a little. When he brooded and sulked, I was alone all over again. Then I remembered why we had to stick together. Why I accepted the risks and sacrifices and self-loathing that came with what we did. Because the only people I had in the whole world did it, and I couldn't be part of their lives if I didn't do it, too.

We pulled up next to the BMW in the school parking lot. This time when I got out of the car, I flashed Rachel a smile, forcing an expression of serenity on my face as I walked past the group. I saw Logan in my peripheral vision, felt his eyes on me. It took effort to avoid looking at him, but I kept walking, letting Parker get ahead of me with his long-legged stride.

I was crossing the quad at the center of campus when a voice called out behind me.

"Grace! Wait up!"

I turned to see Selena and Nina standing near a bank of lockers in the outdoor hallway. Selena said something to the long-haired blonde and then hurried toward me, curls escaping from the loose bun at the back of her head.

I smiled, genuinely happy to see her. "Hey!"

"Hey! How was your day yesterday?"

She fell into step, and we headed for the buildings at the back of the quad.

"It was good. Everyone seems really nice," I said. "What do you have first period?"

"Government. How about you?"

I made a face. "Precalc."

"Ugh. I barely passed Integrated Algebra. Math isn't my thing."

I stopped in front of the building where my class was held.

"This is me," I said. "But I'm glad we ran into each other."

"Me too. I was thinking; would you want to hang out at my house sometime? We could swim if it's not too cold, watch movies . . . whatever."

I smiled. "I'd love to. And actually, I might need a shopping partner. Someone to help me pick out a few things so I'm not hopelessly out of fashion in Playa Hermosa." I batted my eyelashes dramatically.

She laughed. "I think you're doing pretty well, but I won't turn down an excuse to go shopping."

"Great! I'll text you."

I slipped into class as the first bell rang, my mom's voice echoing in my head: *Maybe you can use her.* I felt a flush of shame. But that wasn't what I was doing. I liked Selena. Liked her a lot. I would just keep everything separate, that's all. Keep Logan and Rachel apart from my friendship with Selena. It would be easy. They didn't even run in the same crowd.

By fourth period I almost believed it was possible, and I slid into my seat in AP Euro, feeling more in control.

"Hey."

I looked up at the sound of Rachel's voice. It was confident, with a sharp edge that made it easy to imagine what she sounded like when she was annoyed or pissed off.

"Hey."

"Think I could look at your notes from yesterday?" Rachel asked, smoothing her already pin-straight red hair. "I think I missed some stuff while I was looking for a pen."

"Sure." I pulled the notes out of my binder and handed

them to her. "I don't know how good they are, but you're welcome to them."

She bent her head and started writing. "So . . . you're new here, right?"

"Yesterday was my first day."

"Where are you from?"

"San Francisco."

Rachel looked up. "What brings you to Playa Hermosa?"

"My dad's work."

She wrote silently, like I wasn't there. Finally, she handed my notes back with a chilly smile. "Thanks."

"No problem."

Mr. Stein walked into the room, and I turned uneasily to the front of the class, wondering why Rachel's questions felt less like small talk and more like an interrogation—and if it might be easier to move on to Logan after all.

Ten

I brooded over Rachel the rest of the morning. She was the queen of her little kingdom. It was a given that she would be selective about granting admittance. Still, forging bonds with people was more art than science, and I'd learned to listen to my instincts. Friendships could be built on a shared interest in rescue cats or French fashion, eighties punk rock or video games, bad horror movies or Japanese candy.

At the same time, a mark could seem one way on paper and be completely different in person. I'd been assigned to get close to people who were a slam dunk in the subject files, only to discover that in person we were missing the mysterious brand of chemistry required for fast friendship.

But I'd always been able to overcome it. Failure to connect wasn't in my professional vocabulary, yet that was the only way I could describe the weird vibe between Rachel Mercer and me. Something about the inquisitive shine in her eyes, the appraising tip of her head, told me she would not be an easy mark. I could keep trying, but my gut told me it would be a waste of time.

I decided to move on. Having Rachel on my side might make things easier, but it wasn't absolutely necessary. I would switch gears, focus on the girls Rachel hung out with—Harper and Olivia—and most importantly on Logan Fairchild.

I sat with Selena, Ashley, and Nina at lunch. Ashley and Nina shared a pair of headphones, talking nonstop about a concert they'd attended the week before (Selena's dad wouldn't let her go), while Selena and I planned a Saturday shopping trip. Rachel and her friends still occupied the table near the window, clearly "their" spot. Logan was there, too, throwing a foam football with a couple of guys when the lunch monitors weren't looking.

This time when Logan looked over, I smiled, making a point to meet his gaze across the cafeteria.

Screw Rachel Mercer.

I stayed after school to talk to my English teacher about the upcoming midterm. By the time I headed outside, there were only a handful of cars left in the parking lot. The Saab wasn't one of them.

My cell phone had buzzed while I'd been talking to Mrs. Kryzek, but I'd forgotten to check it when I left the classroom. I pulled it out now and discovered three texts from Parker.

In the parking lot.

Where are you?

Assume you have a ride? Text if you need me to come back.

Sighing, I sat down on the curb. I was texting Parker when a car approached from the left. It was almost in front of me when I recognized the black BMW.

The car stopped, the passenger side window retracting with an electronic hum.

"Hey!" Logan smiled through the open window. "Grace, right?"

I nodded. "Right."

"Need a ride?"

"My brother ditched me, but I can text him to come back."

"Don't bother," Logan said. "I can give you a lift."

I bit my lip, wondering if my heart was beating faster because of the unexpected opportunity to work Logan or because he had such a nice smile.

"I live at the top of Camino Jardin," I finally said. "Is that too far?"

He laughed. "Nothing's too far on the peninsula. Get in."

"Thanks." I slid into the front seat and fastened my seat belt.

Logan maneuvered through the parking lot and pulled onto the main road. Then we were winding our way up the peninsula, the wind blowing my hair around, the late afternoon sun warm on my shoulders as the ocean shimmered on our right.

"Did you move here for your parents' work?" Logan

asked over the wind.

I nodded. "My dad was part of a big IPO. Now he owns a venture capital firm. There are some start-ups down here he wants to invest in or something."

It was vague, but I wasn't worried. Nobody my age was interested in what their parents did for a living. It was probably even more true in Playa Hermosa, where, as long as the new cars, trips to Europe, and credit cards kept coming, no one seemed to care where they came from.

"Sounds interesting," he said.

"I don't really know that much about it," I laughed. "What about you? Have you lived here long?"

He made a tight turn around one of the road's switchbacks. "Born and raised."

Was I imagining the note of regret in his voice? I filed the observation away for later.

"It seems like a nice place to be born and raised."

He glanced over, nodding. "I think you'll like it."

"Yeah?"

His smile was slow, even a little sexy, in a totally-unaware-of-how-cute-I-am way. "Yeah."

We turned onto Camino Jardin, the air suddenly cooler as we entered the shade of the thick foliage overhead. We were almost to the corner when I spotted something in the middle of the street.

Logan slammed on the brakes, and I flew forward, stopped only by my seat belt. I braced myself against the dash as I tried to steady my racing heart.

Logan looked over at me. "You okay?"

"Fine." I trained my eyes on the animal in the road. "Is that . . . ?"

"A peacock," he confirmed.

"What's it doing here?"

He raised his eyebrows. "You haven't seen them yet?"

I shook my head, and the bird suddenly fanned its tail feathers in an iridescent display of blue and green. It stood straighter, elongating its neck as if on alert.

"Apparently, some explorer brought them here in the 1920s," Logan explained.

"It's beautiful," I murmured.

"It is," Logan said thoughtfully. "Although there are people in Playa Hermosa who would disagree with you."

I looked over at him. "Why?"

"Well, they block traffic for one thing, and squawk like you wouldn't believe. There's a big fight about it."

"What kind of fight?"

Logan inched forward, edging around the animal. "There's an ordinance that says you can't hurt them, but some of the neighborhoods want to opt out of it because the peacocks are so out of control."

"It's that one, with the Saab out front." I pointed out my house at the end of the street before turning back to him. "So . . . what? People would kill them?"

Logan pulled to a stop in front of the house. "Or trap them and send them away."

I glanced back at the bird. "That's sad."

"I guess they don't know what else to do." Logan turned to me, his attention shifting away from the peacock. "So there's a bonfire at the Cove on Saturday. You should come. Bring your brother, if you want. I think he's on our basketball team in gym."

"Sounds like fun." I got out of the car. "Thanks for the ride."

"No problem. See you at school tomorrow."

I slipped my hand in my pocket, touching the ID card from Chandler High as I watched Logan drive carefully around the peacock, which was still standing, shell-shocked, as if it had no idea how it had ended up in a paved faux-haven like Playa Hermosa.

Eleven

I settled into a routine of meeting up with Selena in the morning and eating with her and the other girls at lunch. Ashley and Nina didn't say much, but Selena and I never ran out of things to talk about. By the end of my first week in Playa Hermosa, I felt like we'd been friends forever. I was still careful not to say too much, not to step on the toes of my own lies, but I found myself telling her the truth about things, too.

Like the fact that I opened every new book to random pages, reading sentences out of context before actually starting it. And how I hated my nose even though everyone else said there was nothing wrong with it. And that I'd wanted to cut my hair short for years but always chickened out at the last minute.

The confessions were nothing big, nothing that would

jeopardize the con, but they were things I'd held back in the past, if only to preserve some small part of myself to inspect when I started to forget who I really was.

Now I started to feel the truth of it. Of me. Not the part I played in this job or in the last one, but who I *really* was. Like acknowledging things about myself out loud somehow made them—and me—more real. It was exhilarating, confirmation that there was something underneath the Grace who lied and stole. But it was terrifying, too. What if the real Grace didn't want to stay undercover anymore?

By Saturday I was filled with unfamiliar excitement, looking forward to both my shopping excursion with Selena and the bonfire later that night. It worried me. I wasn't used to feeling normal. To being excited about parties and shopping. And it wasn't like I hadn't done the teenage thing before. I'd played more or less the same part in every con.

This was different. Sometimes when I was talking to Selena or smiling at Logan across the cafeteria, I forgot who I was supposed to be, the always reliable script in my mind turning momentarily blank. I had to remind myself that the bonfire was work. *Logan* was work. Even shopping was work. Fun wasn't supposed to be a part of it.

But Logan seemed nice, casting glances my way at school, smiling when he caught my eye. It would have been a lie to say I wasn't interested in him.

I would have to work around it, like I was working around Rachel.

I was in the kitchen Saturday morning, planning my

outfit for the day and heating up a waffle in the toaster, when my dad came in dressed in plaid pants, a golf polo, and a hat.

I laughed. "You're either auditioning for the sequel to *Happy Gilmore* or you're going golfing."

He poured himself a cup of coffee. "I ran into Warren Fairchild when I took a tour of Mar Vista on Tuesday. He invited me to try the club before I join."

"Is it nice?"

He nodded. "Gorgeous. Right on a bluff overlooking the water."

"Perks of the job, huh?" It sounded snide, even to me, which wasn't what I intended.

My dad raised an eyebrow. "Ouch."

I pulled my waffle out of the toaster and poured syrup over it. "Sorry. I guess I'm having a little trouble."

"Because of your new friend?" he asked. "Selena, is it?"

I shrugged. "Maybe."

"Well, you don't have to spend time with her if you don't want to." He was stepping around the issue, not wanting to violate the rule about talking outside the War Room.

"I know. But that's the thing: I do." I cut my waffle, trying to think of a safe way to put my feelings into words. "I think I need it, you know?"

He set his cup in the sink and pulled me close, kissing the top of my head. "We all need things, Gracie. Just be careful."

The words echoed through my bones like sonar. Careful of what? Careful not to be myself? Not to get close to anybody?

But of course that was exactly what he meant. Both of those things and more. There were endless things to be careful about.

"Oh, I forgot to tell you," he said, turning back as he opened the door to the garage. "Warren invited us over tomorrow. The Fairchilds are having some kind of barbecue. Everyone will be there."

I forced a smile. "Great."

I carried my plate to the table and thought about the bonfire. There was no doubt that Logan was interested in me, but our time together was limited by the fact that I wasn't part of the group. At lunch, Logan sat with the guys and Rachel, Harper, and Olivia. I still sat with Selena, Ashley, and Nina, and while I actually preferred it that way, moving to Logan's table was a necessary move on the chessboard of the Playa Hermosa con.

The bonfire was my way in. It was the first time I'd be around Rachel's group for any length of time. I needed to make the most of it. Needed to win over Harper and Olivia and cement Logan's attraction to me. If I had the three of them, I was in. Logan's friends wouldn't care one way or another—guys never did—and Rachel would be so outvoted she'd need a reason to keep me on the outside.

Even a queen needed some kind of consensus if she wanted to avoid an uprising.

I was pulled from my thoughts when my mom entered the kitchen wearing slim black pants and a jade-green blouse that accentuated her eyes. Her hair was pulled back, a more conservative style than the one she usually wore, and her legs looked extra long in four-inch heels.

"Hey," I said, putting a bite of waffle into my mouth.

"Hi, honey." She walked to the window and looked outside. "The flowers around the pool are pretty. The landscapers are doing a good job. Fast, too."

"You look nice." I couldn't have cared less about the backyard. "Where are you going?"

She turned around. "Leslie Fairchild sits on the board of the Playa Hermosa Community Theater. They're having a committee meeting today. I'm going to volunteer, see if I can get to know her. Turns out she's a bit of a homebody."

"How do you know?"

"I got some of the women at the salon talking. Seems taking care of Warren, staying on top of his meds and appointments and all the other things that go along with being married to someone with his condition, is a full-time job."

"But he goes golfing and stuff . . ." I wanted to believe that Warren Fairchild's condition wasn't that bad. That we wouldn't be stealing from someone so mentally ill that it took all of his family's resources to take care of him.

My mom laughed. "He's not paralyzed, Gracie. They just have to control his environment. From what I understand, he can handle familiar places and situations as long as he's on his meds. They just have to keep an eye on him, that's all." She didn't sound at all concerned as she grabbed her handbag off the counter. "Anyway, I have to go. Have fun at the bonfire tonight."

"Thanks." I watched her leave, her words echoing through my mind: *He can handle familiar places and situations as long as he's on his meds.*

What about unfamiliar situations? What happened to Logan's dad then? I pushed the thought away. What happened to Warren Fairchild after we took his gold wasn't our problem.

I took my plate to the sink and ran water over it as I looked out the window, scanning the trees for parrots.

"I thought you were going to the mall?"

I jumped at the sound of the voice behind me. It was Parker, standing there in swim trunks and flip-flops, a blue knapsack in his hands.

"God! You scared me!" I took a deep breath. "I'm picking Selena up in half an hour. You don't need the car, do you?"

He shook his head. "I'm getting a ride with the guys."

"The guys?"

"Logan, David, and Liam. They're teaching me how to surf today."

"Oh, wow . . . you got in before me," I said with a twinge of jealousy.

"Not really. I'm about where you are. They invited me surfing when we won our basketball game in gym, but I wouldn't say I'm in yet." He grabbed a beach towel off one of the hooks on the wall by the kitchen door. "The bonfire should help, though."

"The bonfire?"

"Logan invited me. I heard you were going, too."

Guilt heated my face. "I forgot to mention it. I'm sorry. I would have invited you when I remembered."

Even as I said it, I wondered if it was true. If the slip had been intentional. Parker was good at a lot of things: running recon, cracking locks, and finding ways around alarm systems, working the hottest—and richest—girls in any school. But he was also a little too good at being my slightly older brother. And while I appreciated the concern, I wasn't exactly thrilled with the idea of tiptoeing around his protective gaze.

He looked at me for a minute, like he wasn't quite sure what to say.

Finally, he sighed. "I'm just trying to look out for you."

My heart softened. "I know that."

"I hope so," he said. "Because not everybody who says they care is going to do right by you. It sucks, but it's true."

A car honked out front. For a moment, Parker didn't move. When he spoke again, there was something heavy and sad in his eyes.

"I haven't always done the right thing, Grace. But I'm trying to do it now."

He left me standing there, wondering what he meant.

Twelve

Selena's father was a somber man, dressed in a suit despite the fact that it was Saturday. We made small talk for a few minutes and then Selena and I were off, following the winding road down the peninsula until it picked up the Pacific Coast Highway in Redondo Beach.

Selena teased me about staying on the highway that ran parallel to the ocean. We could get to the Galleria faster through town. But I'd learned to take advantage of the good things my strange life had to offer. I'd moved more times in sixteen years than most people would in a lifetime. I'd said too many good-byes, lied so much I sometimes forgot the truth. But I'd also watched the sun set over the desert. I'd walked the streets of New York City in the fall, felt the bite of cold air, smelled the food from the street carts mingling with hot metal from the subway and the earthy scent of leaves blowing across the sidewalk. In DC, I'd seen the cherry blossoms in bloom. In Seattle, I'd raced across Puget Sound in a speedboat, staring into the depths of a sea so green it was almost surreal.

Now I was happy just to be driving with the wind in my hair, the Pacific on one side, a friend on the other. Selena turned up the music, pointing things out as we made our way toward the mall. For once, I felt free.

We cruised the Galleria, stopping in all of Selena's favorite stores. For the first hour I observed, paying careful attention to how the mannequins were merchandized in the popular shops, making note of the brands and styles Selena gravitated toward. She might not be in Rachel's crowd, but she was Playa Hermosa born and bred.

When I felt like I had a handle on the nuances of Southern California style, I bought a pair of killer jeans, a floral dress, multiple sleeveless tops, a shrunken cardigan, and two pairs of strappy sandals. Then I loaded up on cheap earrings, bracelets, and other accessories at one of Selena's hot spots.

I felt a twinge of guilt handing over the credit card my dad had given me; I would never even see the bill. But all the kids in Playa Hermosa had cards paid for by their parents, even Selena, although she had a limit and was questioned by her father about the charges when the statement came in the mail. Mooching off my parents was part of the cover, like the ocean and the house on the peninsula and the Saab I shared with Parker. I might as well enjoy it. I would have to leave it all behind anyway.

I treated Selena to lunch at a sushi place in the mall, our shopping bags stacked in the seats next to us. We talked about Ashley (habit friendship left over from middle school) and Nina (a neighbor Selena walked with to and from school), our classes, and the difference between fashion and label conformity. We were on our second plate of tuna rolls before I dared to bring up the subject of Selena's mother.

I'd been thinking about it ever since that first conversation in the cafeteria. It had nothing to do with the con. Selena was just so unguarded. Her secretiveness about her mother was a noticeable departure from her usual openness. How could I say we were friends if I didn't know the story behind her mother's absence?

"Your dad seems nice," I started, picking up a tuna roll with my chopsticks.

She smiled. "He is. I mean, he's strict and everything, but I understand it. He came here from Mexico when he was a kid. He's had a hard life. He just wants me to take my future seriously."

"I can see that." I hesitated, suddenly unsure. I was so used to digging for information that it felt dishonest to ask questions even when they had nothing to do with the con.

Selena set down her chopsticks. "You want to know about my mom, don't you?" she asked softly.

"No! Well . . . I mean . . ." I sighed. "I guess I am a little curious. But you don't have to say anything about it if you don't want to."

"What have you heard?" Selena asked.

I looked up, surprised. "What do you mean?"

"Come on, Grace. I know people talk about it. It's okay. I get it. It's weird."

"Nobody's said anything to me. Then again, you're pretty much the only person I talk to."

"What about Rachel Mercer?"

"I hardly know Rachel. She's just someone I sit next to in AP Euro. Besides, why would Rachel say anything to me about your mom?"

Selena took a drink of iced tea. "My mom sort of . . . walked out on us a couple years back."

I inhaled sharply. It wasn't what I'd expected. "I'm . . . I'm so sorry, Selena. That must have been really tough."

She nodded.

"Does she still live in Playa Hermosa? Do you see her often?"

"We haven't heard from her since she left." She gave a sad little laugh. "I actually have no idea where she is."

"Wait . . ." I shook my head, trying to get my head around what she was saying. "You mean she just . . . took off without even telling you she was leaving? Without telling you where she was going?"

"Pretty much."

"Well, that's shitty," I said. And then, in case I'd offended her, "Sorry."

She gave me a sad smile. "No, you're right. It is shitty. It's been really hard for my dad."

"And for you, too, I bet."

She nodded slowly. "It was kind of a big deal. At first we thought something had happened to her when she didn't come home from work. My dad called the police and there was a big investigation. They even suggested she'd been having an affair. Then they found her car at the Cove, and they thought maybe she'd drowned or . . . committed suicide or something."

Her face was so still, so lacking its usual animation, that I suddenly wanted to take it all back. Pretend I'd never asked about her mother. Rewind to when we were talking about friends and clothes and the dubious appeal of Hollister. I felt like a thief. Like I'd stolen the light in Selena's eyes.

But it was too late. I'd already brought it up. And who knows? Maybe Selena needed to talk about it. I didn't have a lot of experience with friendship, but it probably involved more than just shopping. I silenced the voice in my head that urged caution, the one that said sharing secrets was the place where real attachment began.

"How do you know she didn't?" I lowered my voice. "Commit suicide, I mean."

"We got a letter a month after she left," Selena said. "It didn't say much. Just that she didn't want to be a wife and mother anymore. That she needed to take care of herself, and she couldn't do that taking care of us, too." She shrugged. "We haven't heard from her since."

"I'm sorry." The words felt stupid and empty, but I didn't have anything else.

"It's okay. I wanted to tell you before, but it just seemed weird and depressing."

I shook my head. "It's real. And we're friends, right?"

She nodded, the light moving back into her eyes. "Yeah, I think we are."

I smiled, wondering why the words made me feel not just happy, but more than a little scared, too.

After lunch, I dropped Selena off and headed home to get ready for the bonfire. I'd invited her to come along, but she'd opted to stay in and make dinner for her dad. It was probably a good thing. Selena would be a distraction, a violation of my new keep-real-friends-separate-from-fake-ones rule. Inviting her had been reckless.

And reckless was a good way to get us all sent to jail.

I was halfway down Camino Jardin, already planning the night's outfit in my head, when something in the middle of the road caught my eye. It was a peacock, and I slowed down, rolling to a stop in front of it. It regarded me calmly, surveying me with watchful eyes, its tail feathers folded back into a silky train, its large body oddly graceful on slender bird legs. I wondered if it was the same one that had been in the road the day Logan drove me home after school.

On impulse, I put the car in park and stepped slowly onto the pavement, half expecting the bird to flee. But it just stood there, watching my approach. I stopped moving toward it when I was a few feet away.

"Hello," I said softly. "Are you lost?"

It cocked its head to one side, like it was considering

the question. Its eyes were strangely human, brown and knowing.

A car swerved around us, breaking the spell. The bird still didn't move, but I suddenly felt foolish. I was standing in the middle of the road talking to a wild—no, a *naturalized*—peacock like I expected it to answer me back.

Retreating, I got back in the car and drove around it, careful not to get too close. I pulled into the driveway and got out of the car, looking back at the street. The bird was gone.

I shook my head, putting it out of my mind as I hurried to change. I ripped the tags off my new jeans and chose a drapey shirt printed with large flowers. I was turning in front of the mirror, trying to get a good view from every angle, when I heard a low hum coming from the window.

I crossed the room on bare feet and peered through the glass. Someone was singing.

And it was coming from next door.

Scanning the neighbor's backyard, I spotted a figure, his face obscured by a wide-brim sun hat, moving across the grass in plaid shirt and shorts. I could only assume it was the man from the Jacuzzi. He held something in his hands as he sang.

Southern trees bear a strange fruit,
Blood on the leaves and blood at the root,

I watched with fascination as he set down a step stool near one of the trees. He climbed up, lifting a bag to a metal

cylinder hanging from one of the branches. Then I understood: he was filling the bird feeders in his backyard, singing as he made his way from one to the next.

A chill ran up my spine as he continued singing. The crooning was eerie, almost creepy. And what was the song about? Dead bodies? It reminded me of my conversation with Selena, and the image of a car, abandoned at the Cove, suddenly appeared in my mind.

I stood there for a few seconds before moving away from the window, trying to shake the uneasy feeling that had fallen over me with the sound of the man's voice, the disturbing lyrics to the song he'd been singing.

This place was getting to me.

I slipped into my new sandals, fortifying my resolve. I would go to the bonfire. I would get close to Logan and everyone else in their group. I would do my job and I would do it quickly.

Before things got even weirder.

Thirteen

"How was surfing?"

We were on our way to the Cove, Parker driving the Saab while I sat in the passenger seat. A cool breeze blew through the window, and I was glad I'd passed on straightening my hair in favor of the beachy waves I'd been working all week. With any luck, the wind would only make it look better.

"Fine," Parker said. "I mean, I suck, but that was to be expected."

"Did you have fun?"

He seemed to think about it. "Yeah. Logan's cool, and his friends are pretty chill, too."

"That's good."

"It makes it easier," he said. "Liking them."

Turning my head to the window, I thought about Selena. "And harder."

He glanced over at me. "Yeah."

Pulling into a gravel turnout, he continued down a winding road to a lot that sat halfway up the cliff. He parked next to a blue Lexus and rolled up the windows before cutting the engine. Then he turned to look at me.

"You don't have to do this, Grace. Neither of us does."

I met his eyes. "Parker . . ."

He shook his head. "I have money saved. I'd hoped to have a little more, but I think it's enough. We could leave. Start over somewhere. I'd look after you. You're the only family I have."

I looked around. This was definitely a violation of protocol. The windows might be rolled up, but it still wasn't the War Room.

"What about Mom and Dad?" I asked softly.

His hand tightened into fists, the leather bracelets constricting around his forearm. "Cormac and Renee aren't my parents. And they're not yours either."

"They're the only parents I've ever had." I hesitated, trying to find the words to make him understand. "I love them. They make me feel safe."

His laugh was brief and bitter. "You could go to jail, Grace. I wouldn't call that safe."

I stared out over the Pacific, glinting like an endless sapphire, the past flashing through my mind. There had been a few nice families. And then there'd been the ones who weren't bad but whose apathy showed in their eyes, in the way they looked past me, as if I'd already moved on when I was still right in front of them. I'd been able to live with that. What I hadn't been able to live with were the other ones. The ones with cold beds and messy sheets, strong fingers wrapped too tightly around my arms, the slap of a palm against my face.

I turned away from the rest of the memories. Turned toward Parker, like a flower seeking the sun.

"No one's hurting me anymore," I finally whispered. "And I don't want to be alone again."

"You wouldn't be alone. We'd stick together," Parker promised. "And you wouldn't have to pimp yourself out for the fucking con."

I smiled sadly. "You love the con."

He shook his head. "Not like this. Not anymore."

I watched the sun in the distance, almost kissing the water. It would be dark soon.

"We have to take the good with the bad, Parker. It's part of the deal."

"Well, I'm ready to deal myself out," he said angrily. "But I won't do it without you."

I had to swallow around a sudden dread. Around the feeling that Playa Hermosa was the place where all our markers would come due.

The one place we might not escape intact.

We both jumped as someone banged against the driver's side window.

"Dude! What are you doing?" It was the blond kid who hung out with Logan. "Let's go."

"Yeah, man, I'm coming." Parker looked back at me. "Think about it."

I forced my mind back to the job as we got out of the car.

Parker introduced me to the guys as we headed for the path leading to the beach. Liam was the platinum blond, the one who'd banged on the car. There was David, the tall one with exotic eyes and straight black hair, and Raj, small and dark.

Logan wasn't with them.

"Did your brother tell you he got spin-cycled today?" Liam asked as we descended to the beach.

I laughed. "Not exactly."

"Oh, man . . . it was crazy!" Raj said. "I was surprised he still had all his skin when he came up off the bottom."

Parker grinned. "I don't know what you're talking about. I was totally cool."

David patted him on the back. "Happens to all of us in the beginning, dude."

Parker smiled good-naturedly, but I saw the tension in the taut set of his shoulders, the flinty look in his eye that said he was still thinking about our conversation in the car. Still thinking about our escape.

I made small talk with the guys as we continued down the hill, switching back a couple of times and winding our way around the cliff face until we finally emerged onto a protected beach. Behind us, black cliffs seemed to touch the sky. The wall of rock descended to a stretch of silky sand leading to the water, the sun just a sliver above the horizon.

I froze, momentarily stunned by the view.

"Pretty awesome, right?" Parker asked, looking down at me.

I nodded. "Pretty awesome."

"Let's go," he said.

I cataloged the scene as we headed across the sand. A bonfire was already raging midway up the beach, coolers and blankets and folding chairs spread out around it. Four guys played Frisbee while a few hard-core surfers stood near the waterline, peeling off their wet suits after eking every last wave out of the daylight. Music blared from a portable sound dock, and people stood around holding bottles of beer or plastic cups while they talked and laughed. I stood there, taking it all in, as the guys headed for one of the coolers. A second later something smacked against my calf, and I looked down to find a volleyball at my feet. I bent to pick it up. When I straightened with it in my hands, I was surprised to find Olivia standing in front of me. Her dark hair was pulled back into a ponytail and she was dressed in Bermuda shorts and a red bathing-suit top, an ensemble that somehow made her look taller than she already was.

"Sorry about that," she said.

I handed her the ball with a smile. "No problem."

"Thanks." She regarded me with open curiosity before heading toward a group of girls standing around a volleyball net. When she was a few feet away, she looked back. "Want to play?"

"What, volleyball?"

She laughed. "Yeah. We're one short right now."

I looked down at my clothes. "I'm wearing jeans . . ."

"It's fine," Olivia said. "We're just passing the time."

I had to fight the irrational impulse to confess that, other than in an occasional gym class, I'd never played volleyball a day in my life. I scolded myself inwardly. I was acting like a novice. I didn't know these people. They were nothing to me. Nothing but a bunch of spoiled rich kids whose lives wouldn't change a single bit because of our con. Besides, I hadn't spotted Rachel in the group of girls at the net, which made it a perfect opportunity to get to know Olivia. Harper was there, too, staring at us from across the sand.

"Okay," I said. "But I should warn you that I'm not exactly an expert."

"It's cool." Olivia started toward the net. "You're from San Francisco, right?"

I nodded, trying to keep up with her long-legged stride.

"No wonder you don't play," she said as we approached the group. "Too cold up there."

Olivia made the introductions. I recognized some of the girls from school, and they were all warm and friendly, happy to have a sixth person to even out the teams. Harper welcomed me with a nervous smile and we joined forces with Olivia on one side of the net, tossing the ball back and forth amid laughter and good-natured trash talk. The girls gave me pointers as the game progressed, laughing off my mistakes as I tried to keep up with their experienced serves and spikes. I was just getting into a groove when someone spoke from the sidelines.

"I guess you started without me."

The ball fell to the ground as everyone turned toward Rachel, who was wearing white short-shorts and a black bathing-suit top, her hair shimmering like a new penny in what was left of the sunlight.

"We didn't know when you were coming," Olivia explained. She tipped her head at me. "And we picked up a sixth, so we figured we might as well play while we waited."

"Come on, Rach," Harper said, sounding a little desperate. "You can be on our team."

Rachel looked accusingly at me. "The teams will be uneven."

Olivia let out an exasperated sigh. "So? We're just having fun. Besides, it'll be dark in, like, ten minutes."

"I can move to the other side so you can be on Harper and Olivia's team," I offered. It wasn't about Rachel. I was past caring what she thought of me. But it would make me look agreeable to the other girls, which would make Rachel look irrational and petulant in contrast.

"Forget it," Rachel said, tossing her hair. "I'll go." She ducked under the net, crossing to the other side.

I had to fight a triumphant smirk. Plan B was fully operational.

And going pretty well, thank you very much.

Fourteen

By the time we finished playing, my legs burned with fatigue and my arms felt weighted with lead. Now I knew why Rachel looked so great in shorts and a bikini top.

After the game, she took off without a backward glance while Olivia introduced me to everyone on the beach. I wasn't much of a drinker—I had to operate at full mental capacity when I was working—but I took a beer with the other girls and sipped it for show. I grabbed one of the beach chairs and was tipping the cold bottle to my mouth when Olivia plopped down next to me. Harper pulled a chair up on the other side and before I knew it, we were deep in conversation, moving between movies, fashion, guys, and finally, San Francisco. I was relieved I'd done some homework on the Bay Area before getting to Los Angeles and even more relieved that none of the girls had been there for more than a weekend.

As usual, I was lying through my teeth, but at least the odds of getting caught were slim.

An hour later, the party was in full swing, and I watched from across the beach as Rachel moved in on Parker, standing too close and flipping her hair, textbook examples of body language in full-on flirt mode. But there was something else, too. Something watchful in the way she stood, the way she angled her body. Like she was expecting an attack any minute.

Or planning one.

Olivia spoke from the chair next to her. "Don't look now, but someone's found a new target."

I laughed. "Rachel? Or Parker?"

"Neither." Olivia tipped her beer bottle in another direction entirely. "Logan. He hasn't taken his eyes off you since he got here."

I followed the beer bottle until my gaze landed on Logan. He was standing at the edge of the fire, a petite blonde chatting him up as he tried to look interested in what she was saying. It might have helped if he'd actually been looking at her.

But Olivia was right; he was watching me.

I offered him a sympathetic smile. His eyes lit up from across the beach.

"Told you," Olivia said, laughing a little.

It was the perfect segue to the dirt on Logan's romantic past. "He is pretty hot," I admitted. "Does he have a girlfriend?"

"Not right now," Harper answered, running her fingers through her short, dirty-blond hair. "But he does have an interesting dating pedigree."

Olivia laughed.

"That doesn't sound good." I sat back in my chair with a sigh. "Go ahead. Give it to me straight. I can take it."

"He and Rachel were a thing," Olivia said. "Until last year, actually."

"Really? What happened?"

Olivia shrugged. "Logan's a little . . ."

"Slow," Harper finished.

"Slow?"

The subject file didn't say anything about Logan being slow. Captain of the lacrosse team, a 3.9 GPA, and president of the school's charitable Human Services Group didn't say slow. Not to mention the way he'd seemed when we talked, the clarity and intelligence in his eyes when he'd given me a ride home.

"I guess *slow* isn't the right word," Olivia corrected herself. "More . . . chill."

"Everyone's chill compared to Rachel," Harper murmured.

Olivia cut Harper a sharp glance before turning her eyes back to me. "Rachel's just . . . high-strung, you know? She likes to party, likes to go to bonfires in Malibu with people none of us know, sneak into clubs in Hollywood. Crazy stuff like that."

"And that's not Logan's scene?" I asked, watching him

feign interest in the blonde across the beach.

Olivia laughed. "You could say that."

I held her gaze without saying anything. Parker had taught me the tactic. It was instinctual for most people to fill silence with words. Silence made people uncomfortable. Made them feel obligated to say something. If you were patient, if you let the silence sit, most people would blab about anything and everything to make it stop.

"Logan's just laid-back," Olivia said. "It didn't work between him and Rachel. Every weekend, she wanted to find the party, and Logan just wanted to come down to the Cove and play his guitar or hang out at Mike's with the guys."

"Mike's?"

"It's a burger place in the Town Center. We hang there when there's nothing else to do," Olivia explained.

"And when Rachel isn't dragging us all over LA," Harper added, her voice thick with sarcasm and something I could have sworn was resentment.

"So . . . I take it Logan's off-limits?" I had no intention of leaving Logan alone. I just wanted to know what kind of territory I was wading into. "Because of the history with Rachel?"

Olivia thought about it. "I wouldn't say that. They're still friends, and the breakup was basically mutual."

"Besides, Rachel dated Liam after she and Logan broke up," Harper volunteered. "Kind of hard for her to pull the friend card when she went out with one of Logan's best friends less than a month after they split."

"Yeah, but I wouldn't want to piss her off . . . ," I hedged, waiting for the advice I knew would come.

Olivia laughed. "Playa Hermosa's not that big. If you make a point not to date anyone who's dated any of your friends, you're going to be single a loooong time."

I nodded slowly, not wanting to seem too eager. "I guess . . ."

"You could talk to her about it," Olivia suggested.

"I don't really know her that well," I said. "What would I say?"

"Just . . . you know, tell her you're interested in Logan—if you are, I mean—and ask her if she has a problem with it." Olivia nodded, like she was agreeing with herself. "Rachel likes it when people ask her permission for things."

Harper snorted, and Olivia gave her a dirty look.

Hell would freeze over before I would legit ask Rachel's permission for anything, but I could play the game.

I smiled. "Thanks, you guys. You're awesome."

Olivia stood up and performed a mock bow. "I live to serve. Anyone want another beer?"

We declined, and Olivia headed for the cooler. She was just out of earshot when Harper spoke.

"Be careful with Rachel. Seriously."

I looked over at her. "With Logan?"

"With everything. Rachel's smarter than she looks."

"What makes you say that?" My instincts were on full alert. Maybe it was the beer. Maybe it was the conspiratorial girl talk. But something had Harper feeling chatty.

She leaned closer. "Let's just say Rachel has a nose for anything . . . off."

My heart beat a little bit faster, the way it always did when I was onto something. An idea or some piece of information that would help with the con. "Off?"

Harper nodded. "If you go after Logan, even on the sly, she'll find out. She has a lot of experience that way."

"What kind of experience?"

Harper drained the last of the beer in one swallow. I couldn't remember if it was her second or her third.

"Rachel's dad has a way with Playa Hermosa's housewives. Rachel's gotten good at sniffing him out over the years, and it's made her good at sniffing out everything else, too." Harper's voice turned distant. "Even stuff that's none of her business."

I kept my face impassive. No way had I planned to get anything like this. Not so soon, anyway. It was an unexpected bonus. But also an unexpected concern.

I knew what it meant to be surrounded by liars. To be one. It meant that your instincts were honed to see deceit in others. That you believed everyone was riddled with dishonesty. That you were trained to look for all the little tics people performed—most of them involuntary—when they weren't telling the truth.

Basically, it meant that you had a nose for liars.

Which made Rachel a potentially serious problem.

Fifteen

A few minutes after Harper's revelation, she rose from her chair and headed toward the cooler. I hoped she wasn't getting another beer. Judging from her unsteady gait across the sand, it was the last thing she needed.

I scanned the party scene, trying to gauge the timing. Rachel was still deep in conversation with Parker. Logan was smiling politely at the little blonde. Everyone else was occupied with their own agenda: drinking, scamming, smoking, or looking for a hookup. It was as good a time as any. I'd made progress with Harper and Olivia.

Now I just needed Logan.

I stuck my nearly full beer in the sand and stood. Leaving my sweatshirt on the beach chair, I moved into Logan's line of sight, avoiding his eyes. When I stepped into the shadows, I wasn't at all surprised to feel someone fall into step behind me.

"Grace!"

I turned around. "Hey, Logan."

"It's getting a little rowdy back there. Mind if I join you?"

"Not at all." We started walking, the waves rushing up to meet our bare feet. "I've never been down here before."

"It's kind of our spot," he said. "Although I prefer coming here alone."

I inhaled deeply, relishing the cold, salty air. "I can see that. It's probably therapeutic. When there's not a bunch of people getting drunk and stoned, I mean."

He chuckled. "Exactly."

"They seem nice, though," I said. "Your friends."

He thought about it. "Well, they're not all my friends, but . . . yeah. They're mostly cool."

I pulled a strand of windblown hair away from my face. "Mostly?"

He shrugged. "You know how it is. There are a few difficult people in every group."

I thought of Parker. Of his mercurial moods, his resentment of our parents, the self-destructive streak that made it hard for me to sleep when he stayed out too late. That made me think about the scars on his arm and what would happen if he felt too desperate, too alone.

"And every family," I sighed.

He looked down at me. "You don't seem difficult to get along with, so I can only assume you mean your brother. Or is there another . . . challenging Fontaine I haven't met yet?"

I don't know why, but I was happy that he'd remembered

my last name. Or the one we were using right now, anyway. "No, Parker pretty much takes that title in our family."

Logan laughed.

"What's so funny?" I asked.

He ran a hand through his hair. "Nothing. Just . . . Rachel should keep even Parker on his toes."

I smiled up at him. "I kind of got that impression."

"Want to sit?" he said, gesturing to the sand.

"Sure."

I dropped to the sand, and he sat next to me.

I turned to look at him. "Truth?"

"Truth."

"I just about died playing volleyball with the girls. I thought they'd never stop."

He grinned. "Your secret's safe with me."

We sat there for a minute, watching the waves roll in and out. I'd been near the ocean in New York and Seattle, but never like this. Manhattan was too loud, too polluted by humanity to be peaceful, even down by the water. Seattle had been beautiful and serene, but the beaches were mostly rocky, the ocean so cold you had to brace yourself to go for a swim even in the summer.

This was different. The sand was soft, the air clean and fresh. The waves hurried up the sand toward us before withdrawing gently back into the sea.

I should have asked questions. Should have tried to get information to move the job forward. But the sound of the tide was rhythmic, Logan's presence next to me soothing. It all lulled me into a kind of peaceful complacency.

"So what do you think of Playa Hermosa?" Logan finally asked.

I liked the way he looked at me, like there was nothing on his mind but me, no thoughts crowding out our moment together. Like it was just the two of us, stranded on a lonely beach in the middle of space.

"I like it. I mean, we haven't been here long, but so far, everyone seems really nice." Other than Rachel, it was true.

He turned his head to look at me. "Like who?"

"Well . . . you seem pretty nice." I didn't think about the smile I gave him. Didn't try to make it shy or hesitant, to make it fit into the con. It just rose to my lips like a piece of driftwood rising to the surface of the sea.

He raised an eyebrow, a slow smile teasing his lips. "I do?"

"Yeah." I spoke softly, not wanting to break the spell of the moment we'd somehow fallen into.

An ear-splitting crack echoed across the beach, and I jumped, looking back toward the light of the bonfire.

"What was that?"

Logan got up, brushing off his jeans. "Firecrackers. Those dumb-asses are going to get beach patrol down here." He reached out a hand. "Come on, we better go back."

He pulled me to my feet, holding on to my hand a little longer than necessary.

We headed back down the beach, walking close to the waterline, the waves rushing up and over our feet. We were about halfway back to the bonfire when he stopped to pull off his hoodie.

He reached around me, placing the sweatshirt on my shoulders. His fingers sent a ripple of electricity where they brushed my bare skin.

"What's this for?" I asked, looking up into his eyes.

"You were shivering," he said.

"I was?"

"Yeah." He squeezed my shoulders and hesitated, like he wanted to pull me into his arms. Instead he started walking again.

I matched his stride. "Thank you."

When we got back to the fire, everyone was packing up, hurriedly folding up beach chairs and stuffing sweatshirts and towels into backpacks. Liam and Raj were carrying two of the coolers toward the path that led to the parking lot.

Someone pointed down the beach. "Here they come!"

I turned and saw two white lights bobbing on the sand in the distance.

"What's that?" I asked Logan.

"Beach patrol. They comb the beach on ATVs," he explained. "Better head out. They're always trying to bust us for drinking and smoking."

My heart raced. I couldn't afford to be questioned, even by beach patrol. It would be a total violation of the leave-no-proof rule, not to mention risky if someone had caught onto us for the job in Phoenix. And there were only two ways off the beach—up the cliff or toward the approaching ATVs.

Something tugged on my arm. When I turned, Parker was staring into my eyes.

"Let's go, Grace."

"I have to get my stuff. I'll meet you by the path."

Parker nodded silently, hurrying away as I took off Logan's sweatshirt and gave it back to him. "Thanks for the walk. I had a nice time."

"Me too." His eyes lit up. "And hey! I'll see you tomorrow."

"You will?"

"The barbecue? At my house? My dad said he invited you."

I smiled. "Right. I'll see you there."

"Grace!" Parker barked from the rocks near the path.

I pulled my gaze from Logan's and ran.

Sixteen

The Fairchilds lived high upon the peninsula. My dad drove, telling us how beautiful the club was and how Warren Fairchild had already put in a recommendation for his membership.

I sat next to Parker in the back, thinking about Logan. I hadn't stopped thinking about him, actually, since the bonfire the night before. As Warren and Leslie's only child, Logan was key to the con. My ability to get close to him could be the difference between getting out clean with Warren Fairchild's gold and being arrested.

But I wasn't thinking about the con. Not the way I should have been. I was thinking about Logan. About how real he was, vulnerable and strong all at the same time. About how he'd looked at me on the beach, like he knew all my secrets and didn't care, and how his fingers had sent a spark across my bare shoulders when he'd given me his sweatshirt.

About what he would think of me if he knew the truth.

We pulled onto a private street, and the ocean and sky seemed to open up around us. The Fairchilds' house sat alone at the end of the road. It was a Spanish-style structure, and smaller than I'd expected. It looked old, not like one of the giant reproductions I'd gotten used to seeing in California.

"Wow . . ." Parker looked out the window. "This must have cost a fortune."

"Warren and Leslie bought it in the early nineties," my dad explained, pulling through the open gate. "Don't get me wrong; it was still one of the most exclusive neighborhoods in Southern California. But the market was a bit lower then."

My mom laughed as we headed up the long, winding driveway. "So it was ten million instead of the twenty million it would be now?"

"Something like that."

We parked behind a row of other cars and headed for the front door. My stomach was fluttering, although I couldn't tell if it was because this was our first chance to check out the job site or because I'd get to see Logan again.

The walkway was paved with stone, heavily shaded from the trees overhead. I heard a squawk and looked up, catching a flash of brilliant red and blue through the foliage.

I pointed. "I think I just saw a parrot!"

Parker gazed upward, peering through the trees. "I don't see anything."

My dad rang the bell. It echoed through the house on the other side of the door. A minute later, it was opened by a voluptuous brunette, her hair graying at the temples.

"Renee! How nice to see you." Her face was transformed by a generous smile. She opened the door wider. "Please, come in!" Her gaze found my dad. "You must be Cormac. Warren has told me so much about you. Seems he's met his match on the back nine."

"I don't know about that," my dad said, laughing and stepping into the foyer. "Warren's been keeping me on my toes."

My mom introduced us, and then we were following Leslie down a long tiled hallway toward the sound of music and conversation. I tried to put my finger on why I was so surprised. Was it because Leslie, clearly not a devotee of the treadmill, was rounder and softer than my mom? Because she wore a loose, caftan-type garment instead of the fashionable, semirevealing clothes that were a uniform for the other mothers in Playa Hermosa? Or because she seemed unconcerned with the silver threading her hair, in no hurry to get to the salon to cover it?

Whatever it was, I liked Leslie Fairchild immediately.

The unmistakable sound of a party in full swing grew louder as we crossed through the kitchen. A few seconds later we stepped outside. I had to stop myself from gasping at the view.

The lot was huge. A graduated stone terrace stepped down to a lush lawn stretching toward the cliffs, the ocean shimmering in the distance. The property was private, with no neighbors on either side and mature trees reaching into the sky, flowering bushes and vines growing a little haphazardly all around them. I glimpsed the top of a peaked roof at the back of the property and wondered if it was the carriage house I'd seen on the plans of the Fairchild estate.

We stepped into the crowd, and I turned my attention to the party. People stood around in clusters, talking and laughing. Across the lawn, Rachel played badminton with Olivia and Raj.

"Well!" Leslie clapped her hands, leading us to an outdoor bar. "Let's get you something to drink and then we'll make the rounds."

She poured my parents a glass of wine each and told Parker and me to help ourselves to a cooler of sodas. Then she started the procession, leading us around the lawn and introducing us to everyone.

We met Rachel's parents first. Her mother was attractive and slender, her hair a familiar shade of copper. When it came time to shake the hand of Rachel's father, Harrison, I heard an echo of Harper's confession at the beach: *Rachel's dad has a way with the Playa Hermosa housewives.*

I could see it. Harrison Mercer was no balding, overweight dad. Instead his trim figure, dark hair, and bold smile gave him a George Clooney–esque charm that was probably irresistible to the bored women on the peninsula.

Liam's father, Blake, was next. A property developer

planning a green housing initiative, he and his wife also owned the Town Center.

And they were just the beginning. There were movie people and writers and tech-company owners and shareholders. Real estate managers and commercial agents and local business owners. I lost track after a while, content to smile, nod, and observe while the adults did most of the talking.

I still hadn't spotted Logan, so I focused on the property instead, making note of security cameras, walkways, outdoor lights that were probably triggered by movement, and anything else that might help us when it came time to make our move. It had become second nature, almost instinctual, to store my observations, and I wasn't surprised to see Parker's eyes wandering, too.

Once the introductions had been made, Leslie Fairchild led us to a massive grill, where a silver-haired man wearing a Kiss the Cook apron stood over a bunch of smoking meat. He jumped a little when Leslie put a gentle hand on his shoulder.

"Warren, honey," she said gently, "the Fontaines are here."

There were shades of Logan in his father's face. Warren had the same openness, the same attentiveness that made me feel like he'd been waiting all day just for us.

"Cormac!" He reached out and shook my dad's hand. "So glad you could make it." He turned to the rest of us. "And this must be your beautiful family."

"That it is," my dad said. "This is my wife, Renee, and

our kids, Parker and Grace."

Logan's dad shook our hands and insisted we call him Warren. When it was my turn, his eyes seemed to hold mine.

"I've heard a lot about you," he said.

I laughed. "Oh no!"

His eyes radiated warmth. "I assure you that it was all good. My son seems to enjoy your company."

My cheeks were suddenly warm. "Thank you. Where is Logan?"

Leslie looked around. "He was here a minute ago. . . . Oh, here he comes!"

Logan stepped onto the terrace, carrying a plate of raw chicken. I wondered if it was my imagination that his eyes seemed to light up when he spotted me.

"Hey! I was wondering when you were coming," he said.

I couldn't help but smile. Everyone else was so coy when they liked someone, so careful not to seem interested. But here was Logan, grinning at me like I'd made his day just by showing up.

I looked down at the chicken. "Need some help with that?"

"This? Nah, I'm good." He carried the plate over to the grill.

I introduced him to my parents, and after a little small talk Leslie led them off to meet the VP of some big advertising agency.

Logan touched his dad lightly on the arm. "Need anything else?"

I don't know why I was surprised by the concern in his

voice. It was just so genuine. So real. I'd expected Warren Fairchild's condition to put stress on the family dynamic. Instead it seemed to make them closer.

"No, no!" Warren said. "You kids go. Have fun. And if you want to gnaw on some meat, come find me."

Logan laughed, touching his dad lightly on the back. "You'll be the first to know, Dad." He looked at Parker and me. "You guys up for some badminton?"

Seventeen

We traveled a gravel path to the big grassy area at the back of the property. Logan filled us in on the aftermath of the bonfire as we walked, telling us who had been busted by beach patrol the night before. I hoped he didn't notice the tightness in Parker's jaw, the protective gleam in his eyes when Warren Fairchild said Logan liked my company.

We stepped onto the grass, and Olivia and Raj paused their game, greeting us with waves and genuine smiles. Rachel was decidedly less enthusiastic, although she did warm up a bit for Parker.

We spent a few minutes talking before splitting into teams: me with Logan and Olivia, Parker with Raj and Rachel. The game got under way, and I told myself to forget about the con. About casing the Fairchilds' house and the fact that I needed to get close to Logan to further my part of the job. The weather was perfect, warm and dry, a breeze blowing off the water that crashed against the cliffs below. I was allowed to have fun. It was all part of being in character.

Part of fitting in.

We played three games—Rachel, Raj, and Parker taking two out of the three—and went our separate ways. Olivia and Raj got drinks while Parker and Rachel walked toward the edge of the property, sitting on the grass that overlooked the water.

Logan turned to me. "You're not one of those girls who never eats, are you?"

I laughed. "Definitely not."

"Great. Let's eat, then."

He held out his hand like it was the most natural thing in the world, and when I took it, it kind of was.

We got plates of food, and I slipped off my shoes as we sat on one of the ledges built into the patio. The grass was cool and moist under my bare feet, the breeze soft and scented with jasmine. Looking around, watching everyone laughing and talking, I felt strangely content. I was surprised by how low-key it was: Logan's father working the grill, his mother perfectly at ease hosting fifty people with no catering help at all.

"I get the feeling your brother doesn't like me much," Logan said, setting aside his plate.

I shook my head. "Parker's just . . . moody."

Logan seemed to think about it. "I can see that. He seemed so laid-back when we went surfing, but today . . ."

"He had a great time surfing with you guys," I said. "He told me so."

"Really?"

"Yeah. He's just protective."

"Why does he feel like he has to be protective around me?"

Because he doesn't like the idea of our parents using me to steal your dad's gold. Because he is one of very few people in the whole world who care if I live or die. Because he's the only one—other than my parents—who knows how hurt I've been, and he wants to protect me from ever being hurt like that again.

But I couldn't say any of it, so I spoke the other truth instead. The one I'd only barely begun admitting to myself. "I think he knows how much I like you."

"You do?"

I immediately regretted the confession. "Well, I guess I don't know you that well. But I'd like to know more." I laughed. "If that makes any sense."

His smile was slow, reaching his eyes bit by bit. He reached for my hand. "It makes perfect sense."

His fingers fit just right around mine, like they were meant to go together. Like I'd been crisscrossing the country, trying out different states and different schools and different last names, just to make my way to him.

"Logan!"

We turned around, following the sound of his mother's voice from the patio.

"Yeah, Mom?"

"Can you bring some more soda in from the garage?"

"Yep!" He turned to look at me. "You'll be okay?"

"Of course," I said. "Is it cool if I take a look around while you're gone? It's so beautiful here."

"Definitely. I'll find you when I'm done."

He took our empty plates and made his way up the terrace.

I scanned the property. Investigating the house was out. No one was inside, and I'd only just met the Fairchilds today. It would be too suspicious.

The grounds, however, were fair game, and I crossed the lawn and stepped onto the gravel pathway, following it toward the roofline I'd seen through the trees. I passed the grass where we'd played badminton and continued to the side of the property until I came to a narrow drive that seemed to run from the front of the house all the way to the end of the yard.

The trees and bushes were less pruned as I got farther away from the main house, and I reached out a hand, running it over the trailing shrubs and vines that lined the drive, feeling the silky petals of the bougainvillea under my palms. The air grew cooler, the sun blocked out by the trees overhead. I made note of the cameras spaced every twenty feet in the trees and of the gravel, noisy under my feet.

All things we needed to know.

The thought of it made me feel sick. I didn't want to think about conning Logan and his family, stealing from them, disappearing without an explanation. But wishing things were different didn't change anything.

I knew that better than most people.

An aging outbuilding rose through the trees at the end of the path. It looked like an old carriage house, with sliding doors and peeling white paint.

I glanced up at the roofline, scanning it for cameras. There was one in the eaves, aimed at the entrance of the carriage house. I made a point to look around, wanting to seem casually curious to anyone who might be monitoring the camera feed.

From the outside, it didn't look promising as a potential hiding spot for Warren Fairchild's gold. Situated by itself in the middle of the trees, there was no space between walls or other structures for a panic room or safe.

I looked at the sliding doors. The camera made me nervous about going inside, but Logan had given me permission to take a look around. It might be the only chance I'd have to see it without raising suspicion. Besides, this was why Parker and I were so integral to the cons. People might suspect a teenager of sneaking off to make out, of stealing lip gloss from a department store or vandalizing something just for the fun of it. But no one ever suspected us of pulling the kind of jobs that were our specialty. Parker and I made it possible for our parents to blend in with other families. To join school fund-raisers and committees, to snoop around sprawling mansions during barbecues and birthday parties.

Or have us do the snooping for them.

The smell of dirt, old wood, and mildew assaulted my

nose as I stepped inside. I looked around: the far reaches of the building were shrouded in darkness, dust motes shimmering in a single beam of sunlight working its way through the open door. Old windows were stacked against the uninsulated walls, sunlight leaking in through cracks in the wood siding. It was both serene and a little spooky. I was standing there, giving my eyes time to adjust to the dimness, when I heard footsteps behind me.

I turned to find Rachel, standing in the doorway, arms crossed over her chest.

"Doing a little exploring?"

"Rachel . . ." I was grateful for the darkness as guilty heat flooded my face. I recovered quickly. "Logan said I could take a look around. It's amazing, isn't it?" I looked up, making a show of taking it all in while I filed stuff away for later.

"What are you doing here, Grace?" Rachel's voice was cold.

"Just . . . you know, looking around."

"Just looking around, huh?"

I met her eyes, forcing my gaze steady. "That's what I said."

Rachel was quiet as she paced the floor of the carriage house, her eyes scanning the walls halfheartedly, like she'd seen it all before and just needed a place to focus her attention.

"It's weird, that's all," she finally said.

"What is?"

"Your family . . . moving to Playa Hermosa right after

school started, renting a house on Camino Jardin, where hardly anybody rents, being so . . . *interested* in Logan. In all of us."

"How do you know I live on Camino Jardin?"

Rachel stopped walking, her eyes taking on the shrewd, knowing shine that was starting to give me the creeps.

"I know lots of things," she said. "Lots and lots of things."

"What are you getting at, Rachel?"

She flashed a small, chilly smile. "Nothing in particular. Just that when I don't know something, I usually have a way of finding out."

She held my gaze, silence looming between us, an abyss that seemed more impossible than ever to cross. Then she turned around and walked away, leaving me standing alone in the shadowed carriage house.

Eighteen

As soon as we got home, my dad pointed to the staircase. "Upstairs," he ordered.

The rest of the barbecue hadn't been a rousing success. I'd spent my time with Logan, torn between how much I liked being with him and how uncomfortable it was to look over and see Rachel following us with her eyes. Parker hadn't helped, either. By the end of the afternoon he was so sullen he wasn't even going through the motions. He'd barely tipped his head in thanks to Warren and Leslie Fairchild when we said good-bye.

Despite my growing attraction to Logan, I'd been glad to leave.

Now, I trudged up the stairs behind Parker, mentally preparing myself for whatever was coming when we got to the War Room.

Closing the door behind me, I sat down at the little table in the center of the room. Parker was already there, leaning back with his legs splayed out, a stubborn light in his eyes.

Our dad glared at him. "Would you care to explain what that was all about?"

His voice was level, but I wasn't fooled. He was a dynamic, intense person, even when angry. I knew he was really mad when he didn't speak with emotion. It meant he was making an effort to keep it under wraps.

"Nothing," Parker answered, his expression defiant.

My dad leaned in until he was close to Parker's face. "That didn't look like *nothing*. You spent the afternoon ignoring Logan and Rachel instead of being friendly to them, which I might remind you, is *your job*."

"Maybe I don't want this job anymore," Parker said lazily.

"Parker . . . ," my mother warned.

He glanced over at me, and I remembered his words from the parking lot above the Cove: *We could just leave. Start over somewhere.*

He took a deep breath and looked away, like he was remembering, too.

"I'm sorry," he finally said. "It's just . . . Grace is my little sister. I know it's not biological or anything, but I don't like the idea of her having to come on to some guy for the con."

"It's business," our dad said. "We're in this together. Grace understands that."

Parker's nod was slow, his jaw clenched. "It won't happen again."

Our dad nodded. "Good." He pulled up a chair, turning his eyes on me. "Now, how did it go?"

I jumped in to fill the awkward beat of silence. "Logan and I are getting along well."

"How about the house and grounds?" He looked from me to Parker. "Notice anything unusual? Anything that might point to the location of the gold?"

"I went inside once," Parker said, "but Leslie Fairchild was dealing with the desserts and she started making conversation. Then she needed help carrying everything outside and that was the end of that."

My mom spoke up. "I got a quick look around when you were talking to Leslie and Warren about business."

I could only assume she was referring to the fake venture capital firm that was our excuse for moving to Playa Hermosa.

"And?" my dad prompted.

"I only got through a couple of the rooms, but I didn't see anything that would point to a vault or panic room big enough to hold all that gold."

"Did you look behind the paintings?" my dad asked. "Check the bookcases for false fronts?"

"As well as I could with fifty of the Fairchilds' closest friends wandering in and out of the house."

My dad rubbed the five o'clock shadow that had appeared on his jawline. "What about you, Grace?"

"I didn't get a look inside, but I did scope out the old carriage house in back."

"And?"

I shrugged. "It's just an empty room. The walls are wood with no insulation. I could see the sun shining through them, so there's definitely no place to hide a safe or panic room. It looks like it hasn't been used for ages." I hesitated, deciding to leave out my conversation with Rachel. It didn't really change anything. "I did spot cameras in the trees along that old driveway, though. The one that runs next to the grass."

He grabbed the sketch pad and handed it to me. "Show us."

I drew a rough sketch of the Fairchild property, feeling like a traitor with every stroke of the pen. There was the house, the lawn, the big driveway that segued into the narrow, old one leading to the carriage house.

"I spotted them here." I marked the cameras along the drive, finishing with the one right in front of the carriage house. "And here."

"Good." My dad nodded his approval. "Anything else?"

I shook my head, and my mother smiled knowingly. "Well, Logan really seems to like you. I'm sure you'll be invited back to the Fairchilds' soon."

For a split second, pride at a job well done overcame the guilt in my mind.

"How's it going with Leslie Fairchild?" my dad asked.

My mom laughed a little. "Let's just say I'll be volunteering, baking cookies, and covering up my cleavage for the foreseeable future."

"Whatever it takes," he said. "I'm having Allied quote us

a security system like Warren's. Everyone wants what everyone else has in a place like this. Allied will spill the details of the Fairchilds' system if it means a new client. I'm also working on how to transport and sell the gold once we find it. In the meantime, Warren's been generous with his recommendation. I'm expecting the club to approve my application any day. After that, it'll be easy to score more time with him on the course."

"Is he really . . ." I hesitated, not sure which word to use.

"Crazy?" my dad finished.

I nodded. "I guess."

He thought about it. "He has some irrational fears, but I don't think you'd notice if you weren't looking for it."

"Fears?" I pictured the friendly husband and father manning the grill at the Fairchilds'. "Like what?"

"He won't use a golf cart, for one. Insists on walking. He claims he likes the exercise, but he gets nervous when someone else drives by in a cart. And he stares at the electrical wires a lot."

"What do you mean?" my mother asked.

"Just what I said. I'll look over and he'll be standing there, staring at the power lines like he expects them to fall any second. It's a wonder he manages to go anywhere at all."

There was a strange ache in my chest at the thought of it. Warren Fairchild wasn't what I'd expected. He was just a regular guy, struggling with something dark inside himself, which made him more like the rest of us than I wanted to admit.

"Well!" My mom smiled. "It sounds like we're on track."

My dad nodded. "I'd say so. Details are the name of the game now. We need as many of them as possible. About the Fairchilds, their schedule, the house, the security system . . . anything and everything. As always, we don't know what will make a difference when the time comes to make our move. Until then, proceed as planned. And remember"—he leveled his gaze at Parker—"no one talks about the job outside of this room."

Parker nodded stiffly as everyone stood.

I tore out the sheet of paper depicting the layout of the Fairchild property and fed it through the shredder. Our parents were already locked in their bedroom by the time I followed Parker out of the War Room.

"Parker . . ." I didn't know what to say. I wanted to thank him for looking out for me, but all that came out was, "Everything will be all right."

He turned to face me. "Just think about what I said, okay?"

He didn't wait for my answer, just walked into his room and closed the door.

Nineteen

I was heading to my usual table on Monday, surprised to see Selena sitting alone, when Logan waved me over. Liam, David, and Raj were there, and Olivia, Harper, and Rachel. Olivia smiled as Harper moved over to make room. Rachel was the only one who looked less than thrilled. But it didn't matter. Too many of the others wanted me there now.

I glanced from Selena, head bent over a book, back to Logan's table. I didn't have a choice. Infiltrating Logan's group was what I'd been working toward since my first day at Playa Hermosa High. It was my part of the job and one of the most important components of the con.

But Selena was my friend. My only friend. And they didn't exactly grow on trees. Not for me, anyway.

I looked at Logan and mouthed the words *Hold on.*

Then I headed to Selena's table.

She looked up as I approached. "Hey!" She closed her book. "How was the bonfire?"

"Well, I have good news and I have bad news," I said, still standing. "Which do you want first?"

"Um . . ." Her forehead wrinkled with concern. "The good news?"

"The good news is: the bonfire didn't suck as much as I thought it would, although I still wish you would have come with me."

"Oh . . . okay," Selena said. "That *is* good. What's the bad news?"

I let her eyes slide to Logan's table. "They want me to sit with them now, and I'm not going without you."

"Wait a minute. You're asking me to sit with them?"

"No," I said. "I'm asking you to sit with me . . . while I sit with them."

She gave me a half smile. "Kind of sounds like the same thing."

"Well, it's not." I sighed. "Look, you're the best friend I have here. I don't want to lose that just because I'm getting to know other people. And they're not that bad."

She raised her eyebrows. "Not that bad, huh?"

"Okay, Rachel's kind of a bitch." I laughed. "But everyone else is really nice. Besides, Ashley and Nina aren't even here, and I'm pretty sure David's been checking you out."

"Now you're getting desperate."

"Look for yourself if you don't believe me," I said. "Although I don't recommend it."

"Right."

She turned in her seat to look at Logan's table. David was staring right at her. When she turned around, her cheeks were flaming.

"Thanks for that."

I grinned. "Anytime. Seriously, though. Will you come with me? Please?"

She stood with a sigh. "Okay, but I'm not promising it'll be permanent."

"No worries," I said. "This is a contract-free arrangement."

I tried to calm the butterflies in my stomach as I led the way to Logan's table. It wasn't about getting in with the group, about the con. I just wanted Logan to like me, and I wanted everyone to be nice to Selena.

But I shouldn't have worried. After a moment's surprise, everyone moved over and made room for both of us. I chose a seat next to Logan, and Selena took the one across from me.

"Where's Parker?" Rachel asked.

I looked around. "Um . . . I don't know. Probably studying or something."

She nodded as conversation resumed at the table. I breathed a quiet sigh of relief when I overheard David ask Selena what she was reading. Everything would be fine.

Logan smiled down at me. "Hey."

Heat rushed to my stomach as his denim-clad thigh brushed against mine under the table.

"Hey," I said. "Thanks for yesterday. I had fun."

"Me too. My parents like you."

"Really?"

"Yeah." He leaned in, so close I could smell the Mango Madness Snapple, fruity and tropical, on his breath. "So do I."

I smiled up at him and something warm and tremulous seemed to blossom between us.

After that, I was surprised how easy it was, sliding into Logan's group, sitting with them at lunch, hanging out by the BMW in the morning. Even more surprising was how much I liked them. Sure, they were spoiled and a little entitled—Rachel being one of the worse offenders—but they were nice and interesting, too. They welcomed Selena without question, and after some initial shyness, she seemed happy to have a new group of friends. Olivia teased her about her propensity for the clearance rack and Selena teased back about Olivia's shoes costing enough to feed ten third-world children. But it was all in good fun. Selena still said hello to Ashley in the halls and still walked to and from school with Nina, so I guessed the new arrangement hadn't impacted their less-than-wholehearted friendship.

Even the guys seemed happy to have us around, and Raj and Liam parted ways with Logan at the first bell so we could walk to class alone together. After Parker's intensity, it was nice to just be with someone. To be silent in someone's company without worrying that they were slip-sliding toward the depression and self-destruction that always seemed to lurk under Parker's surface.

Rachel was the only one who never quite warmed up, and I got tired of the icy gaze, the surreptitious glances, the flip of red hair. Tired of Rachel acting like I would go away if only she ignored me long enough. Then, just when I was ready to tell her to bite me, I would see that thing in her eyes, that sly and knowing *thing* that made my heart skip a beat for no good reason. A rush of fear would flood my body and I'd have to remind myself to take it easy. To be careful.

By the second week of October, my nerves were shot. Torn between annoyance and anxiety, I finally decided to err on the side of caution by trying one last time to win Rachel over. It might not make a difference to the con, but it would definitely make things more pleasant in the meantime.

Drastic times call for drastic measures and all that.

I made my move on a Friday, inviting Selena, Rachel, Harper, and Olivia over for a hangout and sleepover later that night. I half hoped they would say no—I was a little freaked about the idea of having them all in the house on Camino Jardin—but they were all over the idea. Olivia launched into a plan to give Selena a makeover (over Selena's very public protests), and Harper suggested a clothing swap (after glancing nervously at Rachel for approval).

Rachel just sat there.

"You'll come, too, right, Rach?" Olivia asked.

Rachel hesitated, glancing at me before turning her gaze on Olivia with a smile. "Definitely. Sounds like fun."

Later, when I was saying good-bye to Logan after making plans to get together Saturday night, he tucked a piece of hair behind my ear and smiled.

"You don't have to win Rachel over for me, you know. I don't care what she thinks."

"Yeah, but I do," I said. "You've all been friends a long time. I don't want to be the one who makes that awkward. I just don't get why she hates me so much."

Logan laughed. "She doesn't hate you. She's just . . . Rachel. It takes her a while to trust people. It's crazy, but she'll come around."

I gave him a hug good-bye, his words echoing through my mind. There was no way to tell him that Rachel wasn't crazy at all.

She had every reason not to trust me, even if she didn't know why.

Twenty

I raced home from school and did a quick check of the house. I knew it was irrational. We were careful. Had been trained to be careful. Other than Parker's lapse at the Cove, we never even spoke about the con outside of the War Room, and we definitely didn't leave anything incriminating lying around the house. Our work meant being up close and personal with our marks for weeks or even months. People dropped by, invited themselves over.

Anything could happen.

Still, I wanted to be sure. I'd never had people over before. Had never wanted to risk it. Working an angle meant knowing stuff about everyone else, not letting them in on the details of my own life. I'd gotten good at manipulating people into inviting me places instead.

So why, then, had I invited Selena and the others to my

house? Why risk it when I could have suggested a girls' night somewhere out on the town?

I didn't know, but I'd felt off ever since arriving in Playa Hermosa. Like I was slipping. Like there were details just beyond the periphery of my vision. Things I should be seeing, needed to see, but just couldn't. I was distracted. By Logan and my attraction to him. By Selena and the desire to have a true friend. By Parker and the distance that was wedging itself between us like an immoveable mountain.

I suddenly wanted to call the whole thing off, to tell Selena and the others that I'd changed my mind, something had come up, I wasn't feeling well. But it was too late. They were on their way. I'd just have to make the best of it.

I combed the living room, reassured by the photos of Parker and me with our parents. There weren't many—and they'd been carefully chosen, taken in places that couldn't be identified with all of us looking like we looked now—but it was enough to make the house look like a home.

I had finished my pass of the second floor and was checking the door to the War Room, making sure it was closed, when the first knock sounded from the front of the house. It was Selena, dropped off by her dad. Rachel, Harper, and Olivia followed, and I ushered them inside, trying to calm my nervousness as I showed them the first floor of the house. We ended up in the kitchen, where everyone settled around the island as I poured iced tea. I listened, taking it all in as they talked about school and college and the guys. It was nice. Normal. Even Rachel seemed comfortable, although there was no way to know if it was an act or if she was really coming around.

It was almost five when my mom showed up with take-out salads and sandwiches. I'd sent her a warning text about the sleepover, and she looked calm and unruffled as she unpacked the food. She was regaling us with stories about a woman at the gym who was in her eighties and ran the treadmill dressed head to toe in a hot pink Juicy sweat suit when I noticed Rachel's gaze fixed on something across the room.

I followed her eyes to the massive farmhouse-style dining table near the window. Or, more specifically, to the price tag still attached to one of its legs.

Shit.

I scanned the room surreptitiously, looking for other evidence of our all-new decor. But there was nothing. No way for Rachel to know that all our furniture had come from Mortise & Tenon in Hermosa Beach. Or that everything had been bought a week before we'd moved in, right down to the sheets on the beds, brand-spanking-new.

I needed to chill. Not let Rachel get under my skin.

It was too early for dinner, so we stuffed the food in the fridge and headed out to the pool. It was still warm, and Olivia and Selena wasted no time diving into the deep end. They were animated, splashing each other like kids and floating around on foam noodles, chatting nonstop while Harper sat on the edge, moving her legs idly through the water.

I snagged a lawn chair next to Rachel, clad in a tiny black bikini, her eyes invisible behind the lenses of huge gold-rimmed sunglasses. I didn't bother trying to make nice. It would only backfire with someone like her, so I just sat there, head tipped back to the sun, hyperaware of every move she made.

A few minutes later she spoke without turning to look at me. "You got your dining room table from Mortise and Tenon's."

I opened my eyes, momentarily thrown. "I don't know." I tried to sound bored. "My mom bought it. Our other one was old. No point paying to move it when we could just buy a new one here." I laughed. "Or that's what she told my dad anyway."

"My mom's a designer," Rachel said, turning to look at me. "One of her best friends owns M and T's. I practically grew up in that store. I know every stick of furniture there."

I forced my voice steady. "That's awesome. I don't know much about that stuff. My mom picks out all our stuff."

I thought Rachel was holding my gaze, but I couldn't be sure with the sunglasses. "Where's your restroom?" she finally asked.

"Down the hall by the kitchen, second door on your right."

She flashed me a smile. "Thanks."

She walked away, oozing confidence, her legs long, lean, and just the slightest bit tan. When she disappeared into the house, I closed my eyes and tipped my head back, trying to talk myself down.

A new dining table didn't mean anything. A whole houseful of new furniture—even purchased from the same store at the same time—didn't mean anything. Not in a place like Playa Hermosa, where people redecorated whenever they got bored. Rachel was just a spoiled rich girl, not some kind of all-knowing Confucius.

"Hey!" A voice startled me into a sitting position. It was Olivia, leaning back on the patio next to Selena and Harper. Their hair was still wet, but their bodies were almost dry. How long had they been out of the pool?

"You falling asleep on us?" Olivia asked.

"I guess so." I looked at the empty chair next to me and swung my feet onto the warm patio. "Is Rachel still in the bathroom?"

Olivia shrugged. "I have no idea."

I stood. "I'll go check on her."

I tried to look unhurried as I headed into the house, but all of a sudden, I couldn't quite catch my breath. The instincts I'd honed on the grift were screaming that something was wrong.

I walked through the French doors and made my way down the hall, scanning for signs of Rachel. For the first time since we'd moved to Playa Hermosa, I was a little creeped out by the house.

It was too quiet.

Parker was playing volleyball with the guys, and I had

no idea where my dad was. The bathroom door downstairs was open, the light off. I checked the kitchen, just to make sure Rachel wasn't topping off her iced tea, but she wasn't there, either.

"Rachel?" I continued to the staircase, stopping briefly when I heard the sound of running water.

My mom in the shower of the master bedroom.

My heart beat faster as I walked carefully up the stairs. The sound of running water got louder as I reached the top of the staircase, and I peeked into my bedroom, wondering if Rachel was snooping. It was empty.

I turned down the hall, careful not to make any noise, hoping to catch Rachel in the act of doing whatever she was doing that had brought her upstairs when there was a bathroom right inside the patio doors, second door on the right, just like I'd told her.

"Oh, hey," Rachel said, stepping out of the second-floor powder room.

"What are you doing up here?" I asked.

A triumphant expression crossed her face in the moment before she composed her features into a familiar mask of indifference. "I was just looking for the bathroom."

"Downstairs, second door on the right, remember?"

"Oh! I thought you meant the upstairs hall. Sorry about that." She headed for the staircase, turning back to look at me. "Aren't you coming?"

I nodded. "Yeah, I just need to get some more sunscreen. I'll see you outside."

She turned and made her way down the stairs.

When she was gone, I hurried down the hall, checking the doors to all the bedrooms. Everything was fine until I got to the War Room.

The door wasn't closed all the way.

I thought back, walking through my pre–girl's night prep. I'd closed the door to the War Room all the way. I was sure of it.

I hurried into the room, closing the door behind me. Then I crossed to the table where we'd had our strategy meeting. A wave of panic hit me as I bent to the trash can under the shredder.

It was empty. The pieces of paper, remnants of the map I'd drawn of the Fairchild property, were gone.

Twenty-One

"So . . . what's the deal with you and Logan?"

Olivia's question was innocent enough, but I couldn't stop my eyes from sliding to Rachel, sitting on the floor of the living room while she painted her toenails.

She looked up at me, the tiny brush poised over her pinky toe. "It's not like it's a secret, Grace. You've been hanging out together all week."

I searched her voice for a trace of emotion. Was she pissed? Jealous? I couldn't tell. Her tone was as cool as ever.

We'd eaten dinner in the living room while watching *Mean Girls*. I'd seen it more times than I could count with girls from New York to Seattle. It was classic sleepover fare, and as the movie rolled across the screen, I had flashes of pink bedrooms and blue bedrooms, girls in sweatpants and boxers, pizza and M&Ms. The memories were like ghosts, both close enough to touch and far enough away to make me wonder if they were real at all.

I'd watched Rachel carefully since discovering her breach of the War Room, but she didn't seem any different, and after a while, I convinced myself I was being paranoid. My mom had probably emptied the trash after our meeting. Rachel was just nosy, checking out our house to see how it compared to the other mansions on the peninsula. Even if she had gotten ahold of the map, it would be almost impossible to piece together from the shredder.

"So?" Olivia prompted, grabbing a handful of popcorn.

I shrugged, measuring my response. "Nothing's really happened."

Olivia snorted. "Sounds like that's about to change."

"What do you mean?" I asked her.

"Tomorrow night?"

I looked at her through narrowed eyes. "How do you know about that?"

She grinned. "I have my sources."

"What's happening tomorrow night?" Selena asked.

"Grace is going over to Logan's to watch a movie," Olivia said, putting *watch a movie* in air quotes.

I laughed and threw one of the sofa pillows at her. "Very funny."

"Everyone knows watching a movie is code for making out," Harper said, capping a bottle of sea-green nail polish and blowing on her fingernails.

My stomach fluttered as she said it, which was stupid. I'd

made out with plenty of guys, always in the name of the con. I'd never understood what all the fuss was about. It was fun. Nice. But it was no big deal. So why did my insides flip-flop at the idea of kissing Logan?

"Maybe she wants to make out with Logan." Rachel's voice was even as she wiggled her toes.

Selena cut a worried glance my way.

I met Rachel's eyes. "Would that be a problem? Because I'm not looking to stir things up."

As long as it didn't jeopardize the con, I didn't care if I stirred things up. I was just playing nice, making a last-ditch effort at connecting with Rachel before I gave up on her for good.

Rachel seemed to think about it. "Go for it. I don't want him anymore."

Anger rushed through my body like a renegade wave. She'd said it like Logan was some kind of toy to be tossed aside when Rachel outgrew him. Like he wasn't nice and smart and amazing. Like any girl wouldn't be lucky to have him.

"Your loss." I muttered the words before I could stop them from escaping my lips.

Her eyes flashed emerald fire. "If you say so."

The room descended into an awkward silence. Finally, Olivia moved to grab her phone. "We need music."

She was still playing around, looking for some new band she wanted us all to hear, when Rachel spoke. "Where's Parker?"

There was an air of forced boredom about the question. Like she knew I'd see through it. Like she wanted me to.

I shrugged. "I think he might be out with the guys."

She reached for the coffee table, grabbing one of the fashion magazines my mom kept there. "Maybe I should see if he wants to hang out tomorrow night," she said, idly turning pages. "You know, since it's shaping up to be a date night and everything." She looked up, leveling her eyes at me. "Would that be a problem? Because I'm not looking to stir anything up either."

"Not at all. Parker can do what he wants."

She smirked, turning her eyes back to the magazine as music blasted from Olivia's phone filling the room with electric guitar and synth so loud I felt like I was at a rave.

"You should try this one," Selena said, passing me a bottle of pale pink polish with a sympathetic smile. "It'll look nice on you."

I took it, grateful for the distraction as I twisted the cap off the bottle. So Rachel was stepping up her game with Parker. So what? It was good for the con. The more people we had in play, the better. At least one of us would be on Rachel's good side. And if anyone could handle her, it was Parker.

Still, something about it didn't sit right. I didn't like the idea of Rachel and Parker being tight. It wasn't jealousy. Blood or not, Parker was my brother. It was something else. A protective instinct usually reserved for the times when Parker got lost in his own darkness. He'd always been his own worst enemy, but now I suddenly felt like there might be another threat. Someone who could do even more damage to Parker—and to the rest of us—than he could do to himself.

Twenty-Two

I was sitting at the kitchen table the next morning, flipping through a magazine, when Parker came in holding a wet towel. He set it one of the chairs and headed for the fridge.

"What's with the vans in the driveway?" he asked.

"Allied is here talking to Dad about the new security system." I took in his wet hair and the fine coating of sand on his tan forearms. "Where have you been?"

"Surfing with the guys." His smile was a little sheepish. "I actually kind of like it, although I'll have to get a wet suit if we stay here much longer."

"I'm glad." It was nice to see him enjoy something, and I had a glimpse of him the way he might have been, minus the foster homes and suicide attempts. Just a regular guy, surfing with his friends and scamming girls, applying to colleges and backpacking through Europe.

He pulled out a carton of orange juice and took a swig from it despite the fact that our mom had told him it was disgusting more times than I could count.

"The girls went home?" he asked when he'd drained half of the juice.

I nodded.

He closed the fridge. "How did it go?"

I thought about Rachel's possible breach of the War Room, but it didn't really matter. I didn't have any proof. "Fine. I don't think Rachel's going to come around, but everyone else is good."

"I've got Rachel covered," he said. "She sent me a text this morning asking if I wanted to hang tonight."

"Are you going to?" I asked him.

He looked surprised. "Well . . . yeah. I mean, she's one of the players. As Dad would say, it's my job." He grabbed the wet towel and headed for the stairs. "I'm going to hit the shower."

I sat there, a funny, fluttery feeling in my stomach. *This is why we're here*, I reminded myself. *To get close to Logan and everyone else in his social circle. To learn all we can about them.* Parker was right. We all had jobs to do. We couldn't afford to let personal feelings—good or bad—jeopardize the con.

I headed for the stairs. I had homework to do before my date with Logan. Plus, I needed to find something to wear. It seemed frivolous in the grand scheme of things, but my job was to make Logan like me. To reel him in, as my dad would say. The right outfit would only help.

That's what I told myself anyway.

I glanced into the living room on my way up the stairs. My dad was sitting on the sofa with two of the guys from Allied, pouring over a large blueprint of the house.

"We can also put cameras here and here," one of the men said, touching the paper with his index finger. "Those are the most likely places for a breach."

"I think Warren said he had sensors on some of the windows, too," my dad said. He glanced innocently at the blueprints like he was trying to make sense of them. I watched as he let the silence sit. Waited for the men from Allied to fill it.

"Exactly," the second guy said. "On all of the first-floor windows, in fact."

My dad nodded. "That's right. I'd forgotten. Let's do the same here then."

I continued up the stairs, torn between admiration and disgust. They were talking about Logan's house. The one that belonged to his sweet mother and his sick father. Nice people who'd probably never hurt anyone. Who hadn't cheated or stolen their way to wealth. Who'd just had the good fortune to inherit it, and from the looks of things weren't the worst people in the world to have it.

I took a shower so my hair could dry before my date with Logan, then settled onto my bed with my laptop. Looking at the empty folders on my desktop was weird, even after all this time, but it was standard protocol to wipe our computers after each job. I didn't understand the technicalities. Computers weren't really my thing. But as soon as we finished a job, my dad took our computers, installed a disc, and deleted everything we'd accumulated from our hard drives. Letters, essays, flyers for Drama Club or awareness posters for the Multicultural Diversity Society. All gone like we'd never been part of it at all.

The schoolwork at Playa Hermosa High wasn't as challenging as the work I'd had on the East Coast last year, but I still had two papers to write before Monday, and for a while I forgot all about the con, lost in my essay on *The Scarlet Letter*, glad I'd already read it. The light was starting to fade, blocked by the house as the sun moved over the water, when I heard the humming.

I set my laptop aside and walked to the window, following the sound. It was the man next door, and this time I had a clear shot of his face. I couldn't help being surprised. I'd gotten used to seeing him in shadow, seeing only pieces of his face. Gotten used to the idea that he was being purposefully coy. Which was crazy.

But now he was right there, sitting on a deck chair facing our house, his head tipped back to catch the fading sunlight. His head was bare, wisps of gray hair barely covering his scalp. Although his face was moderately lined, I couldn't tell how old he was. Fifty? Sixty? I couldn't be sure, but I took in the details, cataloging and storing them for later without knowing why.

His body was trim and toned, pale legs emerging from beneath plaid swim trunks and wiry, muscular arms pulling at the white T-shirt that covered his torso. His jawline was slightly shadowed—he hadn't shaved in a while—and his nose was a little crooked, like it had been broken a couple of times and never quite set right.

He seemed at peace, a small smile playing at his lips as he hummed a tune I didn't recognize. It sounded like the others I'd heard him singing, with the same smoky undertone, and I found myself wishing I could hear the words. Like they would offer some kind of commentary—some kind of message— about what was happening with the con, with Parker, with my feelings for Logan.

The back of my neck tingled, and I suddenly had the feeling that he was looking right at me, studying me from behind his sunglasses. That everything he did was deliber- ate, as if he could somehow know I would follow the sound of his humming at that exact moment. That I would come to the window. That I would even care.

Twenty-Three

The gate was closed when I turned in to Logan's driveway. I pulled up to the little box and rolled down the window of the Saab, not sure what to do. I was about to start pressing random buttons when Logan's voice came over the intercom.

"I'll buzz you in. Just pull up in front of the garage."

I didn't have time to respond before the iron gates sprang to life. I glanced once more at the keypad, taking a mental snapshot of it to draw for my dad later, and started up the driveway. The sun hung low in the sky, setting the sea on fire in the distance. The glare produced bursts of light through the trees as I wound my way toward the house. It made it hard to get a good look at the property, and I squinted even behind my sunglasses, trying to keep my eyes focused on the driveway.

Finally the house came into view, and I maneuvered the

car beside a white Range Rover in front of one of the three garage doors. Logan met me on the porch, lined with pumpkins and strung with a garland of autumn leaves. He looked happy to see me, and my heart fluttered a little at the sight of him, barefoot in well-worn jeans and a V-neck tee that was loose enough to be casual but fitted enough to show off his lean muscles.

He smiled. "Sorry about that. I have to keep the gates closed when my parents aren't home."

"It's fine," I said. "Your parents aren't here?"

He reached out a hand as I climbed the steps to the porch. I took it, and a rush of warmth spread from my fingers to the rest of my body.

"They had a dinner. Some kind of charity thing." He stopped, looking a little worried. "Is that okay? Because if you're not comfortable being here alone, we can hit up a movie or something."

I was touched that he'd ask. I was used to doing things that needed to be done. Whether or not I wanted to wasn't usually part of the equation.

"It's fine. As long as they don't mind."

He opened the front door and led me into the foyer. "Not at all. I told them you were coming and that we were going to watch a movie."

"Great."

He closed the door. "Have you eaten?"

I nodded.

"Does that mean you're too full for popcorn?"

I laughed. "Is there such a thing?"

He grinned, leading me toward the kitchen. "You're perfect."

"Can I do anything to help?" I asked.

"Nah. I've got this covered." He pulled out a stool at the big kitchen island, indicating that I should take a seat, and went to work opening cupboards, choosing a big pot and a bottle of oil from the pantry.

"Are you making popcorn or a four-course meal?" I teased, watching him.

He stopped moving. "Don't tell me you've never had real popcorn?"

"And by real you mean . . . ?"

He set the pot on the stove. "Not nuked in the microwave."

I thought about it. "I've had it at the movie theater."

He shook his head. "Doesn't count. Now I consider it my duty to initiate you in the ways of real popcorn."

"Great," I laughed. "A life skill I can really use."

"Trust me," he said, "you'll use this way more than trig."

He moved easily around the kitchen, pouring oil into the hot pan and swirling it in the bottom, waiting for it to get hot before pouring in the popcorn kernels. He put the lid on the pan and turned his attention back to me.

"So do you miss it?" he asked. "San Francisco?"

I had to think about it. Both because we hadn't really come from San Francisco and because, here with Logan in the warm kitchen, my other life seemed very far away.

"Not really." I searched my memory for things I'd learned about San Francisco during my research. "It was pretty, but crowded. Playa Hermosa feels . . ." I expected him to fill in the blank. People usually did. But he just looked at me, regarding me with interest. Like he had all the time in the world to listen. "Apart," I finally finished.

He shook the pan a little as the sound of kernels popping against the pan rang into the kitchen. "Apart?"

"Just . . . separate from everything else, I guess."

"And you like being separate?" he asked.

"Sometimes," I admitted.

He smiled a little, his eyes never leaving mine. "Me too."

The corn was popping full speed, and I watched with fascination as it lifted the lid from the pan, the time between pops slowly dwindling. Logan turned off the heat and grabbed an oven mitt, turning the popcorn out into a big bowl he'd set next to the stove.

"And what about your friends?" he asked, dropping a stick of butter into the still hot pan. "Do you miss them?"

The butter sizzled as I tried to regain my footing. Guys usually liked to talk about themselves, and since the only guys I'd ever dated had been part of a con, I'd been happy to let them. This was different. I had to provide details. Had to make things up about San Francisco and school and friends that hadn't really been friends. And I had to do it with a straight face while looking into Logan's mossy eyes. Of course, I knew I'd be lying on the job. Knew I'd do a lot of it before the con was over and we moved on to another town.

But now, looking into Logan's face, his eyes so attentive, so *interested*, it somehow felt more wrong.

"Not as much as you might think. When you know you're going to move, you try not to get too attached. To anything." It was more true than I wanted to admit. More true than I should have admitted.

He nodded as he poured the melted butter over the popcorn. Then he threw in a handful of salt and tossed it all together with a rubber spatula before pushing the bowl toward me.

"I await your verdict."

I plucked a couple of pieces from the bowl and popped them into my mouth. It was perfect, covered with a thin coat of salt and butter and not at all dry.

He raised his eyebrows. "Well?"

"Amazing," I said. "Completely different from theater or microwave popcorn."

"Exactly!" He opened the door to the fridge. "What can I get you to drink?"

We chose sodas, and he picked up the bowl of popcorn and led me upstairs to the media room. I expected it to be lavish, fitted with a big-screen TV and movie projector and those fancy chairs that lean back, but it was just a cozy room, its walls lined with bookshelves, the floors covered in what looked to be old, intricately designed overlapping rugs.

"Have a seat." He indicated the overstuffed sectional in the middle of the room, and I sat down, setting my soda on a coaster on the coffee table. "What kind of movie do you feel like watching?"

We spent twenty minutes browsing the Fairchilds' DVD collection before settling on *Almost Famous*. We'd both seen it, but it was one of my favorites, and I had a feeling that sitting next to Logan for two hours was going to make concentrating difficult. Better to go with something I'd already seen.

He sat close to me, the bowl of popcorn resting on both our legs, his bare arm brushing against mine. I had to fight to keep a blank expression while inside, a fire began to smolder. I wondered if he felt it, too. If I was just imagining the chemistry between us. But about halfway through the movie, he lifted the popcorn off our legs. His T-shirt strained against his broad shoulders as he leaned forward to set the bowl on the coffee table. When he sat back, he angled his body toward me and took my hand, all pretense of watching the movie gone.

"Grace . . ." He looked into my eyes, and I felt his hand tremble over mine. He opened my fingers, lifting my hand to his mouth and touching his lips to the tender skin of my palm. I had to fight not to gasp as heat rushed through my body like mercury. "I really, really like you."

"I really . . . really like you, too." The words caught in my throat a little, tripping over the desire building in my veins.

He lowered my hand, still holding it as he leaned in, tension pulling between us like a velvet cord. Part of me wanted to run. To get away before it was too late. I think I knew that once his lips touched mine, I'd be lost. But the other part of me was screaming for him. And it didn't matter anyway. A second later his mouth was on mine, and then there was no room for thought. No room for plotting, for the con, for plans of escape.

His lips were gentle at first, his kiss almost chaste. Then his tongue flicked against my lips, sending a lick of fire through my insides. I opened to him like the jasmine that bloomed on the peninsula under the light of the moon. He pulled me closer as he explored my mouth, holding my face in his palms like he wanted to be sure I was real, wanted to be sure I wouldn't disappear.

But I was disappearing. Melting into him, losing myself in his kiss, in the feel of his hands as they moved down my neck, his fingers twining themselves in my hair. For a while there was nothing in the world but us, floating in a universe of our own making. When the fog finally lifted, it was only because the credits were rolling on the movie, the music a little too loud.

I was lying on the sofa, Logan's body stretched next to mine. We were both fully clothed. We'd done nothing but kiss, although that seemed too mild a word to describe how we'd spent the last two hours, how it had made me feel. He dropped a kiss on my nose as he reached for the remote, silencing the TV. Then he pulled me close again, lying next to me on the couch.

Emotion surged through my body as I laid my head against his chest, listening to the soft *thump-thump* of his heart.

"You're shaking," Logan said, hugging me tighter, kissing the top of my head.

"Am I?" I hadn't realized it, had been too caught up in the raw feeling swirling through my body.

"Yeah," he said. "Are you cold?"

"No."

"Then what is it?" he asked.

I shook my head. "I don't know."

He was silent for a minute. "I'm not playing games with you, Grace. You know that, don't you?"

I nodded against his chest.

He pulled back a little, looking down into my face. "I've never felt so . . . drawn to someone. You know?"

"I know," I whispered.

"I can't explain it, but it's like as soon as I saw you, I just knew."

"Knew what?"

He smiled a little. "That I wanted you, of course."

I felt the corners of my mouth lift.

"So what about it?" he asked. "Will you be mine, Grace?"

Nodding was almost a reflex. A formality. I was already his.

Later, we leaned against the Saab, lingering as we said good-bye against the sound of the waves crashing on the cliffs below. I was still a little fuzzy around the edges, like nothing existed beyond the sudden promise of our feelings for each other.

Reality didn't hit me until I was halfway home, navigating

the dark and windy roads of the peninsula. I had agreed to be Logan's girlfriend, and while my mom and dad would be pleased—it would only make getting information on the Fairchilds easier—I knew it wasn't that simple.

Logan made me forget who I was. Why I was here. And if I needed proof of how dangerous that was, I didn't need to look any further than the time we'd spent together. Because while I'd been wrapped up in Logan, I hadn't done a single thing to case the Fairchild estate.

Twenty-Four

The house was dark when I pulled up in front. It wasn't until I stepped into the foyer that I saw the flickering blue light of the TV coming from the family room. I hesitated, guessing at my chances of making it upstairs without being noticed. I wasn't up for conversation. Wasn't up for giving an account of my night with Logan. Right now, it still belonged to the two of us. Once I let my mom and dad and Parker in on all the details, it would be just another move on the game board. I wondered if its magic would hold up to the harsh light of day.

But I couldn't avoid them. Whoever was up was waiting for me to get home. Trying to sneak past them would only look suspicious. I left my bag on the table in the hall and headed for the family room.

Parker was on the sofa, his shadow backlit against the TV.

"How was it?" he asked without turning around.

"Fine." I dropped next to him on the couch. "How was hanging out with Rachel?"

I kept my tone even, hoping Parker wouldn't guess I was evading the question.

He reached for the remote and muted the TV. "Uneventful, more or less."

"More or less?"

He looked around the room, like he wanted to make sure no one was around.

"Don't," I warned, wanting to head off anything that might be against the rules outside the War Room.

He nodded. "I can't quite get a handle on her."

I didn't know whether to be relieved or even more worried than before. On the one hand, at least I wasn't the only one having trouble with Rachel Mercer. But if she was being careful around Parker, too, it could only mean she didn't trust any of us.

"She invited you to hang out," I reminded him.

"I know," he said. "Which is why it's weird." We sat in silence for a minute until he spoke again. "So? What about Logan?"

I shrugged. "It was nice. We made popcorn, watched a movie."

His look was knowing. "That's not what I'm asking."

I took a deep breath, casting a glance at the stairs. "Parker . . ."

We couldn't talk in the family room, and Parker knew it. But if I was honest with myself, I'd have to admit that I was relieved. Relieved that being outside the War Room gave me an excuse to keep private the details of my time with Logan, even if it was just until tomorrow.

He nodded, his jaw tight.

"We'll talk tomorrow," I promised, rising from the couch. And we would, whether I wanted to or not. Parker wouldn't be the only one asking questions about my night with Logan. I looked at the TV, still on mute. "You coming up?"

He kept his eyes on the screen. "In a bit."

"Okay, good night."

"Night, Grace."

I made my way upstairs, trying to stuff down the lump in my throat. For the first time since we'd become family, I was keeping things from Parker. They were piling up between us, making it hard for us to see each other like we used to. Now we were peering around our secrets, around all the things left unsaid, trying to figure out if there was still someone on the other side. I hated it. I just didn't know what to do about it.

I threw on pajamas, washed my face, and brushed my teeth. Then I climbed into bed and turned off the light. The night was mild, the curtains billowing at the open window. I breathed in the moist brine that seemed to hang in the air on the peninsula and thought of Logan. Was he lying in bed, thinking about me, too?

I replayed every moment of the night, from his grin when I'd arrived to the first time his lips touched mine to the heat that had blossomed between us on the sofa. I tossed and turned, remembering the feel of his body, the look in his eyes—part desire, part tenderness—as he'd gazed down at me.

I told myself that it was only natural to get worked up. I was a sixteen-year-old girl. Logan was hot. And nice. It felt good to be held. To be kissed. To be touched. It was biology, that's all.

"He's just a guy," I whispered into the dark. A reminder. "Just a mark."

Twenty-Five

"Now we've got something to work with," my dad said, a familiar gleam in his eye.

It was Sunday morning, and we were sitting at the table in the War Room, catching up on the progress each of us had made during the previous week.

"What did you find out about the security system?" Parker asked.

My dad unrolled a blueprint of the Fairchild house. "The gate's intercom system is monitored by live security. There are cameras in the driveway and at all four exterior corners of the house, also monitored by Allied. The keypads at the front, back, and side doors have to be disarmed within thirty seconds of a breach. The ground-floor windows are also wired, but a breach from one of those gives us two minutes to disarm."

"Two minutes?" I asked. "Why so long?"

"If someone who lives in the house forgets their key, they can get through one of the windows if it's unlocked, but they'd need longer to get to the keypad to disarm the system," he explained.

"Can't we just clip the line on the alarm?" Parker asked.

He shook his head. "It automatically goes off if the line is cut."

Parker drummed his fingers on the table. "Is anything else in the house wired? Any sign of a safe or panic room?"

"I told the installation consultants from Allied that we had a large safe we'd like protected. Told them whatever Warren had was fine. They said as far as they knew, nothing but the doors and windows were wired at the Fairchild estate."

My mom's forehead wrinkled a little like it did when she was thinking hard about something. "But if nothing else is wired, where is the gold?"

"It's there. Warren probably just wants it off the grid," my dad said.

Parker laughed. "Can't say that I blame him. If I had twenty million in gold sitting around, I wouldn't want the dog to know about it, let alone a bunch of experienced security guys."

My dad nodded. "On the plus side, getting onto the grounds and into the house shouldn't be too difficult, and if Warren has kept the location of the gold a secret from Allied and everyone else, once we find it, taking it shouldn't be a problem."

Parker stared down at the map. "Where are the cameras in the driveway?"

"Not sure," my dad said. "Since we don't have a long drive here, I wasn't able to use my keeping-up-with-the-Joneses act to pinpoint the locations, although we have a few of them from Grace's recon at the party. The rest should be easy enough to figure out, especially with Grace visiting Logan. Until then, we should assume they're evenly spaced from the gate to the house."

My mom turned to me. "Speaking of visiting Logan, how did it go last night, honey?"

I steadied my voice, calling up the explanation I'd been rehearsing all day in my mind. "Fine. I mean, we went straight to the kitchen, made popcorn, and watched a movie. I didn't get a chance to see much, and I didn't want to be too suspicious my first time there."

She smiled. "I trust that you know how to handle Logan."

Her words made me feel sick, but I just nodded, hoping the false calm on my face was believable.

"What about the keypad?" my dad asked. "Did Logan disarm the system after he let you in?"

"He did, but I couldn't make out the code over his shoulder."

A lie. I had been too preoccupied with the prospect of spending time with Logan to even try.

My dad nodded. "How did it go with Logan? Is he interested?"

"I'd say so," I said, bracing myself to tell the one truth I had no choice but to tell. "He asked me to be exclusive."

I caught Parker's clenched jaw in the moment before my mom's eyes lit up.

"You worked him fast," she said.

There was admiration in her voice, and I couldn't help wishing we were some other mother and daughter. One where her excitement over Logan's asking me to be his girlfriend was about being happy for me, not gaining access to information that would help us steal from him.

"That's excellent news." My dad beamed. "Now you'll have plenty of access to the house and grounds."

I nodded, not trusting myself to say anything.

"How's it coming with the night guard at Allied?" my dad asked Parker.

Parker shrugged. "I can only assume he's pissed, which is just how we want it."

I wondered what they were talking about, but if my dad wanted it to be common knowledge, he would have explained. Until then, it was none of my business.

"And Rachel Mercer?" my dad asked him. "Your mother said you saw her last night?"

"Yeah, we went to eat at Mike's in town," Parker said.

"And?" my dad prompted.

Parker shrugged. "She seems interested—interested enough to text me to hang out—but she's cagey, too."

"Cagey how?" my mom asked.

"Just . . . difficult to pin down. She asks more questions than most girls. Doesn't want to talk about herself much."

My mom laughed. "Not all women are self-centered, Parker."

If she expected him to protest, she was disappointed. He just leveled his gaze at her without a word. Her eyes turned flinty in the awkward silence that followed.

"We don't really need Rachel anyway," my dad finally said. "Grace is in with Logan. That's what we wanted. Just play it cool with Rachel and we should be fine." He looked at each of us. "Anything else? Any concerns?"

No one said anything.

My dad stood. "Good. Keep doing what you're doing." He looked at me, his gaze steady. "We need that key code, Grace—and we need the location of the gold."

Twenty-Six

"How are things really going with Logan?"

My mom's voice was muffled from inside the dressing room. It was later that day, and I was helping her choose some new things to wear around Leslie Fairchild. My mom didn't really need me—her taste was impeccable—but shopping was one of the ways we spent what she called "quality time" together. I didn't mind. It made me feel normal, and I was always reminded that she was smart and fun to be with. I could have done worse.

"They're fine, just like I said." I used my fingertip to trace circles on the upholstered bench outside the dressing room. I didn't want to talk about Logan. Not like this. Not right now.

"Come on, Gracie. It's no fun without details." She stepped out of the dressing room wearing a turquoise wrap blouse. "Yes/no?"

"There are no details," I said. "We've only kissed." I studied the blouse. "The color might be a little too South Beach."

She nodded. "Agreed." She headed back into the dressing room. "Is he a good kisser?"

I groaned. "Seriously, Mom?"

She laughed. "Don't be a prude. I'm just curious."

"Yes, he's a good kisser," I sighed. "Now can we drop it?"

"Fine." She emerged from the dressing room again, this time wearing a navy blouse with a mandarin collar. "Better?"

I nodded my approval. "Much."

We spent two more hours trolling stores in the mall before stopping for lunch at a faux Italian bistro. Logan texted me, telling me that he couldn't wait to see me on Monday, and I spent the rest of the day with my pulse running a little faster, caught up in a manic euphoria while I counted the hours until I could see him again.

But when I woke up Monday morning, all my optimism was gone. Dawn cast too bright a light on my excitement. I had work to do, especially now that I had a reason to be at the Fairchild house. I couldn't afford to be sidetracked. It was okay that it felt good to be with Logan. I couldn't help that. But I had to be disciplined, put it aside so that I could focus on my part of the job. It was easier to accept with some space between us, without the fresh memory of his mouth on mine, the way he seemed to see all my secrets and not care at all.

I was digging through my dresser, looking for a belt, when I saw the small wooden memento box at the back of the drawer. Paranoia and guilt had gotten the better of me, and I'd returned the ID card from Chandler High to the box at the end of last week. Now I lifted the box out of the drawer and opened the lid, looking down at the card.

Carrying it was dangerous. Worse than dangerous; it was stupid. Because it didn't change anything. Didn't make real the life I'd led in Arizona, despite my feelings to the contrary. But now I wanted it for a different reason. Not to make real the life I'd led there, but to remind me why I'd been there in the first place. To remind me why we went anywhere. Not to make friends. Not to fall in love.

To con people out of their money. To sustain a lifestyle that, while strange, was all I had. All I knew.

I lifted the ID out of the box, slipped it into the pocket of the short floral dress I'd bought with Selena, and headed downstairs to meet up with Parker for school.

He greeted me with a tight "hey" and we headed to the Saab. I wasn't surprised by his attitude. I'd known it was coming ever since my revelation in the War Room that Logan and I were official. Parker wouldn't say anything about it in front of our parents—not after his last altercation with my dad. But we would be alone on the drive to school. I knew the questions were coming.

We'd barely pulled away from the curb when he started up. "Why didn't you tell me?" he asked. "About Logan?"

I sighed. "We were outside the War Room when I came home. I was just being careful."

"You could have told me you were official. It's not a

breach in and of itself."

I glanced over at him. "No, but this is," I said softly.

"We're in the car."

I shook my head. "It doesn't matter." I couldn't even say it was against the rules. Not out loud.

"Whatever."

"Why are you acting like this?" I asked.

He gripped the steering wheel so tightly that his knuckles were white. "I just don't want you to feel . . . pressured."

"Pressured?"

"To do anything you don't want to do."

I turned my face to the window. How could I tell him that I'd felt pressured to do everything up until I'd met Logan? That getting to know Logan was the one thing I'd done because I wanted to?

"It's not like that," I said, trying to be cryptic. "He's a perfect gentleman. It's not like he's going to pressure me into doing anything."

Parker turned into the school parking lot. "It's not him I'm worried about."

I knew he was talking about our parents, but there was only so much I could say outside the War Room. "No one's pressuring me. I'm just . . . getting to know him, that's all."

"Whatever, Grace."

He pulled into our regular spot next to Logan's BMW and got out of the car, walking past Rachel without a word. She watched him go, a mixture of surprise and annoyance on her face. He hadn't even acknowledged her.

Twenty-Seven

I was still rattled when I slid into my desk in AP Euro. Parker was on the edge. More on the edge than I'd seen him since he was first adopted into the family. He was always volatile. But he was also smart. Everything he did was calculated, even the bad stuff, the scary stuff.

This was different.

I had the feeling even Parker didn't know what he would do next. That he was operating purely on impulse, his anger and resentment dictating everything he said and did. Dangerous for anyone on the grift, but most dangerous of all for Parker.

And for those of us in it with him.

I told myself he was just overworked. He needed a break, but he would hold it together until after the Playa Hermosa con. I was sure of it. I slipped a hand into my pocket, fingering the ID card. *It's just a job*, I thought. *Just another job.*

"Where was the fire this morning?" Rachel said, taking her seat.

I looked up, taking in the artfully messy braid, the barely there makeup, the casual-chic ankle pants.

"Fire?" I repeated.

"Someone was in a hurry," she said. "Parker looked pissed."

I rolled my eyes, trying to make light of Parker's attitude. "More like pissy. He's not exactly a morning person."

She nodded, digging in her bag for her notebook and pen. "I heard about you and Logan." She turned and flashed me a smile. It almost looked genuine. "Congratulations."

"Thanks," I said. "He's a good guy."

Her nod was thoughtful. "He is."

Mr. Stein stepped to the front of the class. "Good morning," he said, picking up a stack of papers from his desk. "Today I'll be announcing teams for the first semester project."

I looked at Rachel in surprise. "Project? What project?"

"It's in the syllabus," she said. "It's a third of our grade."

I dug the syllabus out of my binder. AP Euro wasn't supposed to have projects. It was a lecture class, its sole purpose to prepare us for the AP test. That meant notes, not projects.

But there it was, right on the syllabus. One project each semester, worth a third of our grade, just like Rachel said.

Mr. Stein walked across the front of the classroom, handing out pieces of paper to the kids in the first row with instructions for them to pass it back. He explained that we would be grouped into teams before choosing one of three possible projects from the sheet. Then he started naming pairs. By the time he got to me, I knew Rachel and I would be assigned to work together; everyone was teamed up with the person sitting next to them. Way to be original, Mr. Stein.

"Grace Fontaine and Rachel Mercer."

I looked over at Rachel and gave her a wry smile. Now that I was in with Logan, I didn't need her. But she still made me nervous. She was nosy and way too curious. I'd planned to just avoid her, focus on Logan and the others during the times when Rachel and I were forced to be in each other's company. That was going to be a lot more difficult paired up on the AP Euro project.

"Want to exchange numbers?" I asked her on the way out of the classroom. "So we can talk about the project?"

"Sure," she said.

She didn't seem happy about it. I wanted to tell her the feeling was mutual. Instead I recited my number and entered hers into my phone.

"Any idea what you want to do?" she asked as people shoved past us on their way to their next classes.

I glanced down at the sheet. "I don't know. Maybe the historical board game?"

She nodded. "Fine."

"Great," I said. "I'll text you so we can get together."

I left her standing there as I headed down the hall. Letting someone—anyone—walk away first made you the submissive party. And not being submissive to Rachel was a matter of principle.

I met up with Selena at lunch, watching with a smile as she took her position at the table next to David. It was nice to see her happy, to see the light in her eyes when David looked at her. I considered it a victory. Maybe after we left Playa Hermosa, Selena would stay friends with the group. Maybe she would be a little less alone than the girl I'd met reading *White Oleander* that first day.

I sat next to Logan, my pulse jumping a little when he took my hand under the table and leaned in to kiss me on the cheek. I knew what I needed to do. Knew I should listen to the conversation going on around me for information we might use later. Who was going out of town, who'd been woken up by the security team outside their window, whose parents had had a fight about money. It could all come in handy, and it could all be casually revealed at any moment.

But I was too distracted by Logan's proximity, the smell of his cologne, the sound of his voice as he told me about a giant wave he'd caught before school. I reached into the pocket of my dress with my free hand, feeling for the ID, needing the reminder. The pocket was big, meant to be slouchy. At first, I thought the ID was hiding in a corner, that it had slipped into one of the folds of my dress. I fought a surge of panic as I fumbled around the pocket, trying to grasp the plastic edge of the card. Finally, I had to acknowledge the truth.

It was gone.

Twenty-Eight

Wednesday night Parker and I headed to Logan's house. His parents were out again—another charity event—and he had invited everyone over to hang out.

Parker and I rode in silence, the tension that had been building since we got to Playa Hermosa heavy between us. He hadn't said any more about my relationship with Logan, but he didn't have to. I knew why he was sullen, why I would sometimes catch him looking at Logan when he wasn't paying attention. I wondered if anyone else noticed his jittery energy, the way he tapped his foot and bounced his leg when we were hanging out, like he couldn't wait to get away. Did Rachel notice how distracted he was when she talked to him, the way he seemed unable—or unwilling—to look her in the eye? Like she was so far off his radar she didn't even warrant eye contact? Then again, maybe that was a turn-on for someone like Rachel, who never had to work for anything.

The group seemed to read Parker's attitude as moodiness, and while they hadn't shut him out yet, I was starting to wonder how long they'd put up with him.

We turned onto Logan's road, and Parker pulled up to the security gate, waiting for Logan to buzz us in. A few seconds later the gates swung open, and Parker eased down the driveway. This time I scanned the trees for cameras, noting the blinking red lights spaced at forty-foot intervals along the drive.

When the house came into view, I saw that the space in front of the garage was already lined with cars. There was a BMW, a Mercedes, an Audi, and a Saab similar to the one Parker and I shared. I'd offered to give Selena a ride, but she'd been dropped off early by her dad, who had insisted on meeting Logan's parents before he would allow Selena to come over.

Parker pulled next to a red BMW and we got out of the car. I expected to hear music thumping from the house, but it was quiet.

I led Parker to the front door, where we waited for Logan to respond to our knock. He appeared a minute later in khaki shorts and a navy button-down with the sleeves rolled to the elbow. He looked both pulled together and casual, and I had a sudden attack of insecurity, wondering if the long skirt and drapey tank I'd worn were too much. Then his eyes lit up at the sight of me, and all my worry disappeared.

"There you are!" He took my hand and pulled me inside, wrapping me in a hug. When he pulled away, he kept one arm possessively around my shoulder. I stuffed down a rush of pure unadulterated happiness as he gave Parker a casual handshake. "Glad you could make it, man."

Parker nodded. "Thanks for the invite."

Logan shut the door and turned to the alarm keypad. I caught Parker's eye as he tried to glance casually over Logan's shoulder. A second later he gave a small shake of his head, and I knew he hadn't gotten the code. I was both disappointed and relieved.

Logan led us upstairs. I didn't hear anything until we turned the corner into the media room. Music played softly from a sound system set into the wall while Rachel, Harper, and Olivia sat on one of the sofas, talking quietly. Across the room, Selena was playing Cards Against Humanity with Raj, David, and Liam. I don't know what I'd expected. Rich kids raging? Doing drugs? Puking on the floors?

Rachel glanced up at me. I avoided her eyes, thinking about the lost ID.

"Can I get you a beer?" Logan asked.

"Sure," Parker said.

I nodded. "Thanks."

Logan crossed to a refrigerator underneath the bar and pulled out two bottles of Corona. We were all underage, but that didn't mean anything. Not in Playa Hermosa and not anywhere else I'd gone to school. Alcohol was a given at high school parties, and as parties went, this one was pretty mild.

Logan gave us our beers, and Parker ambled over to Selena and the guys.

"Want to play Cards?" Logan asked.

I loved Cards Against Humanity, but I couldn't keep avoiding Rachel. It only made my paranoia worse. Besides, she might not have found the ID at all. True, I'd had it when I went into AP Euro. But we'd been in the hall afterward. People had been shoving past us on their way to class. It could have fallen out of my pocket, been swept up in the mountains of stuff that collected under lockers and behind trash cans every day of the week in any high school.

"Actually, I think I'll talk to the girls for a bit." I smiled. "You go ahead. I know where to find you."

He leaned down, touched his lips gently to mine, and a shiver worked its way up my spine.

"Get a room!" Raj called out.

We laughed, and I headed over to the sofa where Rachel and the other girls were sitting.

Olivia smiled up at me. "Hey, Grace."

"Hey. What's up?"

"We were just talking about prom. We're fighting an uphill battle against a Hearts in Atlantis theme. You should join the committee." She turned to Rachel. "Right, Rach?"

Rachel attempted a smile. "We can use all the help we can get."

I didn't want to join prom committee. Didn't want to plan for a dance that I'd probably never attend. A dance where Logan would lace his hands across the small of some other girl's back as they swayed to the music in a dimly lit room.

"Hearts in Atlantis sounds super cheesy," I agreed. "What else is up for discussion?"

"Let's see . . ." Harper thought about it. "There's Moonlit Forest."

"And Bon Voyage," Olivia added.

I raised my eyebrows. "Bon Voyage?"

"I think it's nautical or something," Rachel said dismissively.

"Buoys and anchors and sailor suits?" I laughed. "Sounds awful."

Olivia nodded. "Right?"

"Moonlit Forest could be nice." I hesitated. "Or . . ."

"What?" Harper asked. "Do you have an idea?"

"What about Midnight in Paris?" I suggested. "Like the movie?"

It wasn't really my idea. Our school in Phoenix had done a Midnight in Paris theme for prom. It had been romantic despite the fact that I was working a mark named Bradley, keeping him busy while Parker got his sister drunk in an attempt to find out the combo to the family safe holding their mother's jewelry.

"Oh, my God, I *love* that movie!" Olivia said.

"Paris is always romantic," Harper said. "Plus, with the movie tie-in, you have the 1920s to play with, too."

"That's true!" I sounded surprised, even though some of the kids in Phoenix had shown up in Gatsby-esque dresses and tuxes.

"See?" Olivia said. "You should join the committee. We need fresh ideas."

For a split second I could see it: brainstorming ideas for the dance, laughing and hanging white lights, getting dressed and putting on makeup together before the guys picked us up in a limo.

"Yeah, maybe," I said faintly.

The pizzas came a while later, and everyone gathered around the coffee table to eat. Parker made a trip to the fridge and pulled out another beer. I couldn't be sure, but he seemed a little unsteady on his feet. I wondered how many he'd had.

Logan and I sat next to each other on the sofa, talking quietly about school and music and college. It was only the second time in my life that I'd had such an instant connection with someone. Parker had been the first, but our connection had been based on tragedy, on loss, on a shared survival instinct. Where Parker and I had huddled together like survivors in a life raft, Logan was pulling me out into the clear blue sea, teaching me that I could swim. That I could live outside the shelter of the boat that was both my refuge and my prison.

After dinner we changed into bathing suits and headed outside to the Jacuzzi. The night was chilly by Southern California standards, the salty spray of the ocean mingling with the chlorine-scented hot tub water. I sat next to Logan, wondering if I was feeling flushed from the hot water or from the strangely intimate experience of sitting close to him while both of us were nearly naked.

I watched the group interact through a surreal kind of haze. I was both part of them and apart from them. I could smile on cue and laugh. I could even participate in the conversation. But I was an actor reciting my lines, playing a part. I felt stupid. Why had I felt like I belonged? I would never, ever be one of them. Would never have that luxury. And I wasn't talking about their money. They were at ease in one another's company, drinking beer and making inside jokes and recounting their shared experiences, in a way I'd never been with anybody.

In a way I would never be with anybody.

Parker took a swig from his beer bottle and met my gaze across the water, steam rising between us like a veil. It was a reminder, and I rose from the water and stepped out of the Jacuzzi, reaching for my towel.

"I'm going to get some water. Does anyone want anything?"

"I'll come with you," Logan said, starting to rise.

"There's no reason for both of us to drip water through your kitchen," I laughed. "I'll be right back."

He eased back into the water with a nod.

I headed for the house.

Twenty-Nine

The lawn was dark, lit only at the edges and along the pathway by the landscaping lights. I let myself into the house through the doors off the terrace. It was strangely quiet, a soft glow emanating from the lights under the cabinets in the kitchen. It could have been any kitchen in any house in any city we'd worked.

I looked around, my mind doing a quick, almost instinctual calculation of the situation. Away from Logan and the others, with the clock ticking, it was easier to remember who I was, and I quickly ran the towel over my body, then wrapped my hair in it to avoid the drip marks that would outline my route through the house.

I moved through the kitchen and into the hallway, my bare feet silent on the stairs as I made my way to the second floor. My mom's search of the house at the Fairchilds' party had been perfunctory. I needed to double-check all the rooms on the second floor, just to be sure.

I started with the media room. I'd have other chances to check behind the closed doors—probably bedrooms—but Logan seemed to use the media room as his prime hangout spot. It might be a while before I had another opportunity to case it alone.

I headed for the walls, lined with bookcases. A large safe or panic room would have to be set into one of the walls, and I felt around the bookshelves, hoping for a break. When that didn't work, I started shuffling books, looking for signs of a hidden room—books that didn't line up with the alphabetical system clearly in place, bumps that might indicate a thick door hidden in the walls, a change in the sound of my fist rapping against the wood as I made my way down the line of shelves. Nothing seemed out of place.

I stood there, staring at the shelves and contemplating the merits of looking closer before discounting the idea. I'd been in the house for at least five minutes, probably a little bit longer. If I wanted a look at the other rooms, I needed to hurry.

I headed for the closed door across the hall from the media room. Its comfortable but nondescript decor suggested a guest room, and I made a quick search of the walls and closet before moving on. I'd made it through another guest room and two bathrooms when I heard the sound of voices. I glanced out the bathroom window and caught sight of Harper and Raj moving toward the house, Logan and the others trailing behind them.

I did a quick scan of the hallway, making sure everything was the way I found it, before bounding down the stairs. Pulling the towel from my hair, I wrapped it around my body and was just sliding onto one of the kitchen stools when the door opened.

"Hey!" Logan said. Worry shadowed his eyes, and he crossed the tile floor. "You okay?"

I dropped my head into one of my hands. "I'm sorry. I wasn't feeling very well."

He laid a hand on my forehead as the others came in. "Did you get your water?"

I shook my head. "I didn't make it that far."

He crossed the kitchen to the sink and filled a glass with water. "Drink," he said, pushing the glass toward me.

"What's up?" David asked. "You okay, Grace?"

"I just felt a little light-headed," I said.

"Probably the hot tub," Harper said, toweling her hair dry until it stood up in short spikes around her pixie face. "Logan's mom likes it hot."

"You want to lie down?" Logan asked. "You can take my room if you want."

"I should take her home," Parker said. He was leaning against the wall, his eyes dark. Logan glanced back at him. "Why don't you stay?" Logan said to him. "I can run Grace home."

Parker's eyes flashed blue fire. Logan was implying he was drunk, and Parker knew it.

"I'm fine to drive," Parker said. "I only had three beers."

Liam clapped him on the back. "Hate to break it to you, bro, but that's three too many to make you a safe driver."

Parker shook off his hand and looked around the room. His eyes fell on Logan.

"Sorry, man. House rules," Logan said.

"I can drive," I said. "I had half a beer two hours ago. And I'm just a little under the weather. I don't have the plague."

"You sure?" Logan asked.

"She's sure," Rachel said, rolling her eyes. "She's not made of glass. If she says she can drive, she can drive."

Logan nodded slowly. "Okay, then."

I got dressed and Logan walked Parker and me to the car. Parker slammed the passenger side door, leaving Logan and me to say good-bye in private.

I sighed. "Sorry about Parker."

Logan gave me a half smile. "Don't sweat it. He just had one too many beers."

"Yeah, but he kind of ruined the mood in there."

He pulled me close. "It was just an excuse to hang out with you. Besides, it's a weeknight. Everyone will be heading home soon anyway."

Wrapping my arms around his torso, I felt the ripple of muscle in his back. I inhaled the smell of him—chlorine and trees, surf wax and the sea—and laid my head on his chest.

"Think you'll be at school tomorrow?" he asked.

I looked up at him. "Definitely. I just need a good night's sleep."

He leaned down and touched his lips lightly to mine. "Feel better, Grace."

I nodded and got in the car.

"And text me when you get home safe." He shut my door.

I reversed and then put the car into gear, starting down the driveway. It was so dark I could only make out the trees lining the driveway. Beyond them, everything was black.

Parker sulked, slouched in the seat next to me. I waited until we'd passed the gates, already open when we got there, to speak.

"What the fuck are you doing?" I asked him softly.

"What the fuck are *you* doing, Grace?" I thought his words were a little slurred. I was glad Logan and everyone else had put their foot down about him driving.

"I'm doing exactly what I'm supposed to be doing." I was careful. Careful not to violate the rules by saying something I shouldn't.

"I'm doing what I'm supposed to be doing, too," he said, glaring at me from the passenger seat. "Looking after you."

"By getting drunk?"

"It was a party," he said. "I thought I was supposed to fit in."

I turned onto the main road leading home. "In case you didn't notice, that's not exactly what you were doing."

"I'll take that as a compliment," he muttered, turning his head to the window.

"You shouldn't," I said. "You're not doing us any good acting this way."

"And you are?"

Anger heated my face, rushed through my bloodstream like a wildfire. "As a matter of fact, yes."

"By being Logan Fairchild's main squeeze?" he sneered.

I turned onto Camino Jardin, surprised by the hatred I suddenly felt for him. "Yes."

"Driving around in the BMW, hanging out at the big house, being wined and dined by Mr. Trust Fund Baby . . . must be tough."

The sarcasm in his voice made me want to slap him. I pulled in front of the house and turned off the car. Then I took a deep breath, listening to the tick of the engine as it cooled.

Finally, I turned to him. "You might not see what I'm doing as important. You might think it's all fun and games, that I'm enjoying my time with Logan. You might even be right. But while you were getting smashed, acting like a spoiled four-year-old, ignoring everyone we're supposed to be working, I was casing the house. I was looking for the gold, for cameras along the driveway." I met his eyes across the darkened car. "What were you doing?"

I got out and slammed the door. He didn't follow me inside.

Thirty

It was a Friday afternoon in early November when I came downstairs to find the Allied installation team packing up and leaving. Selena had talked me into joining her for a walk at the Cove, and I had come home from school to change into jeans and a sweater. I grabbed an apple from a bowl on the kitchen table as my mom closed the front door on the last of the installation workers.

"Is that it?" I took a bite of the apple, avoiding her eyes. It had been two weeks since my argument in the car with Parker after Logan's party, and I still felt guilty about breaking the War Room rule. Parker's attitude, and my own anger toward him, had made me reckless. I considered confiding in my mom, telling her everything—Parker's increasingly sullen moods, his unwillingness to integrate with Logan's group, the darkness that seemed to be eating him alive all over again. But I couldn't do it. I didn't know what my dad would do to Parker, but he'd already been warned. We weren't there yet. Things were still under control. More or less.

My mom nodded, heading for the dishwasher. "I'll show you how to work the alarm keypad before you go. It's pretty simple."

"Great."

"What are you up to tonight?" she asked.

"I'm going to the beach with Selena, and then we're going to grab something to eat," I said.

She raised her eyebrows. "No Logan?"

"We're going out tomorrow night." I couldn't tell her that I needed a break from Logan. Not because I didn't like him, but because I had to brace myself to see him, prepare myself for the war raging almost constantly in my head. The battle between heart and head, a battle that only had one possible outcome.

"That's nice," she said. "Probably better to not to be too available anyway. Keep him interested."

I gave her a halfhearted smile as she ran the tap in the kitchen sink.

"What about Rachel and the other girls?" she asked, loading a few glasses into the dishwasher. "I thought you were focusing on them?"

Her choice of words was appropriately vague, but I knew what she was getting at: She didn't think Selena was important. She wasn't as rich as the others, wasn't as cemented into the group.

"Selena's one of us now," I explained. "Plus, she's played the role of observer for a long time. You'd be surprised what she knows."

I hated myself for saying it, even if it was true. My friendship with Selena wasn't about the con.

My mom nodded. "I can see that."

"What are you up to?" I asked, eager to deflect attention away from myself.

"There's a board meeting for PHCT. We're putting the finishing touches on their annual fund-raiser, which as it turns out, is held at the Fairchild house."

PHCT was the acronym for the Playa Hermosa Community Theater group. It had become a common topic of conversation around the house ever since my mom had joined the board to get close to Logan's mom. So far she hadn't had much luck, and I wondered if Leslie had some kind of bullshit detector that made her suspicious of my mom. Deep down, I think I was rooting for Leslie, hoping she would somehow steer clear of the toxic manipulation that was part of every con.

"That sounds nice," I said.

My mom laughed. "If hanging out with a bunch of bored housewives is what you consider nice."

Isn't that what you are? I thought. I bit it back, shaking my head against the tide of hostility that that seemed to be seeping from my pores, leaking like an oil spill contaminating the waters of my relationship with my mom. She wasn't doing anything wrong. Nothing the rest of us weren't doing, anyway.

I reached over and gave her a spontaneous hug, startling her as she shut the door to the dishwasher.

She laughed. "What's that for?"

"Just a reminder that I love you."

"I love you, too, Gracie." She gave me a squeeze and smoothed my hair. "Have fun tonight."

I grabbed my bag and the keys to the Saab and headed outside. I had no idea where Parker was, but he'd left the car, so I figured it was fair game. I was almost to the driveway when I heard the crooning from next door.

> They said someday you'll find
> All who love are blind.

I hesitated, feeling the draw of the fence. Why was I compelled to look? The man next door had nothing to do with me. With us.

I hurried past the fence and to the car.

After I picked up Selena, we headed to the Cove. I parked, and we snaked our way down the cliff and stepped onto the empty beach. The sky was heavy with clouds. They hung over the ocean, turning the water steely gray, blocking out what little sunlight remained in the day. I zipped up my jacket and stuffed my hands in the pockets.

"It's quiet," I said.

She nodded. "It's the weather. And the time of year. After October, everyone kind of hunkers down for the winter."

I laughed. "It's not like it's super cold or anything."

She smiled. "Says the girl from San Francisco."

It was a reminder of my betrayal, and my laughter faltered. "So what are you saying? You guys are wimps in SoCal?" I joked.

"Basically. Most of the parties will be held indoors now, or on someone's patio." She looked around as we made our way to the water's edge. "It's why I like it so much this time of year."

I looked around and smiled. The fact that Selena preferred overcast skies and an empty beach was just one more sign that we were kindred spirits.

It was too cold to take off our shoes, and we walked just out of the water's reach, the rhythm of the waves like a mantra, slowly calming the endless loop in my head. The one that was always rehearsing what to say next, rehashing what had already been said, plotting my next step. Selena's company helped, too. She had never even asked about Parker, about the way he'd acted at Logan's party. It was one of the things I loved about her: she had no need to label or define things. They were what they were.

We walked in silence until the Strand, a stretch of concrete that ran all the way from the Cove to Malibu, was in sight. Then we turned around and headed back the way we came.

"I think about her a lot when I come here," Selena suddenly said.

I looked over at her. "Your mom?"

"It's silly, especially since we know she's living a new life somewhere."

"Yeah, but for a while, you thought she disappeared here," I said.

"I hardly remember what it was like to have her around," she admitted. "I think I just miss the idea of her, you know?"

I nodded. It was exactly how the concept of normal was for me: a vague notion, an almost memory of the way things were supposed to be.

She stopped walking and turned to me. "Anyway, I want to give you something." She held out her hand. Two silver bracelets sat in her palm, each with half an interconnecting heart dangling from the chain. "She bought these when I was fourteen. One for her and one for me. She . . ." Selena took a deep, shaky breath. "She sent hers back with her letter."

I looked down at the bracelets, trying to think of something to say that would ease Selena's pain. My mom and I might not be biologically related, but she would never, ever do to me what Selena's mother had done to her.

"I'm sorry," I said. "You deserve so much better. But I . . . I can't accept it. It's too much."

"I hope you will. Because for a long time, I felt alone, and now . . . well, not so much. Because of you." She smiled. "And I kind of miss wearing mine." She slipped one of the bracelets onto her wrist and held the other one out to me. "Think of it as a friendship bracelet."

I took it from her hand, torn between gratitude and guilt. "Thank you."

I didn't deserve it. Didn't deserve such an important

symbol of Selena's friendship. But not taking it would hurt her, and that was something I wasn't willing to do. Plus, I wanted it. Wanted the tangible reminder that I was connected to something—to someone—real.

We put the bracelets on, holding our wrists out to admire them. She grabbed my arm as we headed back to the cliffs. By the time we got there, it was almost entirely dark.

"I don't know about you," Selena said as we huffed our way up the trail toward the parking lot, "but I feel like I've earned some cheese fries."

I laughed. "Totally."

Thirty-One

Mike's was packed, and we stood at the front, scanning the crowd for an open table. It was the first time I'd been there, but it could have been any burger joint in any city in the country, complete with pleather booths, scuffed linoleum floor, and an old Space Invaders game against the wall.

Selena pointed to a couple of tables at the back. "Everyone's here."

I followed her gaze. Logan was taking a drink from his soda glass while Liam laughed next to him. Raj and Olivia scribbled on the back of one of the paper menus, and Rachel was deep in conversation with Harper and David. They looked completely at ease, like it was a scene they'd played out a hundred times before. It made me feel my apartness all over again. I was just a guest star, a walk-on in the television show of their lives. They got to really live it.

Logan glanced around the room and caught my eye. A grin lit up his face, and he immediately stood and headed toward me.

"Hey, you!" He leaned in and kissed me on the lips, right in front of everyone. "Your face is cold." He rubbed my shoulders. "Did you get my text?"

I shook my head, pulling my phone from my bag. "When did you send it?"

"About a half hour ago," he said. "I wanted to see if you were up for hanging with us tonight."

I looked at my phone, seeing the unread text. "We were at the beach. I don't think I get a signal down there."

He put his arm around me. The smell of his cologne, light and a little spicy, caused something to stir in my stomach. Something warm and familiar but exciting, too.

"You're here now," he said. "Come on. We'll make room." He led us back to the table, making small talk with Selena as we went. I liked that about him: the way he never left anyone out. The way he seemed to like everyone.

"Hey, hey! The gang's all here!" David said when he spotted us. He grabbed a chair and pulled it next to him, gesturing to Selena that she should take it.

She smiled shyly and sat down. "Thanks."

Everyone shuffled a little, and Raj moved to the other side of Logan so that I could take his seat.

"You look a little windblown," Rachel said. "What have you two been up to?"

"We went for a walk at the Cove."

She nodded, the lift of her eyebrows making it seem like there was something shady about taking a walk on the beach.

"Where's Parker?"

It occurred to me that it wasn't the first time she'd asked me the question. In fact, it seemed she was always asking, always noticing that Parker wasn't around. I was surprised she still cared after the way he'd blown her off. Then again, I didn't know everything Parker did. Maybe he hadn't blown her off after all.

"I have no idea," I said. "He doesn't exactly keep me up to date on his schedule."

She nodded and went back to her conversation with Harper, but I was unsettled. Not by her question. I was used to those by now. But part of me had assumed Parker was with Logan and the guys, especially since he'd left the Saab parked in front of the house on Camino Jardin. If he wasn't here, and he wasn't at home . . . where was he?

I sent him a quick text and pushed my worry aside. He was probably working whatever angle my dad had him on at Allied. He'd be home when I got there.

Selena and I added two orders of cheese fries and two Cokes to the check, and we spent the next hour and a half talking and laughing with the group, arguing over which eighties songs to play from the kitschy jukeboxes at every table. I was filled with an unfamiliar brand of contentment. Surrounded by Logan and the others in the cocoon that was Mike's, the rest of the world was far away. It almost seemed possible to continue being friends with Harper and Olivia, with Raj and Liam and David. Continue getting closer to Logan, the con some far-off end in the distance, a little blurry and a lot less real than what was right in front of me.

By the time I got home, it was after eleven. I was surprised to find my dad sitting at the kitchen table, a glass of what looked like his favorite Scotch in front of him.

He looked up when I came in. "Hey. How was it?"

I put my bag down and sat across from him. "Fine. Selena and I took a walk and then we met up with the others at Mike's."

There were questions in his eyes, but I knew he wouldn't ask them outside the War Room. He glanced behind me.

"Where's Parker?"

My stomach lurched. "I thought he was here."

"Haven't seen him all night." He took a drink from his glass. "Maybe he's out with Rachel Mercer."

I swallowed the lump in my throat. "Yeah, maybe." Standing, I leaned down and kissed his cheek. "I'm going to bed. Good night."

"Night, Gracie."

I trudged up the stairs and got ready for bed. Then I turned out the light and slid between the sheets, my mind churning. Parker wasn't with Rachel, he wasn't with the guys, and he hadn't taken the Saab. If he'd been working on Allied, my dad would have known about it.

So where was he? Panic bubbled up inside me. Could he

have left? Abandoned our parents—and me—like he'd been planning?

I shook my head in the dark. Parker wouldn't do that. Whatever had happened between us, however tense things were, he wouldn't leave me behind. I knew it. Knew him.

Then I thought about the words sung by the man next door:

> *They said someday you'll find*
> *All who love are blind.*

And suddenly I wondered how well I really knew Parker. How well any of us knew one another.

Thirty-Two

I was on my way out of the house the next morning when I spotted Parker through the crack in his bedroom door. He was sprawled facedown across his bed, still dressed in jeans and a T-shirt. It was after ten. Usually he would be up, sitting at the kitchen table and reading the business section. He must have been out late.

I nudged the door open a little more with my foot and peered around the room, eager for clues about his whereabouts the night before. His jacket was tossed haphazardly on the chair near the bed, the carpet covered in muddy boot prints. They led to his boots, which looked like they'd been pulled off in a hurry, tossed so that they landed a few feet apart, half under the bed.

I hesitated, torn between wanting answers and wanting to put off another confrontation. The idea wasn't appealing, especially since Rachel had texted early this morning asking if I was up for working on our AP Euro project. The thought of spending time alone with her tied my stomach in knots, but the saying "Keep your friends close and your enemies closer" was a cornerstone of every con. Besides, if Rachel had picked up the ID in AP Euro, she would have confronted me with it. And even if she hadn't, the ID wasn't proof of anything. We could have been in Arizona before San Francisco. People moved all the time.

I took a deep breath, trying to calm myself down, and pulled Parker's door closed.

Rachel lived a couple of miles away, farther up the peninsula on a bluff overlooking the sea. Her house was bigger than Logan's. Unlike the aged bronze of Logan's gate, the one outside Rachel's property was buffed silver. The house was newer, too, although I'd guess a lot of money had gone into making it look like the houses that were original to the peninsula, most of them built in the 1960s and 1970s.

Rachel buzzed me in at the gate, and I continued up the driveway. The house stood in the middle of a gigantic stretch of lawn. Other than a few well-placed palm trees, there was no foliage. Nothing to create shadow or mystery. It was a diamond, glittering under the showroom lights, carefully positioned to look as shiny as possible.

I parked the car and made my way to the door. The bell echoed throughout the house in a long series of rings. A few seconds later, footsteps sounded on the other side of the door just before it was opened by a youngish woman with dark luminous skin and deep brown eyes.

"Miss Fontaine?" the woman asked.

"Yes."

She opened the door wider. "Please, come in. Miss Mercer is waiting for you in the kitchen. I'll show you the way."

Miss Fontaine? Miss Mercer? Did Rachel's family seriously have a maid? It was hard to tell. The woman wore plain black pants and a white shirt, and while it wasn't everyday wear for most of the people on the peninsula, it wasn't exactly traditional maid attire either.

I followed her down a hallway lined with terra-cotta tile to the back of the house. Like most of the houses I'd seen in Playa Hermosa, the kitchen looked out onto a backyard with a pool and enough patio furniture to outfit an entire living room. At the doorway, the woman turned to me with a smile.

"Here you go," she said, turning to leave.

"Thanks, Graciella," Rachel said. She was standing at the kitchen island, her laptop open in front of her as she poured two glasses of what looked like lemonade. "Thirsty?"

"Sure." I walked into the room, careful not to look around. The slate countertops, custom tile backsplash, and commercial-grade appliances were standard for the rich. Even noticing them could be a red flag for someone like Rachel, who would expect me to be used to it.

She pushed one of the glasses my way and took a drink of her own, eyeing me over the top of it. The silence was like a vacuum, sucking all the air outside the room. It got under my skin, and I had to remind myself who I was, what I'd spent the last few years doing. It's not like I was an amateur.

"Want to work outside?" she finally asked. "We can turn on the patio heaters if it gets cold."

"Sounds good."

She picked up her laptop and we headed for the patio just outside the French doors. She dropped casually into one of the wicker chairs, setting her drink and computer on the coffee table in the middle of the seating group. I chose the love seat across from her and pulled my laptop out of my bag.

"Any ideas for the board game?" she asked.

"A few," I said. "The instructions say we should pattern it off a game we know. I was thinking maybe Monopoly? Depending on the era we decide to work with, we could have players buy different commodities?"

She picked up her computer. "True. Or different pieces of land."

We tossed ideas back and forth, finally agreeing to focus on the Reformation. She was surprisingly agreeable. Not exactly friendly, but minus the super-icy vibe I'd gotten used to. I wondered if she'd finally given up on freezing me out. Maybe she realized how futile it was now that Logan and I were official and I was in with the rest of the group.

We'd been working for about an hour and a half when Graciella came out with a plate of gourmet cupcakes. Rachel closed her laptop and reached for one of the cupcakes, her hand hovering over the plate until she finally chose what looked like red velvet.

"So how are you liking it here?" She glanced down at Selena's bracelet on my hand. "You seem to have settled in quickly."

I set my computer aside and chose a vanilla cupcake with lilac-colored frosting. I didn't really want it. I just wanted to keep my hands busy. I was still a little off-balance, still wondering if this was really Rachel being friendly or if she was just on some kind of bipolar upswing.

"I like it." I laughed. "It's a lot warmer than San Francisco."

She nodded. "How long did you live there?"

"Not long."

She finished the cupcake and set the wrapper down on one of the dessert plates Graciella had left. "Sounds like you move around a lot."

"You could say that."

"Where did you live before San Fran?"

"Atlanta," I answered. We'd never worked in Atlanta, which was kind of the point.

"How was that?" she asked.

I smiled. "Sticky." Not hard. The whole South was hot and humid.

She nodded. "Where else have you lived?"

I recited a few of the cities we'd never lived in, then laughed with a shrug. "I can hardly remember them all."

Winging it wasn't exactly protocol. Our backstory was airtight, rehearsed both individually and as a group when we'd been in Palm Springs prepping for the Playa Hermosa job. But that was before Rachel. Before I'd lost the Chandler

ID card. I'd broken a big rule by keeping it and carrying it around. I didn't want to make it worse by handing her any of the cities we'd worked in, but if she had picked up the ID, I didn't want to rule it out and look like an outright liar either. Better to be vague, hedge my bets.

"Crazy," she said. "It must be kind of exciting, though. To be able to reinvent yourself so often."

I smiled. "Not really. I mean, this is me. It doesn't really matter where we live. It just sucks having to make new friends all the time."

"I wouldn't know. I've only ever lived here." She stood. "I'm running to the ladies' room. Can I get you anything while I'm up?"

"No, thanks."

She headed back inside, shutting the French doors behind her. I sat there, feeling like a rock was lodged in the pit of my stomach. There was nothing overtly suspicious about her line of questioning. In fact, it was less intense, more conversational than the questions she'd lobbed my way when we first met.

Somehow the thought didn't comfort me. I couldn't help feeling like she was up to something, like her newly pleasant demeanor was a facade for the suspicion she'd been so open about until now. If I could play the game—working to win Rachel over for my own agenda—it stood to reason that she could, too. And if I wanted to know something about someone, wanted them to slip up because I suspected them of lying, I'd have a better chance of getting information by being nice than by alienating them.

I stared at Rachel's laptop on the outdoor coffee table. If she was suspicious, would there be something on her computer? Something that would tell me if she had anything substantial?

Glancing back at the doors off the patio, I confirmed that the kitchen was empty. I guessed she'd been gone about a minute, and I looked at the clock on my computer to mark the time before I set it aside and reached for Rachel's laptop.

I opened it, waiting a few seconds for it to reconnect to the house's Wi-Fi before clicking on her open tabs. There were several shopping sites, a Wikipedia page for Martin Luther, YouTube, Spotify, and email.

I looked behind me to make sure I was still in the clear before scrolling through her emails. There weren't many. A couple from teachers about school, something from the volleyball coach about tryouts, a link from her mother about a sample sale in the garment district, and a few others that were obviously spam.

I ran through my options. I could check her browsing history, but that would take time, and she had already been gone four minutes. It would have to wait.

Skimming the tabs again, I clicked on the open Wikipedia page. Then I hit the Back button. It returned me to the browser page, and my attention was immediately pulled to the name flashing in the search bar.

Grace Rollins. The name I'd used at Chandler High School.

The name on my old ID card.

Thirty-Three

Logan picked me up at five and we headed to Santa Monica. I was almost manic with anxiety, my nerves crackling like a live wire. I'd made a point to stay at Rachel's, discussing our project, after she'd come back outside, but all I could think about was the fact that she had my old ID card.

And now she knew about my alias.

"You okay?"

Logan's voice pulled me from my thoughts, and I looked over, trying to smile.

"Fine. I was just thinking about the project Rachel and I are working on for AP Euro."

"How's that going?" he asked.

"Not bad, actually. I think she might be warming up to me."

"By which you mean she's a number four on the bitch scale instead of a ten."

"Well, maybe a five."

He laughed, and I couldn't help but smile. His laugh was deep and warm, as genuine as everything else about him. My pulse quickened a little as I looked at him, his faded jeans and button-down shirt fitting him just closely enough that I could make out his athletic legs, his muscular arms and shoulders.

He navigated the car up the Pacific Coast Highway toward the Santa Monica Pier. The windows were down, the sunroof open on the BMW. The setting sun streamed in from the beach on our left, casting everything golden as it reflected off the water in the distance. I tried to focus on the moment, to be present. But I felt Rachel's suspicion like hot breath on my neck.

I had no one to thank but myself. The rules were in place for a reason. My mom and dad had been on the grift long before Parker and I came along. They'd established the rules to protect us, and I'd put us all at risk for some kind of childish reassurance, for the kind of false security people like us couldn't afford to believe in.

Logan parked in one of the lots near the beach and we walked up to the Third Street Promenade. He'd made a reservation at a seafood place, and we settled into a plush booth. We were halfway through a meal of stuffed snapper and grilled vegetables when he surprised me by reaching across the table and taking my hand.

He smiled into my eyes. "I'm happy you're here, Grace."

"I'm happy, too," I said softly, suddenly shy.

"Mostly, I'm happy you're with me."

I smiled. "Me too."

He sighed a little and looked down at the table.

"What is it?" I asked.

He shook his head. "I don't think I knew how lonely I was until I met you."

"Lonely?" I'd imagined Logan a lot of things. Lonely hadn't been one of them. "But . . . you have so many friends. And your mom and dad . . ."

"Yeah, but the guys and I talk mostly about surfing. And girls." He blushed a little. "We don't really talk about serious stuff."

"And your parents?"

He took a deep breath. "I guess you could say they are the serious stuff."

"How do you mean?" He had no way of knowing that I was fully aware of his dad's condition. My question was just one more lie between us.

He fidgeted with his water glass. "My dad's kind of . . . sick."

"Sick?" I hesitated, giving it time to seem like it was sinking in. "With what?"

His laugh was a little sad. "A lot of things, actually. Bipolar disorder, paranoid schizophrenia . . ."

I could see the pain in his eyes. Worse, I saw shame there, and I knew it was because he was worried about me. About what I would think of him and his family.

I squeezed his hand. "I'm sorry, Logan. Is it . . . manageable?"

"More or less. He's been institutionalized a couple of times, but he's been home for over two years now. This course of meds seems to be doing the trick. So far, at least."

"That's good," I said. "But it still must be hard for you and your mom."

He nodded. "Even when he's good, I think we're both always wondering when the tide is going to turn, you know?"

"Yeah." Parker hadn't been diagnosed with anything, but I knew what it was like to watch and wait. To wonder if something small would set him back, maybe take him from us for good.

"Because of Parker?" Logan asked, as if reading my mind.

My nod was slow.

Logan laughed a little. "Sucks to be the normal ones, right?"

"Definitely." I laughed with him, surprised either of us could find any humor in the situation.

"Well, now we have each other," he said, his eyes never leaving mine.

I'd never wanted something to be more true.

He paid the bill and we wandered down to the pier. It was cold and dark, the lights from the boardwalk and Ferris wheel reflecting off the water, making it look like the sea was strung with thousands of Christmas lights.

Logan looked up. "How do you feel about Ferris wheels?"

"I've never been on one," I admitted.

"Seriously?"

"Seriously."

"Well, we have to fix that right now," he said, pulling me toward the ticket booth.

We got our tickets and stood in line. Logan put his arms around me from behind, pulling me close while we waited our turn. Surrounded by flashing carnival lights and squealing children, Logan's warm body against mine, I almost felt normal. When it was our turn, we ascended a small flight of stairs to a metal platform under an empty Ferris wheel seat. A man with a scraggly gray beard and clear blue eyes lifted the safety bar, and Logan took my hand as I climbed into the seat. It rocked slightly as I sat down, and I had a moment of vertigo where the sky and sea tilted. I clutched the side of the seat, fighting a wave of panic. Then Logan was next to me, his arms around my shoulders, and everything seemed to steady.

The bearded man smiled his encouragement and lowered the safety bar before putting his hand on a big metal lever. My stomach lurched as we were swung backward. We stopped a second later as the man assisted passengers into the next seat, a step that was repeated several more times, each one taking us higher and higher into the night sky, the sea receding farther and farther below us.

Finally, the Ferris wheel lurched to life and stayed that

way, swinging us up and up, closer to the top. I clutched the side of the seat with one hand and grabbed Logan's knee with the other, terrified to look beyond the safety of our little bucket.

"Grace," Logan whispered in my ear.

I dared a glance up at him.

He smiled. "It's okay. I've got you. Look around."

But I couldn't tear my eyes away from his. Secure in the safety of his gaze, the way he looked at me that said everything would be okay, I was too scared to look anywhere else. I shivered, and he kissed the top of my head, pulling me close. Heat seeped from his body into mine.

"Look, Grace," he said softly. "It's all for you."

And that time I did. I saw the sweep of beach, a smudge against the darkness of the sea, as it curved in and out, all the way to the cliffs of Playa Hermosa in the distance. The lights on the water from the pier gave way to the mystery of open sea that went on and on. And far below, people laughed and shrieked, lost in their own wondrous moments.

"It's beautiful, isn't it?" Logan said in my ear.

I looked up at him with a smile.

It was. And so was he.

Thirty-Four

I was still light on my feet when we headed back to the car hand in hand. High above it all, Logan and I had been in a world all our own. I still felt a little untouchable. Like nothing in the world could hurt us.

We were almost to the car when Logan slowed his pace. "What the . . . ?"

"What's wrong?" I looked around, following his gaze.

He was looking at the BMW, parked about fifty feet ahead. At first I didn't know what he was seeing, but a second later my eyes adjusted to the dark and I caught sight of the hooded figure, bent down near the driver's side window.

"Hey!" Logan shouted, hurrying toward the car. "What are you doing?"

The figure straightened, turning toward us. I couldn't make out the person's face in the split second before he took off sprinting in the opposite direction.

I followed Logan, stopping a few feet away when I caught sight of the damage. Someone had keyed the driver's side, and a deep gash ran all the way from the rear tire well to the front bumper.

"Oh, my God . . . ," I said.

"Stay here, Grace." Logan took off after the man.

"Logan!" I looked around, not sure what to do. "Be careful!"

A gust of wind blew in off the ocean, and I wrapped my arms around my upper body, scanning the parking lot, suddenly aware of how alone I was. I don't know how long I stood there before I heard footsteps pounding the pavement in the distance. I peered into the darkness. A rush of adrenaline hit my system as a figure came into view beyond the streetlight casting a weak yellow glow across the pavement. Could it be the vandal coming back to do more damage?

I braced myself to run. The promenade wasn't that far away, and we'd passed plenty of people walking to and from it on our way to the parking lot.

But a second later the figure emerged under the streetlight. It was Logan.

I hurried toward him. "Are you okay? What happened?"

He bent over, panting, trying to catch his breath. "I found a cop. They're going after the guy. Told me to wait here."

I nodded, looking back at the car. "Who would do something like that?"

"I don't know. Let's just hope they catch him."

We walked back toward the car. We'd been waiting about ten minutes when the blue and red lights from a police cruiser passed over the parking lot. It pulled behind the BMW, and a uniformed officer emerged from the driver's side. She was small, her dark hair pulled back into a short ponytail.

"You the owner of the car that was vandalized?" she asked us.

Logan nodded.

The woman turned toward the squad car, and a tall man got out of the passenger side. He opened the back door.

"Let's go," he ordered.

I narrowed my eyes, trying to get a better look at the person in the back of the cruiser. He stepped out, head bowed, posture defiant.

The male officer tugged off the hood that concealed the suspect's face in shadow.

"Parker?" I said it almost without thinking.

"You know this guy?" the woman asked me.

I nodded, glancing quickly at Logan before turning back to her. "He's my brother."

She grabbed hold of Parker's arms, cuffed behind his back, and tugged him toward me. "What are you doing messing with your sister?" She shone a penlight in his eyes. "You drunk? High?"

"Should we test him?" her partner asked.

She shook her head. "Nah, he's clean." She looked at me, tipping her head at the BMW. "This your car?"

"It's mine," Logan said softly.

I searched his face, fear welling inside me. Not because I was worried about the con, worried that Parker had blown all my work with the mark. Not for any of the reasons that should have had me afraid.

I was scared because I didn't want Logan to think less of me. Didn't want my association with Parker to change the way Logan saw me.

The woman held out her hand. "License, insurance, and registration."

Logan went around to the passenger side and opened the door. He dug around in the glove compartment before returning with some slips of paper. He handed them over to the woman.

"Run them," she said, handing them to her partner. He went back to the squad car. "You guys have some kind of beef?" she asked, looking from Logan to Parker.

"Not that I was aware of," Logan said.

Parker had yet to say anything.

We stood in awkward silence until the male officer returned with Logan's documents. "He's clean," he said, handing them back to Logan.

The woman sighed. "You want to press charges?"

Logan didn't even hesitate. "No. It's fine."

She glanced back at the car before turning to Logan. Her expression as she shook her head said it all: *Any seventeen-year-old with a BMW can afford a new paint job.*

She looked at Parker. "You got a free pass this time. Looks

like you should be nicer to your sister's boyfriend."

She returned to the police cruiser with her partner, and they got in the car and pulled slowly out of the lot.

"Parker . . . ," I started.

He turned around and started to walk away.

"That's it?" I shouted at his back. "No apology? No explanation?"

But he just kept walking. I watched him go, waiting until he'd disappeared into the shadows to turn to Logan.

"Logan . . . I'm so sorry. I don't know what's gotten into him."

He shook his head and took a step toward me, pulling me into his arms. "It's okay. It's not your fault. You're not responsible for Parker."

I laid my head against his chest, his words echoing through my mind. It wasn't true. Our parents had taught us well. Taught us that the only way to make it unscathed out of a long con was to stick together no matter what. We were responsible for each other.

All of us.

Thirty-Five

I left the house early Sunday morning before anyone else was awake. I'd spent the night in a kind of half sleep, drifting in and out of consciousness, floating in that space between dreams and the endless loop of my thoughts. It was six thirty when I finally gave up, and I threw on a pair of jeans and a sweatshirt before letting myself quietly out of the house.

I didn't have a destination in mind. I just needed to move. I headed down Camino Jardin, turned onto another residential side street, and kept on going. The morning was damp, a light mist falling from an overcast sky. The smell of the sea was heavy in the air, the ebb and flow of the tide audible in the distance. Every now and then a flash of color caught my eyes from the trees. I thought about the parrots, making themselves a home in the only one they had. I wondered if they were happy here.

Parker hadn't been home when Logan had dropped me off, although the door to his bedroom was closed when I left this morning. I knew I should tell our parents about his behavior. It was erratic, a danger to us all. But I wasn't sure I could do it. Wasn't sure I could put the job—or even my own security—before Parker.

And that's what I'd be doing, because if my dad believed that Parker was jeopardizing the job, he would find a way to eliminate Parker from the equation, pay him to leave or hold something over his head to get him to step back.

And then what? After the Fairchild con, we'd move on. There would be no Logan. No Selena to cushion the blow of my loneliness. We needed each other, Parker and I. My isolation had never been more palpable. Normally, I would talk to Parker about my problems. Now he was the problem, and I had nowhere to turn.

I was turning the corner, ascending one of the peninsula's steep hills, when I saw the figure coming toward me. Shrouded by the mist, almost blending into the early morning twilight, there was something familiar about the gait, the slight stoop to the shoulders. He was only a few feet away when I realized it was Parker, wearing the same hoodie he'd been wearing the night before when he'd vandalized Logan's car.

He slowed down as I approached. "Hey."

"Hey," I said.

"Mind if I join you?"

I shrugged, and he fell into step beside me. For a few minutes we walked in silence, our companionship like an old friend in spite of everything that had happened.

"I'm sorry," he finally said.

I glanced over at him. Even in profile, I could see the dark circles under his eyes, his sallow complexion. "For what you did to Logan's car or for jeopardizing the job?"

We were outside the War Room, out in the open where anyone could hear. But somehow I couldn't find the energy to care.

He looked at me. "For putting you in that position."

"I'm not the only one exposed here," I said.

His eyes were unwavering. "You're the only one I care about."

I shook my head. "And what do you think would happen to me if the job went bad? If something happened to you or Mom and Dad?"

His laugh was bitter. "Trust me, you'd be fine without 'Mom and Dad.'"

We came to a dead end, the sidewalk stopping at a chain-link fence. A field of brush lay past it, and beyond that the ocean. Parker bent down, lifting up a piece of the fence that had been cut. I ducked under it and waited for him to follow, the unspoken language of longtime allies flowing between us. Following a path through the overgrowth, we stopped at the edge of the cliff, the water frothy and violent below us.

I dropped onto the ground and looked out over the sea.

"We're all in this together. If one of us goes down, we all go down." I paused, trying to figure out where things had gone so wrong. "I guess I just don't get it."

He looked at me. "What?"

"What's changed? Why now?"

His gaze tracked the seagulls gliding in circles over the water. "I see how you look at him," he said softly. "At Logan."

The flush of humiliation warmed my face, as if he had unearthed my deepest secret, laid it bare for us to inspect and analyze.

I didn't look at him. "Haven't you ever liked someone? Gotten attached?"

He was silent so long I wondered if he'd heard me. "There was someone once."

I looked at him, surprised by his honesty. "Who?" I thought back, trying to guess. "That girl in Seattle? Maya Richardson?"

Maya had been Parker's mark. I'd spent a lot of rainy afternoons with her younger sister, Lacey, watching movies in the family room with a fire blazing in the giant fireplace. They had been nicer than a lot of our marks.

He shook his head. "Her little brother, Ben."

"Ben?" I only vaguely remembered him, a small, quiet boy with dark, glossy hair and eyes that had seemed too big for his delicate face.

Parker nodded. "I played basketball with him when it wasn't raining, built LEGOs in his room when it was.

He . . . well, I think he looked up to me."

"You told Mom and Dad that Maya and Ben were close," I said, remembering. "That you could get on her good side by spending time with her little brother."

"It wasn't a lie," he said.

"But that's not all there was to it."

"No." He hesitated. "He was so innocent. It was like . . ." He shook his head. "I don't know. Like seeing myself. The kid I could have been if I'd had parents with boring jobs and a house in the suburbs, the kind who put out presents from Santa at Christmas and pretend to eat the cookies left by their kids."

"Was it hard?" I lowered my voice. "Stealing from them?"

The job had been simple: steal the savings bonds purported to be somewhere in the house. After two months of snooping, Parker had found them in a couple of shoe boxes at the top of the parents' closet.

He picked up a rock and tossed it angrily over the cliff. "Turns out the bonds were for Maya and Lacey and Ben. For college. Their parents had been buying them since the kids were born. They weren't even rich."

Dread swept over me. It was the dread of sudden realization, like I'd been swimming in the shallow end only to extend my legs and find that the bottom was nowhere to be found.

"But you took them anyway." We'd stuck around Seattle for two more months, but no one had ever said a word.

I wonder how long it took the Richardsons to realize the bonds were gone.

He looked at me. "I lost something on that job, Grace. Some . . . I don't know, some part of me that still believed I was redeemable. That believed I could be someone else someday. And it was because I stole from Ben. Because I cared about him and I stole from his family anyway."

I didn't know what to say. It had never occurred to me that Parker had a conscience about what we did. His loyalty to our parents had been less than enthusiastic, but he had never openly questioned their motives until we came to Playa Hermosa. Until it had been to protect me.

"I'm sorry," I said. "I didn't know about Ben, about the Richardsons. But this is the deal. It always has been. You've never minded before."

"That's not true." His voice was dangerously low, an undercurrent of anger running through it. "I've never liked the way they use you. The way they use us."

"They're not using me," I said. "I've profited from our jobs. So have you."

He continued looking out over the water. "Yeah, well, we've lost, too."

"Maybe. But that's life. And this is who we are."

His eyes bore into mine. "What if it isn't?"

The words struck a chord, some long-buried part of myself snapping to attention.

Maybe, maybe, maybe . . .

But no. I couldn't afford to think that way. Not now.

We were in too deep.

I shook my head. "You can't just change the rules in the middle of the game."

"I don't want to change them," he said. "I want to stop playing."

"Parker . . ."

"Come with me, Grace. That's all I'm asking. You don't even have to stay with me if you don't want. I just want you to . . . to have a chance."

"A chance at what?"

"Another life. A better life."

"What about you?" I asked. "Don't you want that, too?"

He looked away. "I think it might be too late for me."

My heart seemed to skip a beat. "Don't say that. You're only a year older than me. If I have a chance, you do, too."

"I'm not like you, Grace. I don't have an endless supply of hope, of optimism."

"You think I don't lose hope? I don't feel despair?"

He turned toward me. "Then come with me. Before it's too late."

I thought about it, tried to imagine it. Parker and me somewhere else. On our own. No more lying. No more running.

"I'm not saying no," I said. "I just . . . I can't think about it right now. Let's finish this job. Then we can figure out what's next. Can we do that?"

"You'll think about getting out?"

I nodded. "But Parker . . . you have to stop what you're doing. You're shining a light on the whole family. And neither of us will get out if we're exposed now."

"I'm sorry," he said. "I've been at loose ends. But I can hold it together until the end of this job. I *will* hold it together."

"Promise?"

He put his arm around me and pulled me close in a brotherly embrace. "I promise."

Thirty-Six

By Thanksgiving, I was starting to breathe easier. Parker had been less confrontational, and while he was never overjoyed to see me with Logan, he was civil. He had even apologized, offering to pay for the damage to Logan's car. It wasn't necessary—Logan had told his parents he'd been a victim of random vandalism—but he had appreciated the offer. They'd shaken hands and that had been that.

We had a quiet Thanksgiving at home with my mom's notoriously bad turkey and famously good sweet potatoes. Parker and I worked together on the stuffing. Afterward, I drove to Logan's house for a low-key dessert with his parents. The more time I spent with them, the more I liked them, and I found myself avoiding them despite the fact that they were always warm and welcoming. When I was alone with Logan, it was easier to shut everything else out, but that was a lot harder to do while looking into Warren Fairchild's haunted eyes, watching Leslie touch his shoulder reassuringly as she passed by.

The Saturday after Thanksgiving I put on my new jeans and a slouchy sweater and headed to Selena's house. The guys were at Liam's, breaking in a newly released video game, and Selena and I had agreed to go with Rachel, Olivia, and Harper to a beach party in Malibu. After hearing one too many stories about Rachel's wild nights in LA and Hollywood, I'd offered to drive. I didn't want to be at her mercy if I wanted to leave. Plus, Selena had lied to her father, telling him we were going to dinner and a movie, and her cover story depended on making curfew.

She was waiting in the driveway, wearing black jeans that accentuated her curves and a thick white sweater under a leather jacket. As always, her hair was barely contained in its ponytail, curls springing out around her face like they had a mind of their own.

"Hey!" she said, sliding into the passenger side. "I hope you brought a jacket. It's going to be cold down by the water."

"I did." I put the car into gear and headed for Olivia's house. "And didn't you say beach parties were over for the year?"

She shrugged, reaching for my iPod on the console. "They practically live on the beach in Malibu. Or so I've heard."

"How'd it go with your dad?" I asked.

"Good." She changed the song and put the iPod down. "We have no problem as long as I'm home by midnight."

We picked up Olivia and Harper, and I laughed as they piled into the backseat, fighting over who was going to sit in the middle once we picked up Rachel.

"She is going to *hate* sitting back here," Harper said with what I thought might be a note of satisfaction.

"Yeah, how did you get her to let you drive?" Olivia asked. "She never lets us drive."

I felt a childish twinge of satisfaction. "I told her Parker wanted me to have my own car in case the cops showed up."

"You pulled the Parker card?" Olivia laughed. "Good one."

"So she really likes him?" I asked. I knew they texted and had been out a couple of times, but Parker was otherwise close-lipped about how far things had gone between them.

Olivia leaned forward between the two front seats, and I caught a whiff of her perfume, expensive and French. "I think it's more the chase, you know? Rachel's not used to having to work for it."

"Work for it?" I repeated, turning onto Rachel's road. "Seriously? We're talking about my brother here."

"Sorry. You know what I mean."

"Guys usually fall all over themselves for a shot with Rachel," Harper explained from the backseat. "I thought she was going to die of embarrassment when Logan broke up with her."

"Logan broke up with her?" I don't know why I was surprised.

"Yep," Olivia said. "Gave her the old 'it's just not a good

fit' line. Like he was firing an employee. She was totally humiliated."

I let that sink in as I turned onto Rachel's street and stopped at the end of the driveway. I used the call box, then waited as the gates swung open.

Rachel was standing near the garage, looking completely comfortable in spite of her silky pajama-like pants and loose tank top. Her only nod to the cold was a cardigan draped over one arm.

Olivia opened the back door. "Ready to partay?"

Rachel rolled her eyes. "Only if you move over. There's no way I'm sitting in the middle."

We all laughed as Olivia moved to the center of the backseat.

There wasn't an exact address to type into the Saab's GPS, so I left the peninsula and followed Rachel's directions up PCH toward Malibu. Harper complained that it was the long way, but Rachel insisted it was faster than driving inland to the freeway only to work our way back out again to get to the beach.

As we headed up the coast, I began to relax. It was oddly intimate being crammed into such close quarters, the car dark except for the lights on the dash. Selena dished about David, telling us how his voice had shaken when he met her dad and how he'd asked permission to kiss her after they'd gone to a movie the night before. We talked about Liam's reported hookup with a quiet girl no one seemed to know and about a locker raid that had busted two of the school's top students for possession of Adderall. In between, they passed around Harper's compact mirror, freshening powder and reapplying lip gloss. We'd been driving for nearly an hour when Rachel finally told me to slow down.

She leaned forward, gazing out the window past Harper, her eyes combing the beach. "There," she said. "Park up ahead by those other cars."

"Where are we?" Harper complained. "And how do you hear about this stuff?"

Rachel didn't answer.

I pulled into a turnout at the side of the road and parked behind a silver Lexus. When I cut the engine, music drifted in through the closed windows. A bonfire lit up the beach below us, everything dark outside its perimeter of light.

"You sure this is the right party?" Olivia asked.

"It's somebody's party," Rachel said, opening her door. "And I *need* to get out of this car."

"Wait . . ." Harper slid out after Olivia. "Are you saying you didn't know if there was a party here? That we weren't invited to this one?"

Rachel waved the questions away. "There's always a party up here. And it's a public beach. It's not like they can kick us out."

"You always do this," Harper huffed.

Selena stood next to me as I locked the car.

"Is this cool?" she asked me softly.

I looked around. The bonfire was on an empty stretch of beach, the water on one side, a giant hill leading up to the road on the other. The party seemed pretty low-key, with less than fifty people sitting around the fire. Someone laughed, and it was carried up to us on a rush of wind.

"I think so," I said. "And if it's not—I dangled the keys in front of her—"we can always leave."

Rachel pulled a bottle of vodka from her shoulder bag. "Let's go." She headed to the beach with Olivia and Harper.

"I can't believe we're doing this," Selena murmured as we fell into step behind them.

I smiled reassuringly despite the fact that my nerves were clanging like a wind chime. The success of any job relied on controlling the elements of the con. We'd been taught to know our marks and the other players, weigh the odds, assess the risk of any situation before making a move. The bonfire at the Cove had been easy, almost controlled. A mile from home with people we'd carefully researched in attendance, it was only the details that were unknown. Would I have a chance to talk to Logan? Would I get the opportunity to win over Rachel?

Now I knew nothing about the situation we were walking into, and I braced myself for anything.

Thirty-Seven

We descended to the beach using a set of concrete stairs built into the hill. The music got louder, the hum of conversation audible as we stepped onto the sand. Now that we were closer, I heard the thread of two different songs—one playing through a minispeaker propped up on a cooler, the other strummed softly on a guitar by a long-haired guy near the fire. The smell of pot mingling with salt water hung over the beach, and several of the kids turned nervously our way as we headed toward them.

"Hey!" Rachel held up the vodka and stepped into the light cast by the fire. "We heard there was a party here. Did we come to the right place?"

The guy with the guitar set it aside and took a joint from the muscle head next to him. "What's the password?" he asked on the inhale.

"Um . . ." Rachel looked around, her eyes landing on the bottle in her hand. "Vodka?"

The long-haired guy stood up, opening his arms expansively as a smile lit his face. "How'd you know?"

Laughter and a few halfhearted cheers went up around the fire as everyone introduced themselves. The long-haired guy was Waldo (after Ralph Waldo Emerson, he claimed when Rachel laughed), but I was too busy processing the scene, trying to detect possible problems, to remember all the other names thrown my way.

They offered us beer from the cooler—Selena and I passed—and we found seats on the sand and in a smattering of beach chairs around the fire. Everyone was nice, lubricated by copious amounts of weed and no small amount of beer. They were all friends from Malibu High, and I listened as they compared it to Playa Hermosa, seeming to find some kind of rich-kid kinship with Rachel, Olivia, and Harper.

An hour later, Olivia was deep in conversation with a jock wearing a Malibu High jacket and Selena was talking about summer-abroad programs with the olive-skinned brunette sitting next to her. Rachel stood, linking hands with Waldo, the guitar-playing stoner. They walked off, disappearing into the darkness beyond the fire.

I turned to Harper. "Is she seriously going to make out with Waldo?"

Harper turned her eyes to the fire, something wary settling over her delicate features. "Rachel's different when she's not in Playa Hermosa."

"Different how?"

She leveled her gaze at me, her eyes cold. "You don't really think she's the Rachel she shows to everyone at home, do you?" I noticed the same angry edge to her voice I'd heard that first night at the Cove. "Rachel would never be seen with someone like Waldo in front of Logan, in front of her parents."

"What are you saying?" I asked. "She's two-faced?"

Harper's laugh was brittle. "That's a nice way of putting it."

I turned back to the fire. I didn't believe for a minute that Rachel was trapped in some kind of rich-girl wonderland, forced to be someone she wasn't by the expectations of her family. There was something too gleeful in the way she switched roles. The way she kept everyone off-balance. Like a high-strung toddler who got some kind of subconscious pleasure from keeping everyone on edge, wondering what she'd do next.

"Hey, Grace, let me have your keys?"

I looked up, surprised to see Rachel standing over me with Waldo. "My keys?"

"We're going on a beer run," she said. "And since you insisted on driving, I need your keys."

"Um . . . I don't think my parents would like it if someone else drove my car." I stood up. "Besides, you've been drinking. I'll drive."

She sighed. "I had half a beer an hour ago. I'm completely sober. Don't be a baby. Just give me your keys."

The conversation had grown quiet around us as everyone watched our exchange. I felt suddenly self-conscious, like the goody-goody in a group of delinquents.

"The sooner you give me the keys, the sooner I'll be back," she said, extending her hand.

She wasn't going to let it drop. I could either give her the keys or draw even more attention to us by continuing to argue with her in full view of everyone on the beach.

Reluctantly, I reached into my pocket and withdrew the keys. I put them in her hand. "If you wreck my car, Parker will kill you."

Her laugh echoed off the water. "Whatever, Grace."

She skipped off toward the stairs, red hair streaming behind her like a brightly colored banner, with Waldo in tow.

"Did you seriously just give her the keys to your car?" Selena hissed.

"I didn't know what else to do."

"It's fine," Olivia said, dropping next to me onto the sand. "She'll be back."

A girl with short, dark hair had picked up Waldo's guitar. We listened as she strummed, the notes soft and slightly melancholy. It was cold, and I hunched down into my jacket, trying to calm my nerves, telling myself that Olivia was right; Rachel would be back. It's not like she was a car thief. I didn't know how much time had passed when I noticed the faint cast of blue and red near the stairs.

"What the . . . ?"

"Cops!" someone shouted.

A police cruiser was parked on the road near the stairs, and two uniformed figures were descending to the beach.

I jumped to my feet amid a flurry of activity: blankets thrown over shoulders, half-smoked joints and beer bottles buried in the sand as everyone dispersed, heading away from the stairs toward some unknown exit.

"What do we do?" Selena asked, her eyes a little wild.

Olivia shrugged. "Nothing we can do without a car." She eyed the cops heading our way across the sand. "Just play it cool."

I watched the police officers—one tall and stocky, the other small and wiry—get closer. They stopped in front of us, the little one surveying us with shrewd blue eyes.

"What are you doing out here, ladies?" he asked.

"Just waiting for our friend," Olivia said. "She had to take someone home."

The big guy raised his eyebrows. "You don't have a ride?" The look in his eyes said he'd been expecting a routine party bust, and a fresh note of panic thrummed through my body.

"We do," Olivia said. "She'll be right back."

"Why don't you girls come on up with us," he said. But it wasn't really a suggestion. We had no choice but to follow.

We trudged up the stairs, my heart pounding in time to our footsteps on the concrete. I tried to talk myself down. This was no big deal. I had a valid California driver's license in the name of Grace Fontaine. I hadn't even been drinking. And if the police wanted registration and insurance information on the Saab, I could give it to them when Rachel came back. Worst case, she didn't come back in time, and I'd call my parents. They wouldn't be happy I'd called attention to myself, but I'd been working, worming my way into Logan's crowd like I'd been assigned. It happens.

We reached the police car, and the smaller officer—I saw now that his name tag said Gutierrez—held out his hand. "Let me take a look at your IDs."

We handed them over. Olivia and I had driver's licenses, Selena had a learner's permit, and Harper had only her school ID.

The cop named Gutierrez glanced at them. "Stay here."

He headed for the police car, slid into the driver's seat, and shut the door while we stood awkwardly next to the bigger cop. I couldn't quite make out his badge, but he seemed bored, which was a good sign.

A few minutes later Gutierrez reappeared. He handed us back our IDs, then looked at his watch. "I'll give your friend ten minutes. After that, we have to take you in and call your parents. I'm trying to give you a break, but you're minors. We can't just leave you standing out here by the road."

I glanced at Selena, feeling responsible for the terror in her eyes. The rest of us would get off easy if our parents found out we'd been at a random beach party in Malibu. Selena would be grounded for life.

Time seemed to stretch long and dark; the lights from the police car cast a kaleidoscope of blue and red across the pavement. It seemed like ten minutes had passed ten times over by the time I heard the sound of a car approaching on PCH. We all turned toward it, relief flooding my body as it slowed to a stop at the side of the road.

Rachel got out of the driver's seat. There was no sign of Waldo.

"Hey!" She flashed a smile that would have been more at home at a fund-raiser, like nothing at all was wrong. Like we weren't standing by the side of the road, minutes from being taken to the police station because she'd insisted on taking my car. "Sorry about that!"

Gutierrez held out his hand. "License and registration."

Rachel dug around in her bag. "I can help you with the license part, but it's my friend's car."

"I'll get the registration," I said, heading for the Saab.

I held my breath as Gutierrez looked over everything. "You girls go on home now," he said. "It's not as safe as you might think to be out on an empty beach at all hours."

Rachel smiled. "Yes, sir."

I snatched the keys from her hand and headed for the car. No one said anything as they piled in, the police car still parked in front of us. I had just started the car when Rachel opened the back door.

"Hold on," she said. "I forgot my sweater on the beach."

"You have got to be kidding me," Selena muttered.

The door slammed shut, and we watched as Rachel headed for the stairs to the beach, waving breezily at Gutierrez, who had once again stepped out of the police car.

"Is she serious?" Harper said.

"She's Rachel," Olivia said. "You know how she is."

"I'm tired of making excuses for her," Harper said. "Let's just be honest—sometimes she's a fucking bitch."

The atmosphere was thick with shocked silence in the moment before we all started laughing.

Thirty-Eight

I was waiting for Logan in the school parking lot the following week when I finally googled the name I'd used in
Arizona. I'd been putting it off, afraid of what I would find.
Afraid of what Rachel might have found when she'd done
her snooping. But I was suddenly feeing brave. Or resigned,
at least. Whatever Rachel might know, it was better to find
out so I could deal with it.

I sat on the curb in the parking lot and pulled up the
browser on my phone. I typed in the name *Grace Rollins,* trying to remember if I'd done anything of note at Chandler
High School. Anything that might put me in the local paper
or on the school website.

I scrolled through three pages of results before I modi-
fied my search to *Grace Rollins Chandler High School.*

And there it was. One hit on the district website's online
newspaper. I clicked through and started reading.

Several Chandler High School students spent Saturday afternoon packing food boxes for needy area families. The food was gathered by Linda Tucci, Chandler High School's food bank coordinator, and donated by Sav-Mor and Peterson's Food Mart. "It feels good to help people who need it," said Grace Rollins, Chandler High School student and food bank volunteer.

I scrolled down, looking for a picture. There wasn't one, and I breathed a sigh of relief. Letting someone quote me was sloppy, even if it was unintentional, but without a picture, there was no way to prove I was the same Grace Rollins quoted in the article.

Still, Rachel hadn't said anything, which meant she either hadn't found it when she'd done her own snooping or she knew she didn't have enough to force a confrontation. I just needed to play it cool. Not let my paranoia throw me further off my game.

"Hey, beautiful. Come here often?"

I followed the sound of the voice and realized Logan had pulled up in front of me, the BMW sporting its glossy new paint job.

I laughed. "Not really. Today's just your lucky day."

I slid into the passenger seat and shut the door. My heart stuttered a little when he leaned over to kiss me. His lips lingered on mine as his hand slid gently down my neck.

The spell was broken when someone honked behind us. We smiled, our lips still touching.

"You're quite the distraction, Grace Fontaine," Logan murmured.

I was momentarily disoriented by the sound of my last name. Fontaine, not Rollins. Grace Fontaine.

We talked about school as we headed to Logan's house to set up for the PHCT fund-raiser that weekend. My mom hadn't been kidding; it was a big deal. There would be a silent auction, a live band, catered dinner service, and an open bar.

Leslie and Warren were in meetings, finishing up a few last-minute details, and I had offered to help Logan prepare the house for the onslaught of wealthy locals, all of whom were spending a pretty penny for the opportunity to bid on vacations to Fiji, rare bottles of wine, and private plane charters.

But it wasn't the party that made me nervous. It was what I had to do.

The Fairchild con was a big one. It was expected that it might take a little longer to get everything we needed to make our move. But I had feelings for Logan. Real ones. I was past the point of deluding myself that I could escape with my heart intact. I didn't know when it had happened: maybe on the Ferris wheel, at the top of the world. Maybe in the parking lot when he'd let Parker go. Maybe even that first night on the beach, when it had seemed like we were the only two people in the world.

But I had fallen for him. Hard. It was too late to keep my distance. I could only hope to get out with enough of my soul intact to scrape myself back together again when it was over. And that meant getting the job done fast.

We pulled up to the gates in front of Logan's house, and he entered the pass code before continuing up the drive. I tried to slow my breathing, focus on what needed to be done.

Get the pass code to the alarm.

Find the gold.

Logan took my hand as we headed up the walkway to the front door. His touch was like a brand, marking me for what I was.

A traitor. A liar.

Slipping one hand in my pocket, I reached for my cell phone, waiting for Logan to deactivate the alarm. I'd given up trying to see the code over his shoulder. He was too tall. I might never get a clear view of the keypad.

Instead, I'd decided to record it. The keypad in the Fairchild house was exactly like the one Allied had installed in our rental on Camino Jardin. If I couldn't see the pass code, I might be able to re-create it by matching the beeps each button made when they were pressed.

Logan shut the front door and reached for the keypad, his shoulders blocking it from my view like always. I opened my phone and pressed the button for Record, hoping I'd gotten it right, that all the times I'd practiced working my phone blind would pay off.

A second later Logan turned toward me with a smile. "You sure you don't mind helping today?"

I mustered a smile as I pressed Stop on the phone in my pocket. "Not at all."

The caterer was in the kitchen with a couple of people, scoping out the fridge and planning countertop prep space in advance of Saturday's party. Logan and I went to work, setting up tables and chairs on the massive lawn at the back of the house and hanging the garlands, glossy lemon leaves woven with white peonies, for decoration. We would wait to put the tablecloths on until the day of the event, but I could already see that the total effect would be simple and elegant.

Logan was in the carriage house, pulling out some iron-stone buckets his mother wanted to use for flower arrangements, when I finally got a few minutes to myself in the house. I'd offered to help him, but he'd given me a giant stack of linen napkins to fold instead, and I'd planted myself at the coffee table in the living room and waited for him to leave.

As soon as he was out of sight, I hurried upstairs. I needed to find the gold, and I hadn't had a single opportunity to be alone in the house since Logan's party a few weeks before.

I checked my phone so I could mark the time and started with the rooms I'd missed on the second floor. My face burned with shame, my heart thudding wildly in my chest as I searched the master bedroom. I hated going through Leslie and Warren's things. Hated opening their dresser drawers, moving their clothes, searching their closet.

And in the end, it was all for nothing. The gold wasn't there.

I hurried to the other rooms, making sure to rule them out before moving on to the ground floor. It didn't take me long to search it. There was the living room, three powder rooms, a laundry and mud room, and the kitchen. Most of the rooms didn't have a likely hiding place for a panic room or safe big enough to hide Warren Fairchild's gold. I concentrated on the enormous living room, glancing over my shoulder as I moved books and knickknacks, focusing on the walls, looking for a hidden panel or doorway.

Logan had been gone for nearly fifteen minutes when I finally gave up. He would be back any second. As far as I could tell, the gold wasn't hidden inside the house. The three-car garage was the only place I hadn't looked, but it would have to wait for another time.

At least I had a recording of the pass code for the alarm.

I sat down on the couch and hurriedly folded napkins. I'd only gotten through six of them when Logan reappeared, arms full of stacked metal pails.

"How's it going?" He glanced at the pile of napkins on the coffee table and laughed. "Wow . . . You might be even slower at that than me."

I forced a smile, my pulse still racing from my speed search of the house. "Right? I think I tried folding them five different ways before I finally picked one."

He set down the buckets and kissed the top of my head. "The caterers will refold them anyway. My mom just wanted to keep them from wrinkling in the meantime."

"Now you tell me," I laughed.

He pulled me to my feet. "What do you say we take a break, and then I'll help you with the rest of those."

I wrapped my arms around his waist and looked up at

him. "I could go for a break."

"Want to order pizza?" he asked.

"Pizza sounds great."

He called in the order and came around to the couch, where I was still trying to make progress with the napkins. "Forty minutes."

I nodded. "What do you want to do while we wait?"

He sat down and pulled me closer, looping a piece of my hair around one of his fingers. His arms slid around my waist. Our faces were only inches apart, and all of a sudden we were back on the beach, the only two people in the universe.

I pushed away thoughts of the grift. Of all the work I had to do. All the lies I still had to tell. It was the way it had to be. The only way I could manage the dual roles of Logan's girlfriend and betrayer.

He smiled. "I'm pretty sure we can think of something."

I let go of everything as his mouth claimed mine.

Thirty-Nine

"I don't know if this will help, but it's all I could think of," I said, pushing my phone across the table toward my dad.

We were in the War Room the night before the PHCT fund-raiser. It was the first chance I'd had to tell them about recording the Fairchilds' pass code. I still felt a twinge of shame thinking about it.

"What is this?" my dad asked.

"It's the pass code on Logan's alarm system," I explained. "I can't see over his shoulder, but I thought we might be able to match up the sound of the buttons with the keypad here at home."

My mom looked impressed. "Great idea, honey."

My dad took the phone. "I'll send the file to my computer. I can probably enhance the sound before I get to work on it."

He tapped my screen a few times and handed the phone

back to me. "Nice work, Gracie. Any luck with the gold?"

I shook my head.

"No sign of a safe or panic room anywhere in the house?" Parker asked.

"No, and the garage is all I have left." I looked at my parents. "What about you guys? You've been playing golf and lunching with Warren and Leslie for weeks. Haven't you been able to get anything out of them?"

"Other than some dates when they might be out of town long enough for us to move the gold, I've got nothing," my mom admitted.

"Warren's about as close-lipped as they come," my dad added. "Which shouldn't come as a surprise. The only reason he has the gold in the first place is because he's so paranoid."

"I'll check the garage during the fund-raiser tomorrow," I said. "Maybe there's a panic room between it and the house or something."

My dad nodded, turning his attention to Parker. "How are things at Allied?"

"Proceeding as planned," Parker said.

For weeks Parker had been disappearing with the black backpack at all hours of the night. My curiosity finally got the better of me. "What exactly are you doing there?" I asked.

Parker looked at my dad. He nodded his approval.

"Turns out there's only one night guard monitoring the Playa Hermosa accounts from Allied's facility," Parker said.

"He can't leave his post, so he calls local police if there's any suspicious activity. I'm working to make sure we can get him away from the monitors when it comes time to take the gold."

"How are you doing that?" I asked.

Parker smiled. "By having a little fun with him."

"What kind of fun?"

Parker drummed his fingers on the table, like he wasn't sure how much he wanted to tell me. Finally, he answered.

"I've been vandalizing the area outside Allied."

I shook my head. "Why would you do that?"

He leaned forward. "I make sure the guy can see me, and then I spray-paint something where he can see it. But he can't do anything about it, because he can't leave his post."

"Yeah, but can't he call the police?"

Parker leaned back with a shrug. "Sure. Probably has. But I'm long gone by then. And it's a relatively harmless act, so I doubt they spend much energy trying to find me."

"But how will this get him away from the monitors when it's time to take the gold?" I asked.

"That's the night I'm going to give him a chance to catch me."

Suddenly I understood. Parker was playing cat and mouse with the guard. Baiting him in clear view and then disappearing before he could do anything about it. The night we took the gold, Parker would linger, give the guy a chance to catch him.

"What if he doesn't come?"

"He will," Parker said. "But if he doesn't, I'll pull out all the stops until he can't help himself."

I nodded. It wasn't foolproof, but it wasn't bad.

"We're getting closer," my dad said. "Your mom might have a private buyer lined up for the gold. Now all we have to do is find it."

Forty

The gates were open, the driveway and lawn packed with cars when we got to Logan's house Saturday afternoon. I was a little surprised by the open access to the grounds, but then I saw the black-suited men strolling the perimeter of the property and I understood: the Fairchilds had hired private security to keep an eye on things during the fund-raiser.

The professional side of me was a little thrilled by the discovery even as regular me shrank from the knowledge. We were swiftly reaching the point of no return. The only reason the famously self-sufficient Fairchilds would hire a contingent of security guards was if they had something to secure. And if there was gold on the property, we were going to steal it.

We parked the car and followed the signs that read Playa Hermosa Community Theater Annual Silent Auction to the backyard. My mom greeted people along the way like an old friend, playing the part of rich, charitable housewife to the hilt. Her efforts at fitting in, gaining the trust of her elite so-called peers, had clearly paid off. Dressed in a subtly slinky emerald-green dress that draped perfectly around her slender knees, she was the picture of classy affluence.

I'd chosen a white shift that offset my now-dark hair and brought out the deeper tones in my blue eyes. But where my mom had opted for strappy heels, I'd gone with gold sandals. I never understood how she managed to walk across the grass in heels without sinking into the dirt, but she made it look easy.

My dad looked handsome in a dark blue suit, and Parker was every bit the rich surfer boy in perfectly tailored chinos and a snug white button-down with the sleeves rolled, bracelets encircling his tanned wrist, a hemp cord visible at his neck.

"Cormac! Renee!" Leslie greeted us as we rounded the corner to the backyard. "Welcome!" She turned to Parker and me. "Parker, don't you look dashing. And Grace, lovely as always." She laughed. "My son has good taste, if I may say so."

There were smiles and laughter as everyone made small talk. A moment later, my mom followed Leslie over to another group of newcomers. My mom had a way of making herself at home with housewives all over the country. She knew how to look good enough to fit in without causing feelings of jealousy or rivalry. She knew how to show enough knowledge to be an asset while still asking questions, still making the mark feel needed and admired.

But I could tell from Leslie Fairchild's body language that she wasn't quite comfortable with my mother. Leslie stood just a little too far away from my mom, her head tipped to the left while my mother stood on her right. My parents weren't kidding; the Fairchilds were tough to crack.

Which meant it was all up to me. All riding on my relationship with Logan.

I didn't see Logan, so I headed for Selena and David, talking near the bar that had been set up to the right of the string quartet playing softly at the edge of the lawn.

"Hey!" I said, giving Selena a hug. "You look fantastic!"

She looked stunning in a simple black dress that skimmed her body and ended demurely below the knee. Her hair was pulled back in a loose, high bun, ever-present curls escaping around her face.

She blushed. "You too. But you always look amazing."

We talked for a minute about the crowd and the decorations. Everything had come together perfectly, white lights twinkling in the garlands, linen napkins sitting atop pristine tablecloths on the tables that dotted the lawn. It somehow managed to be welcoming while being in perfect taste, just like the Fairchilds.

Olivia and Raj joined us, and I used the added conversation as a distraction to scan the crowd for anything interesting. Everyone was drinking and mingling, their voices a hum over the classical music coming from the quartet. I turned my attention to the security contingent, wondering if their location might give up some clue about the gold, but they didn't seem to be concentrating on any specific area of the property.

"Hey, beautiful." The words were spoken softly in my ear, and I turned to find Logan standing behind me, his eyes filled with that special light he seemed to save just for me.

"Hey, yourself," I said, standing on tiptoe to give him a kiss on the cheek. "You look so handsome."

And he did. Unlike the other guys, he wasn't wearing suit pants or chinos. Instead he wore dark, tailored jeans and a black sport coat over a V-neck T-shirt. The effect was one of effortless class, and I marveled that while he never looked like he was trying too hard, he always managed to look better than any other guy in any room.

He grinned. "I have to stay on my toes next to my gorgeous girlfriend."

I shook my head, laughing even as my cheeks got warm. "Stop sweet-talking me."

"It's not sweet-talking if it's true," he laughed.

"Okay, you two," Raj said. "Break it up."

We all laughed and went our separate ways. David took Selena to meet his parents, while Raj and Olivia headed across the lawn to join Rachel. I looked around, wondering what had become of Parker. I didn't see him, and I had to force the knot of concern out of my stomach. Parker had been okay since our conversation that foggy morning after he'd vandalized Logan's car. Besides, he'd promised to keep his cool through the rest of the Fairchild con.

Logan slid an arm around my waist, pulling me a little bit closer. He leaned down, whispering in my ear. "You up for an escape?"

Forty-One

We stuck to the tree line as we followed the gravel pathway leading to the back of the property. We didn't want any of the others to see us and mistake our getaway for a chance to ditch the adults en masse.

The sun was setting over the ocean, and the wind that blew in off the water wasn't balmy anymore. The temperature had plummeted at least five degrees since we left the lawn. The hired party help had been turning on lights and patio heaters when we left. Looking around the path, everything rendered in shades of twilight gray, I suddenly wished for light and warmth.

"You cold?" Logan asked, his hand over mine. He pulled off his jacket without waiting for an answer and draped it over my shoulders.

"Thanks."

The carriage house came into view in the distance, a throwback to another time. Unlike the rest of the Fairchild house, the outbuilding wasn't well maintained. The white paint was peeling, the old wood siding splintering from years of damp, cold, and heat. Still, it was beautiful, and I took a second to admire it as Logan pulled me into its shadowy interior. Knowing we'd already ruled it out as a possible hiding place for the gold, and without Rachel breathing down my neck, I could truly appreciate its abandoned desolation.

"Did they really used to keep carriages in here?" I asked, turning in a circle, watching the play of shadow on what little light remained.

He nodded. "You can tell from the way the doors slide back and forth, like barn doors."

"It's amazing." I looked at him and smiled. "Really beautiful."

He laughed.

"What's so funny?"

He shook his head with a smile. "I don't know any other girl on the peninsula who would think so. It's all custom tile and skylights."

"Don't get me wrong," I said. "I love a lot of the houses up here. But the newer ones can be a little . . . sterile."

He walked slowly toward me, his eyes never leaving mine. Taking my hand, he led me across the room to an old workbench against one of the walls. He leaned on it, pulling me gently against him. I laid my head on his chest, listening to the gentle beat of his heart.

He stroked my hair, leaning in to kiss the top of my head. My breath caught in my throat, and a rush of hot wind sped through my body as his hands traveled to my neck, down to my collarbone, spreading to my shoulders, bare under the slender straps of my dress. My head fell back as his lips touched the sensitive skin near my ear.

"Grace . . . ," he murmured, his breath hot against my skin.

My breath caught in my throat as his lips moved down my neck. He tenderly kissed the corners of my mouth before touching his lips to mine. Then there was no room for gentleness, no room for anything but the passion building between us, as undeniable as the waves crashing on the beach in the distance.

His lips plundered mine, his fingers sliding into the hair at the back of my head, his free hand moving over my body as he explored my mouth with his tongue. He was consuming me, and I offered myself up to him without hesitation. Without reservation.

We were back on our beach. Back in space.

When we finally pulled away, we were both short of breath. His eyes were glassy, dark with desire, and he pulled me close in a ferocious embrace, burying his face in my hair.

"I'm sorry. I'm sorry, Grace."

I put my hands on either side of his head, forcing him to look at me. "Why are you sorry?"

"I'm moving too fast. I don't want you to think I'm playing

you. I just . . . I've never felt like this about anybody."

"Hey," I said, touching my lips softly to his. "You're not the only one."

"I'm not?"

I shook my head, warning bells clanging in my head. Not because of what I was about to say. Because I meant it.

"I feel it, too. I just don't know what to do about it." My voice broke, and I realized with horror that tears were stinging my eyes.

"Hey, hey, hey . . . ," he said. "We don't have to do anything about it. We'll just take it slow. We have all the time in the world."

I wrapped my arms around his torso, holding him close, trying to memorize the feel of his body against mine, the smell of his cologne, the hard plane of his chest under my cheek. Resisting the urge to tell him he was wrong. We didn't have even close to all the time in the world.

And that's when I noticed it. The windows behind Logan were new. Unlike the splintered siding with its chipped paint, the window frames looked freshly coated with polyurethane, the glass clean and clear.

It didn't make sense. The gold couldn't be in the carriage house. The exterior walls were visible on all four sides. There were no adjoining buildings to hide a panic room, no shelves or paneling that could be home to a safe big enough to hold the gold.

I turned in Logan's arms, leaning my head back against his chest, trying to make it seem like a natural way to calm the fire between us as I looked around the carriage house with fresh eyes. He wrapped his arms around my waist and pulled me close.

The walls of the carriage house were just like I remembered; nothing could be hiding there. I scanned the floor, my eyes coming to rest on the rubber mat. It looked to be commercial grade, the kind that might be in a restaurant kitchen. But it was slightly off-center, and there was something else, something glinting on one of the sides.

I looked harder, willing my eyes to focus in the half light of what was now full-on dusk. It took a few seconds, but then I got it. Hinges. The mat was askew, and underneath it, on one of the edges that wasn't lined up quite right, metallic hinges shone just enough against the drab concrete floor to be noticeable now that I was really looking.

There was some kind of door underneath the mat.

We'd been wrong all along. Warren Fairchild hadn't hidden his gold in a safe or a panic room.

He'd hidden it in a bunker.

Forty-Two

I had a hard time focusing on the rest of the party. Rachel was friendly but aloof, making it impossible to tell how much she knew, how hard she was going to push to get at the truth.

People laughed and talked, marveled at the freshness of the salmon and lobster, the quality of the champagne. Money was raised for the PHCT; compliments were given to the Fairchilds for another successful fund-raiser.

But it all went by in a blur. When I wasn't thinking about the possible discovery of the gold, I was thinking about Logan, transported back to the moments when we'd been alone in the carriage house, the feel of his mouth on my skin, his hands on my body.

Parker caught my eye toward the end of the night as he slipped from the house, and I knew from the expression on his face that I wasn't the only one with a discovery to share.

It was after midnight when we got home. Still, we trudged up the stairs to the War Room. Details might be lost overnight, given over to the haze of sleep. We needed to debrief while everything was still fresh.

The door was barely closed when Parker and I spoke in unison.

"There's nothing in the garage," Parker said.

"I think the gold is in the carriage house," I said at the same time.

My dad held up a hand. "Whoa." He looked at me. "Did you say what I think you said, Grace?"

I nodded.

"I thought we established that the gold couldn't be in the carriage house," my mom said.

"That's because we were looking for a panic room or a safe, something that could be hidden in the walls."

"And?" my dad prompted.

"It's not in the walls," I said. "It's underground. At least, I think it is."

"Under the carriage house?" my mom asked.

"I think so."

"But none of the houses up here have basements," my dad said with a perplexed expression.

"Maybe it's not a basement," I suggested. "Maybe it's a bunker."

My mom lifted one delicate brow. "A bunker?"

Parker nodded. "It makes sense. Warren's super paranoid,

right?" He continued without waiting for an answer. "If he were stockpiling supplies for a catastrophe, he'd want something disaster-proof."

"Tell us what you saw," my dad instructed.

I explained the setup in the carriage house, the new windows, the hinges in the floor.

My dad turned to Parker. "And you're sure there's nothing in the garage?"

"I'm sure. I had almost half an hour to check it out. There's nothing there."

My dad took a deep breath. "Okay, then. Let's assume Grace is right and the gold is in the carriage house. We need to confirm it. Along with this." He pushed a piece of paper across the table.

I looked at the six numbers written on it. "Is that the pass code to the Fairchilds' alarm system?"

"I think so. The tonality matches the keys to our system, but there's only one way to find out for sure." We were all quiet, waiting for the other shoe to drop. "Someone's going to have to test it."

"Someone?" Parker asked.

"I think it makes the most sense for Grace to do it. She—"

But he didn't get any further before Parker interrupted. "No way. What if it's wrong?"

"Then she'll run like hell." My dad's eyes were steely.

"No fucking way," Parker said. "I'll go."

"Grace knows the house better than you do. And she can double-check the bunker while she's there, too."

"The alarm keypad is right by the front door. It's not going to take a rocket scientist to find it and test it out," Parker said.

"We can both go," I said. "One of us can test the alarm and the other one can double-check the bunker."

"That works," my dad said.

"The Fairchilds will be out of town Friday night for a family wedding," my mom said. "We can do it then."

Her use of the word *we* got under my skin. There was no *we* in this job. At least not this part of it. Parker and I would have all the exposure. We were the ones who'd have to cover for them if we were caught. But that was the con. It's not like it was anything new.

Parker sighed in resignation. "Fine." He glanced at me. "But we stay together. That way if it's wrong, we can beat it out of there at the same time."

I nodded, feeling a little sick. I don't know if it was the idea of breaking into Logan's house or the looming end of our stay in Playa Hermosa, but I suddenly wanted to freeze time. To stay in the here and now, where Logan still cared about me and I hadn't yet committed an unforgivable betrayal. Where everything that had been done could still be undone.

Forty-Three

We were in the kitchen the next morning, eating a late pan-cake breakfast made by my dad, when the doorbell rang. We froze, looking at each other. It was Sunday morning. We weren't expecting anyone.

My mom got up and headed down the hall, hurrying back to us a moment later. "It's Harrison Mercer." And then, as if any of us needed the reminder, "Rachel Mercer's father."

"Well, open the door," my dad said.

She nodded and left the kitchen. Parker met my eyes over the business section spread out in front of him. A few seconds later I heard the front door open.

"Harrison! How nice to see you!" My mom's voice, slightly muffled, carried through the house. "What brings you here on this lovely morning?"

I strained to listen, catching only the murmur of their

voices and a few scattered words before footsteps sounded on the tile floor.

"Look what the cat dragged in!" my mother joked, entering the room with Harrison Mercer.

My dad stood, a smile washing over his face. "Harrison! How are you? Would you like a cup of coffee?"

But I already knew this wasn't a social call. I could tell from Harrison Mercer's pained expression, the worry lines in his normally smooth brow.

"No, thank you," he said.

"Cormac," my mom said, "Harrison has something he'd like to speak to us about." She turned to Rachel's dad. "Shall we go to the living room?"

Harrison nodded. "That's fine."

It was obvious from the way the three of them left the room that Parker and I weren't invited. I sat there, my heart thudding painfully in my chest, adrenaline flooding my body as I contemplated all the things Rachel Mercer's dad could want to talk to my parents about.

I shrugged when Parker raised his eyebrows in silent question.

Turning my head toward the hall, I listened to the voices in the living room, hoping for some kind of heads-up. But everything was a little muffled, and I could only make out snippets of conversation.

". . . sorry to have to do this," Harrison said.

And then my dad. "Don't be . . . What's . . . your mind?"

After that it was a series of whispers, an occasional word

finding its way through the halls of the house. Fifteen minutes passed before my mother appeared in the doorway, her face tight with something that could have been fear or anger. I didn't know which would be worse.

"Come with us," she said, leveling her eyes at me. "Both of you."

I followed Parker out of the kitchen and into the living room. My dad sat in one of the upholstered chairs while Harrison looked on from the sofa. Parker and I sat at the other end of the couch.

My mom reached into her pocket. When she held out her hand, she was holding my Chandler High School ID and a folded piece of paper. She opened it, and I was shocked to see the assembled remnants of the Fairchild property map glued carefully onto it. It wasn't perfect, but it was close enough. Despite my feelings about Rachel, I felt a burst of admiration. I couldn't imagine the kind of persistence it must have taken for her to piece it together.

"You're fortunate to have Rachel as one of your new friends," my mom said, casting a smile at Harrison. "It seems she's a good one."

I searched her face, trying to get a feel for which direction we were headed. "What . . . what do you mean?"

Harrison spoke up. "My daughter can have a bit of an overactive imagination. Somehow she got it in her head that you"—he laughed a little—"that you had something to hide."

My mom set the ID card and map down on the coffee table. "Your father and I explained to Harrison that we haven't been the best parents lately, what with the move to Arizona followed by the quick turnaround in San Francisco." She sighed. "It's not easy chasing your dad's next big deal."

Harrison glanced sheepishly at me. "I'm sorry. I wasn't aware you were adopted."

"It's no problem at all," my dad said. "Now that the paperwork has gone through, Grace is officially a Fontaine."

My mind was calculating, cataloging the story my parents had told: that my Chandler ID card listed me as Grace Rollins because I was adopted. That we'd lived only briefly in Arizona before a quick stop in San Francisco. Then, Playa Hermosa.

"And I certainly understand your wanting to duplicate what the Fairchilds have done to their property. Landscaping is a language all its own. I let Andrea take care of that stuff," Harrison said with a wave, referring to Rachel's mom.

I glanced at the map, grateful for my quick-thinking parents. Drawing the Fairchild property as an example for the landscapers was a better excuse than I could have managed.

"Well!" Harrison rose. "I'm sorry to disturb you on a Sunday morning. I told Rachel that I would look into her concerns. As I'm sure you know, she and Logan Fairchild were an item for a while. I think she still has a soft spot for him. I figured she was off base. We all enjoy having you here."

There was hand shaking and more small talk, but I barely managed to nod and smile in the right places.

I was in trouble. We all were.

Forty-Four

"What the fuck were you thinking?" My dad was practically shouting, as close to losing it as I'd ever seen him.

I dropped my head into my hands, wishing I could disappear into the floor of the War Room. "I'm sorry."

"Stop saying you're sorry," my mom said, her voice soft. "Just tell us why you did it. Why on earth would you keep that ID card, let alone carry it around with you?"

I glanced at Parker, wondering if he was as pissed as everyone else. There was nothing but sympathy in his eyes.

I looked at my mom. "I don't know. I just . . . it's hard sometimes," I finished softly.

"What's hard?" my dad demanded.

"All of it!" I shouted. "Making new friends every four months and lying and moving and keeping our stories straight and saying good-bye."

"That's the job, Grace." My dad's voice was firm.

"Well, she didn't exactly sign on for the job, did she?" Parker's voice was low and hard.

"She did," my dad said, danger in his voice. "She signed on when she agreed."

Parker folded his arms across his chest. "After you adopted her. Did you really think someone who'd been in the foster system, someone who'd waited years for a family, would walk away when she finally got one?" He shook his head with disgust. "She was just a kid. You knew exactly what you were doing. With both of us. We were your biggest con."

For a minute the room seemed wired, ready to blow, a bottomless silence opening up between us. Then my dad got up, pacing to the window. He turned his back on us.

I looked over at my mom. She was chewing her lip. It was a small gesture, but it gave away her nervousness. I wondered if it was shame or anger that colored her cheeks.

"Well, it's too late now," my dad said without turning around. "We're too close to abandon the job."

"And it would only bring us unwanted attention," my mom agreed. "Better to stay the course. Get it done and get out."

My dad rubbed the five o'clock shadow at his jawline. "We'll have to leave right after we get the gold. With the Mercers on our tail and the link to Arizona, we can't afford to play dumb for a few weeks after the theft like we usually do."

I swallowed hard. It was my fault we'd have to make

a quick getaway. My fault we were under the magnifying glass.

"What about Rachel?" I asked, trying to focus on the problem at hand.

My dad turned around. "What about her?"

"What if it's not enough? What if she's still suspicious?"

"Then she can be suspicious," my dad said. "She's done all she can do."

"For now," Parker said. "But Grace is right; what if she pushes the issue?"

"She's only going to seem crazy if she does that now," my mom said. "Something tells me she's smart enough to know that."

"Right, which means she's smart enough to see through the explanation you gave Mr. Mercer," Parker said.

My dad crossed the room and planted his hands on the table. His gaze was piercing, his eyes too bright.

"Well, then," he said, "we better get back to work. The sooner we get the gold, the sooner we can be out of here. And I think we can all agree that sooner is better than later."

Forty-Five

I stared out the window as Parker sped to school the next day. He was driving too fast, inviting unwanted attention with a possible speeding ticket, but he didn't seem to care. The earth was rumbling under our feet, the veneer cracking on our carefully constructed facade.

He pulled into our usual parking spot and cut the engine. For a minute we just sat there, watching Logan and the others mingle around the BMW.

"You okay?" Parker asked softly.

"Fine," I said. "Thanks for going to bat for me."

"No thanks necessary. You reap what you sow. And Cormac and Renee are reaping big time."

I shook my head. "It was my fault. I violated protocol."

He exhaled in a rush of air. "Do you hear yourself? You 'violated protocol'? Does that sound like something a normal sixteen-year-old would say?"

I reached for the door handle. "Normal for us."

I exited the car before he could say anything else and plastered a smile onto my face as Logan came toward me. I didn't know whether to be scared or relieved that Rachel wasn't standing with the others. I was torn between wanting to keep her in sight and wanting to pretend she didn't exist. Wanting to pretend none of it existed.

I moved through the day in a haze, trying not to feel guilty every time I looked at Logan. Every time he looked at me. I braced myself to see Rachel in AP Euro, but I still felt my cheeks flush when she entered the room. Now I was sure about her suspicions. And she knew I knew.

All the cards were finally on the table.

She dropped something in front of me on the way to her desk. "Here are my ideas for the project." She slid into her chair and leaned over just as Mr. Stein walked to the front of the room. "Nice performance with my dad, by the way. But I don't buy it."

I took a deep breath and shook my head, hoping the gesture passed for *you're crazy* instead of *why can't I shake you?* I spent the period rehearsing explanations and comebacks for what was probably an inevitable confrontation with Rachel. When the bell rang, she followed me out of the room.

"Whether we like it or not," she said behind me, "we're going to have to finish this project together."

I turned toward her, stepping aside so the flood of kids trying to get to class didn't mow us down. "Tell you what:

why don't you do the explanatory essay and I'll put together the board game. We can hand it in at the same time."

She was silent for a minute. "It must be hard."

I sighed. "What are you talking about, Rachel?"

She shrugged. "I just think it would be hard to be around someone who's onto you, that's all. Someone who doesn't buy your little story."

I stepped closer to her, my earlier insecurity morphing into anger. True, I'd been off my game since the beginning in Playa Hermosa. I'd made mistakes. Violated the rules. All of that was on me. But I still couldn't help wanting to blame Rachel. She'd been all over me from the very beginning. It hadn't helped. And who was she? Nobody, that's who. A spoiled peninsula princess who had a hunch. That's all.

"You know what's hard?" I stood so close to her that she leaned back a little. "Dealing with someone who's so crazy that she clings to a delusional fantasy. Someone who's so miserable, so ashamed of Daddy's sexual forays, that focusing on her little fantasy world is preferable to real life."

Her mouth dropped open, her eyes widening in shock. I was surprised, too. I wasn't a mean person. I didn't hurt people intentionally. Not like this, anyway. But I had reached my limit. Everything that could go wrong had. I was on the defensive at a time when I couldn't afford to be anything but offensive. When I couldn't afford to be distracted by what Rachel Mercer believed. What she might tell someone else.

"I don't know what you're up to," Rachel said, recovering, "but I promise you I'm going to find out."

"Or maybe you're just going to realize that you were wrong all along." I turned and walked away, waiting until I'd turned the corner to duck into a bathroom as the late bell rang for next period.

I rushed into the last stall and slammed the door, leaning my head against it. My pulse was racing, the blood rushing through my veins so fast that I felt light-headed. All the fear and uncertainty of the past couple of months—the past few years—welled up inside me, fighting to escape the confines of my skin.

I took a few deep breaths, concentrating on the sensation of the cold metal door against my forehead, the slow intake of breath, the measured exhale. I told myself it would be okay. Rachel had nothing but accusations. Accusations that had been addressed by the perfectly logical explanations my parents had given Rachel's father.

But deep down I knew it wasn't that simple. A light had been shone on us. All of us. There would be no easy end to the Playa Hermosa con. No quiet slinking away explained as another opportunity for my dad, another chance to back a promising new company. We would steal Warren Fairchild's gold and leave without a word. And when it was all said and done, Rachel would come forward.

Then everyone would know what we really were.

Forty-Six

"Logan . . . stop." I laced my fingers with his, moving his hand from its position on my stomach to a safer zone up by my shoulder.

We were on the beach, wrapped up in a blanket and each other the night before he and his parents were leaving for his cousin's wedding in Santa Barbara. Things had been heating up between us, our deepening emotional connection only adding to the physical fire that seemed to build every time we were alone. I wanted him. More than I'd ever wanted anyone. But the last thing I needed was another reason to feel connected to Logan Fairchild. Another reason to make it hard to say good-bye.

"I'm sorry," he said, running his hands through my hair as he dropped gentle kisses on my forehead, my temples, my nose. "I don't want to rush you."

I nodded, trying to swallow around the lump that had lodged itself in my throat. "I know. And it's not like I don't want to. I just . . . I want to be sure, that's all. I don't want to ruin what we have by moving too fast."

"I understand, although I hope you know that nothing could change the way I feel about you." He pulled me close so that my head rested on his shoulder.

The rush of waves on the beach was a match to the rush of blood through my veins, the desire that threatened to pull me into the too-deep waters of my feelings for Logan. I couldn't afford to go there. I'd drown for sure. Was already drowning.

And he was wrong. There were things that could—that would—change the way he felt about me.

We were packing up, folding the blankets and stuffing everything back into the bag we'd brought with us, when he said something that almost stopped my heart.

"I'm sorry about Rachel."

I looked up at him, trying to mask the fear thumping through my body. "What about her?"

He shook his head. "She told me about her theory. Or her nontheory," he added sarcastically.

I sighed. "Which theory is that? The one where I'm here to usher in the apocalypse or the one where I'm secretly working for the IRS, gathering data on the illegal tax loopholes used by the residents of Playa Hermosa?"

He laughed. "She can be a little . . ."

"Crazy?" I volunteered, rooting for the power of suggestion.

He nodded slowly. "Yeah. And high-strung."

"It's fine," I said, brushing sand off my clothes. "I get it."

"You do?"

"Yeah. She still has a thing for you, I move in, she doesn't like it . . ." I shrugged. "And we're different. We move a lot because of my dad's job, I'm adopted . . ."

It wasn't a lie. Not exactly. But it wasn't the whole truth either, and I hated myself for that.

He came over and wrapped his arms around me, looking down into my eyes. "You didn't tell me," he said softly.

"Because it's no big deal. I was in foster care for a while. My parents adopted me. It took some time for the paperwork to come through. . . . It's not something I talk about."

It was the closest I'd ever come to telling the truth about myself.

He brushed the back of his hand against my cheek. "Okay, but I'm here to listen if you change your mind."

I smiled. "Thanks."

We grabbed our stuff and headed up the beach, taking the winding pathway back to the car. Logan talked about the beach in summer, about how nice it was, how warm. He talked about teaching me to surf and going to Catalina Island. He talked like this was just the beginning.

I smiled and nodded, but I knew the truth. This wasn't the beginning he imagined.

It was the beginning of the end.

Forty-Seven

It was after midnight when we headed on foot to Logan's house. There was only one road leading away from the Fairchild property, and we didn't want the Saab spotted if anything went wrong. Plus, we'd have more options without the burden of a car. We could even descend to the beach, although the thought of making our way down the craggy cliff face in the dark made me light-headed with dread.

There was an occasional flutter and rustle in the trees overhead, but otherwise the neighborhood was hushed. Christmas lights winked on porches, and the air had a sharp edge as the wind blew in off the water. Despite my gloves, I stuffed my hands in my pockets as we hurried through the neighborhood, trying to stay in the shadows.

I wasn't nervous. Not about getting in and out anyway. We'd broken into plenty of houses to gather information.

The Fairchilds' security system was a little more high-end, and they were a little more high-profile than some of our marks, but the plan wasn't complicated. We didn't even need to deal with the gate since we weren't taking anything this time. We'd hop the fence instead, sneak our way onto the property—avoiding the cameras along the driveway and at the corners of the house—and break in through one of the windows. Then it would be a race to disable the alarm. If we had the wrong code, we were screwed. Things would go south fast and we'd have to beat it out of there.

But if we had the right one, we would proceed to the carriage house, where we'd try to confirm the presence of the bunker and the location of the gold. If we could get into the bunker easily tonight, we would do it, just to make sure the gold was there. If we couldn't, we'd case the security protocol around it so we could plan a way in the night we made our move.

"You ready?" Parker said softly as we rounded the corner onto the Fairchilds' street.

"Yep."

We walked in the shadows of the bougainvillea plants that lined the sidewalk. I was glad this part of the peninsula, the most expensive in Playa Hermosa, was so isolated. There were only two other properties, both set back from the road and both marked by security gates like the Fairchilds'.

We approached the gates warily, giving wide berth to the camera mounted at the top of one of the posts. Once we were past the gate, we continued to the curve of the cul-de-sac, veering off the sidewalk and into the trees that surrounded the Fairchild property. I breathed a sigh of relief when we were off the street. In the trees, we'd be invisible to anyone making a late-night ice cream run or taking their dog for a walk.

"Let's go a little farther," Parker whispered. "We want to hit the house in the center of the west wall, out of range of the corner cameras."

I nodded and followed him farther into the trees. We walked for about three more minutes before cutting up toward the fence that surrounded the grounds. Once there, we had a clear view of the property and our position in relation to the cameras at the corners of the house.

"A little farther," I said, using my hand to signal the direction. "We're too close to the southwest corner."

"Agreed."

We continued along the fence until we were halfway between the southwest and northwest corners of the house. It was as out of range of the cameras as we were going to get.

"Let's time," Parker said softly.

I nodded, and we both watched the cameras as they scanned the property, moving slowly back and forth. After the cameras had made ten full cycles, I looked at Parker.

"I've got thirty seconds."

"Me too." He looked up at the iron fence. "It's going to be tight, especially with the fence. Can you do it?"

I thought about it, counting as I imagined pulling myself

up and over the top of it, sprinting across the lawn. "I think so."

"You have to be sure."

"I'm as sure as I can be," I hissed.

"Fine," he said between clenched teeth. "I'm just saying."

He bent down, making a sling for my foot with his gloved hands. I stepped into it, wobbling a little as he lifted me up into the air. When the top of the fence was within reach, I grabbed on and pulled myself up. Parker's hand dropped from my foot, and I teetered on the fence for a second before gaining my balance. Once I felt steady, I hoisted one leg, followed by the other, over the top. After that it was a simple drop to the ground.

I stepped aside, looking at Parker through the fence.

He took a few steps back and ran at it, launching himself up high enough to grab onto the top rail. He made swinging over it look easy. He was on the ground in seconds.

"Let's do it," he said.

Turning toward the house, I scanned for windows out of range of the cameras.

"That one," I said, pointing to a window almost midway between the two corners of the house. "Should be the living room."

He nodded, and we focused on the cameras, watching their slow rotation of the grounds, waiting for them to line up a gap we could run through. After a few cycles, I had it.

"After this next one," I said quietly, watching. "Five . . . four . . . three . . . two . . . go."

We sprinted across the lawn side by side. I kept my eyes on the cameras the whole way, just in case we were off on the timing. But it was about right; the camera on the southwest corner was just swinging back toward us when we reached the house.

We plastered ourselves against the stucco, catching our breath, watching to be sure the living room window we were aiming for wouldn't have visibility on either of the cameras.

"Looks good," Parker said. "Let's go." He slid a few feet toward the window and pulled out the glass cutter from the holster-style pack on his chest. "Where are the locks?"

"Center."

He flipped the glass cutter open and made a small circle at the top center of the glass. Pulling a cloth out of his pocket, he held it carefully up to the window, tapping gently. When the circle of glass began to dislodge from the rest of the window, he gave it a thunk with his index finger. It fell way with a tiny pop.

I held my breath. If it survived intact, we could glue it back in on our way out, and it would be a long while before the Fairchilds knew someone had broken in. If the glass fell and broke, the Fairchilds would know they'd had a break-in. We'd take some stuff to make it look like a garden-variety theft, but odds were good that the alarm code would be changed and we'd be back to square one.

I didn't hear it shatter, but that didn't mean it hadn't.

Parker reached a hand through the empty circle, feeling around for the window latch. There was a faint sucking sound as the window released from the weather stripping.

Parker replaced the glass cutter and positioned his hands on the window frame. He looked over, raising his eyebrows. Once he opened the window, the clock would be ticking on the alarm.

I nodded, and he pushed up on the frame.

Forty-Eight

We were up and over the window ledge in less than thirty seconds. It took us twenty more to race to the alarm keypad in the foyer, and I took a few moments to catch my breath, repeating the alarm code I'd memorized before leaving the house. I didn't want to make a mistake.

When my hands were steady enough, I reached out and punched the keys.

8-3-6-0-1-2

Time seemed to stop as I waited for the red status light to change to green. I didn't dare move, didn't dare look at Parker. I was ready to take off running when an almost inaudible beep sounded from the keypad. The light turned green.

I exhaled noisily. "Jesus."

"Let's check out the glass before we go to the carriage house," Parker said.

We made our way back to the living room, using Parker's penlight to scan the ground for the piece of glass he'd removed from the window.

"Careful where you step," he warned.

I was beginning to wonder if it had rolled under the desk, or even the sofas near the TV, when I spotted a glimmer on the carpet.

I pointed. "There."

Parker shone the light in that direction. There it was: an almost perfectly round piece of glass about six inches in diameter.

I picked it up while Parker removed the auto-glass adhesive from the pack. I held the circle up to the flashlight.

"Nice. Not a single crack," I said. "We got lucky with the carpet."

I held the glass while Parker ran a thin line of adhesive around its edges. After that he had to work fast to replace it before the glue dried. It wasn't easy. We had to get the glass back in position without letting it fall through to the other side, and I stood on the desk near the window, trying to help him line it up before we pressed it into place.

When it looked like we had it right, he tipped the glass gently into the empty spot in the window, careful not to press too hard. He shimmied it a little, trying to get it just right before the adhesive dried. Finally, he stood back.

"I think that's it."

I leaned in for a better look. It was almost seamless. There was a very small ring around the piece of cut glass, but I didn't think anyone would notice it in passing.

"Looks good." I held out a hand to Parker. "I'll finish it."

He handed me a small bottle filled with blue liquid and the cloth he'd used to tap out the cut glass. I sprayed a little of the cleaner on the cloth and wiped the glue residue off the window before hopping down off the desk.

"Carriage house?" he asked, putting everything back in the pack.

I nodded, leading him through the house to the kitchen.

"Time," Parker gave the command, and we watched the cameras at the back of the house, waiting for a gap. When we had the timing right, we sprinted across the lawn until we reached the back wall of the carriage house.

This part of the property was in shadows, which was why we'd used it as an approach. The camera aimed at the carriage house entrance prevented us from using the door, so we repeated the procedure we'd used on the window in the living room.

This time we weren't as lucky, and we heard the unmistakable sound of breaking glass as the circular piece fell to the carriage house floor.

"Fuck," Parker muttered.

"We'll deal with it when we get inside," I said. "Just go."

Parker opened the window, then waited for me to crawl through before following. We landed on the concrete floor and immediately spotted the broken glass a few feet from the window.

"There are some old windows leaning against the walls.

Maybe we can borrow glass from one of those?" I suggested.

Parker sighed. "I'll look."

I hurried to the center of the carriage house to the gray floor mat. It wasn't off-center anymore, and I wondered who had been out here. And why. Did Warren Fairchild check on his stash now and then? Did he add to it?

I pulled back the mat and dragged it aside. I'd been expecting the hole in the floor, but it still shocked me to see it. Ten feet wide by ten feet long, it was a lot bigger than I'd thought it would be. Big enough to require two doors instead of one, probably because one would be too cumbersome for one person to lift.

I walked around the doorway in the floor, cataloging details. The double doors were made of what looked like steel. They were designed to meet in the middle, to fold back against the floor when open. Three metal bands—one at the bottom, one in the middle, and one at the top—ran across both doors. Each one was sealed with a hefty padlock.

I looked more closely, sure I'd missed something. There was no way Warren Fairchild's gold was secured with a bunker and three padlocks.

"That must be it."

Parker's voice made me jump. I looked over my shoulder to find him standing behind me.

"There's no way the gold's in there," I said.

"What do you mean?" he asked. "That has to be it. You said you searched the house, and I ruled out the garage."

I stared at the doors. "Yeah, but . . . padlocks? If Dad's

right, there's twenty million dollars worth of gold down there. It doesn't make sense."

"That's exactly why it does make sense."

I looked at him. "What are you talking about?"

"This is a guy who stockpiles gold bars to prepare for a potential catastrophe. The same guy who's worth millions but wires his house with a low-tech security system monitored by local rent-a-cops and then doesn't even attach said system to the bunker holding his gold."

"That's what I'm saying; maybe it's not down there."

Parker shrugged. "I think you're wrong. But there's only one way to find out."

I tipped my head at the padlocks. "Those are going to need some big bolt cutters. We can't do it now. He'd know someone was here."

"We'll execute as planned. Come in when they're not home, cut the padlocks off, and be prepared to take the gold. If it's not there, it's a standard B and E. No harm, no foul."

A seed of hope blossomed inside me. If the gold wasn't there, we wouldn't have to steal from Logan and his family. Nothing that mattered, anyway. We'd still have to leave Playa Hermosa, but maybe I would be able to live with myself afterward.

"On the plus side," Parker said, bending down to replace the mat over the double doors, "we're done for tonight."

"Did you find the old windows?" I asked.

He nodded. "Already replaced the glass. We're good to go."

"Wow, you're fast."

He grinned. "I'm a pro."

We exited the carriage house through the window, lowering it carefully to be sure the new piece of glass didn't fall out. Then we hurried back across the lawn, avoiding the cameras.

We stuck to the walls until we reached the living room window. We'd left it open, and I kept watch while Parker climbed in to reset the alarm. He reappeared a minute later, hurrying out the window and shutting it while counting, careful not to exceed the two-minute delay.

Window securely closed, we timed the cameras and raced across the lawn. My heart pounded in my ears as I scrabbled over the fence and waited for Parker to land behind me. When he did, we hurried into the trees, anxious to be away from the Fairchilds' cameras.

I took one look back at the house and grounds. The next time I was here this time of night, it would be to steal the gold. And it would be the last night I'd be in Playa Hermosa.

Forty-Nine

"Are you going to eat that or play with it?"

I looked up at Selena, sitting next to me in the cafeteria as the rest of the group talked and goofed off around us. "Both?"

She looked at me questioningly, and I realized that there were downsides to having friends. To having someone know you.

I took a halfhearted bite of my salad, hyperaware of everything going on around me. Logan's hand on my knee under the table. The holiday lights winking around the cafeteria in celebration of the upcoming winter break. Harper and Olivia bickering over some kind of archaic fashion rule.

It had been two weeks since our recon mission at the Fairchilds' house. I'd spent most of my free time with Logan, trying to act normal. But inside, I was screaming against the ticking clock of my time in Playa Hermosa. My time with Logan and Selena.

Plans for the night of the theft were under way, and my mom was working to verify the Fairchilds' schedule with Leslie, hoping for a two-day period when the whole family would be gone. Anything less and it would be tough to make a clean getaway before it was discovered that the gold was missing.

I glanced over at Logan, and he leaned down, leaving a gentle kiss on my cheek. Something painful tugged at my heart as I looked into his eyes, saw the light there that was meant for me. I wondered if he saw the same thing in my eyes. If later he would think everything I said was a lie, or if he would remember the way I looked at him and know some part of it had been true.

I glanced away as he went back to his conversation with Raj across the table. I couldn't help smiling as my gaze fell on the others. Olivia and Harper, engaged in their heated debate about clothes while Rachel rolled her eyes next to them. Raj, leaning over the table, talking to Logan with intensity about a new video game. David, on the other side of Selena, holding her hand under the table.

I would miss them. Even Rachel, in some strange way. She was a pain in the ass, a royal bitch sometimes. But she cared about her friends, was even willing to look crazy for them. She had gone to bat for Logan when it counted, even if he didn't realize it yet. That made her a better person than me.

They weren't perfect. They had problems. Made mistakes. But they were real, and the authenticity of their lives suddenly stood in stark contrast to the shiny facade of my own.

I'd created a facsimile of a life. It had seemed real when I hadn't looked too hard, like one of those books with two images—one on top that seemed complete until you lifted it to reveal the detail underneath.

I don't know why I hadn't noticed it before. Maybe Parker had been right. Maybe I had been too young. Too grateful to have a chance at a real family. Too afraid of what I would find—and what I'd have to do about it—if I looked too hard.

Now I had, and nothing seemed any clearer for the revelation.

My phone buzzed in my pocket. I pulled it out, surprised to see a text from my dad.

Meeting 3:00pm

I looked at Parker, holding his phone. He met my eyes, the wordless communication we'd developed on the job moving between us.

It could only mean one thing: it was time to make our move.

Fifty

I knew the plan was in motion the minute I got home. The atmosphere was charged, full of expectation, like the air in the moment before a thunderstorm.

"Are we all set?" Parker asked, the moment the door to the War Room was closed.

"As set as we can be." My dad gestured to the table. "Sit, and we'll go over everything."

Parker sat down, nervously tapping his foot. "Do we know when the Fairchilds will be gone?"

I swallowed my annoyance. He was too eager to see the job come to a close, totally insensitive to my inner conflict. He had nothing to lose. No good-byes to say. His friendship with the guys was a surface one, and Parker had never been interested in Rachel beyond the job.

"In a manner of speaking," my dad said.

I looked from him to my mother.

"Warren and Leslie are staying in Burbank for a charity gala and golf tournament this weekend," she said.

"What about Logan?" I asked.

She took a deep breath. "He isn't going."

"Then it will have to be another weekend," I said.

My dad shook his head. "Impossible. They don't have another event scheduled for the next two months. We can't afford to wait. Besides, everything is in place. We need to move."

"We can't just take the gold with Logan home," I said. "And I doubt I can keep him out of the house long enough for you guys to do it."

"You don't have to," my mom said.

"Then what's the plan?"

I knew I wouldn't like it when my mom cut a glance at my dad before returning her gaze to me. Like she was seeking his last-minute support.

"You'll be at Logan's the night of the theft. We have a mild sedative that you—"

"A mild *sedative*?" I interrupted.

"It will just put him to sleep for a while," my dad said. "Long enough for us to get the gold."

I folded my arms over my chest. "I'm not drugging Logan."

"Yes, you are." My dad's tone was firm, his gaze unflinching. "It's what has to be done to complete the job."

"I can't do it," I said, desperation creeping into my voice.

But even as I said it, I knew I would do what I was told to do. Our safety and freedom depended on it.

"Yes, you can, honey," my mom said gently. "I know it's hard. I know you have . . . feelings for Logan. But it has to be done. We all risk exposure if we stay here much longer."

"And might I remind you," my dad added, "that your carelessness is partly to blame for that."

I was hit with a fresh wave of guilt. He was right. I was the one who'd kept—and carried—the ID card. I was the one who'd let Rachel Mercer wander the house the day she'd found the shredded map of the Fairchild estate.

I glanced at Parker, but he was silent. He wasn't going to bat for Logan. He was on Team Get Out Now, whatever it took.

"What would it do to him?" I heard the defeat in my own voice. Hated myself for it.

My mom's shoulders relaxed a little. "It's just Valium. It'll put him to sleep for a few hours and he'll wake up good as new."

I was still thinking about it when my dad launched into the plans for the night of the theft. "You'll hang out with Logan on Friday, wait until just before midnight, and slip the Valium into his drink. Parker will be at Allied, waiting for our signal."

"What signal?" I asked.

"We have to carry cell phones on this one, Gracie," my mom said. "It's risky, but it's the only way to keep in contact with everyone so spread out. If any of us gets picked up, it's

SOP for getting rid of it."

Standard Operating Procedure for getting rid of a cell phone was to surreptitiously submerge it in a body of water or to remove the memory card, snip it into pieces, and take a hammer to the cell phone. Depending on the resources available at the time.

"You'll text me when Logan's out, and I'll text Parker," my dad continued. "Parker will get in front of the guard he's been taunting at Allied, make him think he has a shot at catching him." He looked at me. "Then Parker will double back to Allied and put the Fairchild cameras on a loop. Once we know he's done, you'll buzz us in through the gate using the alarm keypad."

"Where will you and Mom be all this time?" Asking the question meant defeat. He'd pulled me into the plan, forced me to visualize it, to be a part of it. With every question I asked, every suggestion I made, I was that much more committed.

Psychology 101.

"We'll be waiting in the truck near the cliffs," he said. "We'll start to move when I get the all clear from Parker, and we'll be at the gate when you buzz us in. Be sure to close it behind us so the neighbors don't get suspicious."

"Then what?"

"Then you'll put on the mask we give you—"

"Mask?" We'd never worn masks before.

He nodded. "We'll all have masks. Eventually, they'll know it was us, but we don't want to give them anything we don't have to, just in case."

I heard the rest of his sentence in my mind. *In case we get caught. In case it goes to trial. In case the loop on the cameras goes awry and the footage is used as evidence.*

"We can take them off once we're inside the carriage house, away from the cameras," my mom added, as if such small consolation somehow made everything else okay.

"We'll back the truck up to the carriage house," my dad continued. "Then we'll break the locks on the bunker and start unloading the gold."

"If it's even there," I said, still half hoping it wouldn't be.

"It's there," he said.

"What about Parker?" I asked.

"Parker will keep watch at Allied, make sure they're not suspicious that their cameras have been tampered with. When we have the gold loaded, we'll text him a location and pick him up on our way out of town."

"And that will be it?" I say. "We'll leave straight from the Fairchilds' house?"

"That's the plan," my dad said. "Both of you need to be packed." He leveled his gaze at me. "No mementos, Gracie."

I chewed my lip.

My mom spoke next. "I'll drop your father at a dummy car and he'll take you and Parker to the safe house while I make the gold drop to our buyers. We'll meet up after that."

"Wait . . . we're splitting up?" Parker asked.

"It's the smartest thing to do in this case," my dad said. "Your mom is the one who arranged for the sale of the gold.

These are her contacts. The rest of us shouldn't be exposed if we can help it."

"Then what?" Parker asked.

"We'll leave the country," my dad said. "It's all arranged. But we can talk about that once we're clear."

Because it wouldn't do to have one of us picked up knowing where the others were going. Better to wait until we were all free and clear before divulging our destination.

I reviewed each step, each piece of the plan taking me further away from Logan. From the first life I'd had that had seemed real.

"You'll have to get yourself invited to Logan's Friday night," my mom said. "Can you do that?"

I nodded. I wouldn't even have to ask. If his parents were out of town, he'd want to spend time alone with me. He always did. I'd played him to perfection.

There was no pride in the knowledge.

The rest of the week passed quickly under the duress of my impending good-bye. I wanted to hold on to it. To make every cafeteria lunch and gossip session with Selena last. To memorize the feel of Logan's hand in mine, of his steady presence as we walked the Playa Hermosa campus on our way to classes.

By Thursday night I was in a state of emotional panic. Tomorrow I would say good-bye to Selena and the others, although they wouldn't know it was good-bye. I would see Logan. We would cuddle on the couch and watch movies.

And then I would drug him and steal from him.

I was lying in bed, trying to coax myself to sleep, when I heard the voice outside my window. I held still, listening more closely, trying to figure out who it was. I thought it might be my dad or Parker, but a few seconds later I realized it wasn't either of them.

It was the man next door.

I got out of bed and crossed to the window, careful to stand to the side in case he happened to be looking my way. The house was dark, and I turned my attention to the backyard, wondering if I'd imagined the voice. The outdoor lights were off, too, the yard empty.

I was just about to go back to bed when I saw a faint orange light glow in the dark near the trellis. A cigarette. And then, again, the man's voice.

"Does it surprise you? He's always left too much to chance."

I leaned closer to the window, straining to hear.

"Patience is a virtue," he said, his voice soft but firm. "And in this business, a necessity."

I tried to imagine the kind of business suited to such a weird guy. Dealer of exotic animals? Manager of elderly musicians? Hot tub aficionado?

"Yes, yes. I'm aware." The man's voice was curt. "They'll come to me when they're ready. When they must." A pause. "Good night."

I moved away from the window and crept carefully back to my bed. As if the man were superhuman. As if he could somehow hear and see me through the walls.

I wished suddenly that I'd snooped closer to home. Now I would never know the identity of the man next door, never know why he spoke so cryptically to the birds or sang creepy old songs. He would always be the crazy guy who'd lived next door to us in California.

Just one more of Playa Hermosa's unanswered questions.

Fifty-One

I moved through Friday in a kind of overstimulated haze. Everything felt both immediate and further away, like I'd already left it behind. When Rachel sat next to me in AP Euro, looking perfect as usual, I didn't even have the energy to check my own hair, to worry about whether I was in character, whether I looked the part. I wasn't even sure what that was anymore.

Or if I cared.

"Here's the essay," she said, handing me a stack of papers.

"Thanks. I have the board game, too." I pulled it out of my bag and handed it to her. I scanned the essay while she looked over my part of the project.

"Looks good," she said.

"Thanks. This too. Do you want to hand it in or should I?"

She shrugged. "Whatever."

If I'd had a nickel for every time Rachel had said *whatever*, we wouldn't have had to steal Warren Fairchild's gold.

"You can do it," I said, handing the essay back to her.

She stacked the essay on top of the cardboard I'd used to create our board game on the Reformation. Then she turned around and faced forward like I wasn't even there.

At least there wouldn't be any sappy good-byes with Rachel Mercer.

About halfway through lunch in the cafeteria, I made a show of taking off my sweater.

"Why is it so hot in here?" I complained.

"Um, probably because of the two hundred sweaty, hormone-ridden teenage bodies crammed together like sardines," Selena said.

I laughed. It was more difficult than usual. "Good point. Think I can keep this in your locker until Monday?"

It wasn't an unusual request. Selena's locker was one hall over from the cafeteria. Mine—assigned later because I'd transferred in after the start of the school year—was halfway across campus and nowhere near the rest of my classes.

"Sure. Want me to take it so you can walk with Logan?"

"Nah, I'm seeing him tonight. I'll walk with you."

A few minutes later the bell rang, and Logan walked with Selena and me out into the hallway. He leaned down to give me a quick kiss.

"I can't wait to see you tonight," he whispered.

His breath near my ear sent a shiver up my spine. "Me too."

He walked backward a few steps, still smiling, before he turned and disappeared into the crowd.

Selena grinned wickedly. "Things must be heating up between you and Mr. Perfect."

I tried to smile. "You could say that."

"I'll trade you details with Logan for details with David," she said.

"That, my friend, is a deal."

We turned the corner, and I slipped Selena's bracelet off my wrist and dropped it into the pocket of my sweater. By the time she found it, she'd probably hate my guts like everyone else. But at least she'd have her mother's bracelet.

"Let's have it," she said when we reached her locker.

I handed her the sweater. "Thanks."

"No problem. Just don't forget to get it before Wednesday."

It took me a minute to realize what she meant: winter break started Thursday. I imagined everyone waking up Christmas morning, opening presents in their pajamas, texting friends to compare gifts. I had no idea where I would be, what I would be doing. And while our next stop was always a little vague for obvious reasons, this was different. We'd be in another country. And we'd probably never be able to come back.

She shut her locker. "Want to do something tomorrow?"

I nodded. "Sure."

"Great! Text me." She turned to go.

"Selena?"

"Yeah?"

People were milling around us, rushing to class before the late bell. There was so much I wanted to say. So much I wanted to tell her.

"I just . . ." I swallowed hard, trying to keep it together. "I'm not sure if I ever told you how much your friendship has meant—how much it means—to me."

She smiled. "I feel the same way. I don't know what I ever did before you came here."

"You did just fine," I told her. "You're better than all of these people put together. Don't ever forget it."

Her smile faltered a little. "Grace . . . is everything okay?"

I forced a laugh. "Yeah! Sure! It's the holidays." I shrugged, rolling my eyes. "I guess it makes me a little sappy. I just wanted you to know how much I love you."

She threw her arms around me. "I love you, too, girl! Now stop. Before you make me cry and stuff."

"Deal!" I held out my hand. "We're all business from here on out."

She slapped my hand away before turning to go. "You're ridiculous."

"Takes one to know one," I called after her.

I was still standing in the empty hall when the late bell rang.

Fifty-Two

I packed up my things and left them in my room. It was time to go to Logan's.

I looked around the house as I made my way down the stairs. I would miss the high ceilings, the tile floors that were always cool underfoot, the way the sunlight streamed in through the west-facing windows in the late afternoon. I wondered what the next house would look like. If it would be cold or warm there. If it would have an ocean or lake nearby.

I walked out without looking back. Looking back only made things worse.

Parker was sitting on the porch when I stepped outside. He looked up at me, eyes hidden behind the lenses of his sunglasses.

"All set?" he asked.

I nodded and headed for the car.

We didn't want the Saab sitting in the Fairchilds' driveway in the morning, and we'd have our hands full with the truck and dummy car we would use to meet up with my mom when it was all over. Parker would drop me off at Logan's and my dad would deal with the Saab.

I realized suddenly that I wasn't quite sure what that meant, how it all worked. In fact, there was a lot I didn't know. I'd put too much power in the hands of my parents. If I decided to stay—if I decided not to leave with Parker—that would have to change. I needed to start asking questions. To start making decisions for myself.

I looked up at the house next door as I slid into the passenger seat.

"You okay?" Parker asked as he started up the car.

"Peachy," I said.

He put the car in gear and pulled away from the curb. He didn't speak again until we were on the main road leading to Logan's house.

"I'm sorry, Grace."

I kept my eyes on the ocean, the familiar strip of shimmering blue satin that seemed to go on and on. "For what?"

He sighed. "I know I've been a pain in the ass. But I also know you really liked him. Logan, I mean."

"I really liked all of them." We were both speaking in the past tense. Like Playa Hermosa was already behind us.

"Even Rachel Mercer?" he asked.

"At least she's real."

"Grace . . ."

I glanced over at him, struck by the sadness in his voice. "What?"

"You're real, too. Don't let Cormac and Renee and the way we've been taught to live make you think otherwise. You did what you had to. We both did."

"I could have said no," I said softly. "I could have refused."

"When you were thirteen? Fourteen?" He shook his head. "This has been such a huge mind fuck, you don't even realize it yet. But someday you will. Someday you'll look back and see who the real villains were."

I turned to the window. I didn't want to have the same fight with Parker. Not now. I had to get my head in the game. Had to be ready to execute my part of the plan. If one of us screwed up, it could mean failure for the whole job. And failure meant jail. Or worse.

I took a deep breath as Parker turned onto the Fairchilds' street. The property came into view, and I spotted Logan on the other side of the iron gate.

Parker turned to me as we approached. "Everything will be okay, Grace. I'm going to get us out of this for good, I promise."

"I can't think about that now," I said as the car came to a stop. "Just be careful. Whatever happens, we'll figure it out together."

"Promise?"

I tried to smile. "I promise."

He nodded. "You have the Valium?"

I touched the vial in my pocket. "Yeah."

"See you on the flip side."

The gates were already swinging open when I stepped outside the car with my bag.

"Hello, you," Logan said, walking toward me.

I smiled. "Hello."

He looked over my shoulder and stepped around the car, extending a hand to Parker. "Hey, man. Wanna catch some waves Sunday morning?"

Parker took his hand. "Sure."

"Cool." Logan retreated. "See you at the Cove."

"Sounds good." Parker met my eyes. "See you later, Grace."

Logan waited for Parker to go before hitting a button on the keypad at the head of the driveway. The gates swung shut with a quiet hum.

I looked over at him. "You didn't have to come to the gate."

"It wasn't a problem," he said. "I couldn't wait to see you."

"Same." My stomach twisted with regret.

He took my hand. "You hungry?"

"Sure."

We walked in silence, the setting sun casting dappled shade through the trees alongside the driveway. The sky was a watercolor painting, streaked with orange and pink and violet as twilight took hold of the day.

Logan armed the alarm as soon as we entered the foyer and then shut the door behind us.

"How do you feel about pasta?" he asked, leading me

into the kitchen. Fresh garlands hung over the cabinets, and a minitree sat on the counter, lights winking against the encroaching darkness.

"Who doesn't like pasta?"

He pulled me into his arms. "I knew there was a reason I loved you," he said before giving me a quick kiss.

I swatted playfully at his chest, swallowing the lump of emotion that had risen in my throat at his use of the *L* word. Stupid. It was just a figure of speech.

We worked together in the kitchen, Logan preparing his mother's homemade tomato sauce while I chopped greens and vegetables for a salad. I'd never cooked with anyone other than my family, and I was surprised how comfortable and easy it was, the two of us moving around each other like we'd done it a thousand times before.

Logan went to the media room, and a couple of minutes later music streamed from the speakers hidden above the kitchen cupboards. We sang along, and every now and then Logan would take my hand and spin me around the kitchen.

When the food was done, we sat side by side at the island, talking about the holidays. Logan told me about his traditions, about Christmas Eves by the fireplace, sugar cookies left out for Santa and carrots for his reindeer, trees with the lights left on all night. When he asked me what I remembered, I took bits and pieces and tried to weave them together into something that resembled a normal childhood.

We loaded our dishes into the dishwasher and wiped off the counters. We were getting ready to go to the media room for a movie when Logan asked if I wanted some wine.

I fingered the vial of crushed Valium in my pocket. "Sure."

He pulled a bottle from the wine cooler and studied the label. "I have no idea if this is any good. Do you know anything about wine?"

"Not a thing," I laughed. "I'm sure it's fine."

He poured two glasses, handing me one of them, and we headed upstairs.

The media room was dark, lit only by the colored lights on the massive tree in the corner. Logan used the dimmer switch to turn the lights on low.

"Want a fire?" he asked. "It's getting cold."

"That sounds nice."

He crossed the room to the big stone fireplace. "Why don't you look for a movie while I get this going?" he suggested. "If you can't find anything, we can stream something."

I set my wineglass on the coffee table and opened the armoire's massive double doors. I tried to focus on the titles in the Fairchilds' DVD library, but my mind was all over the place. I was acutely aware of Logan a few feet behind me, of how easy it would be to turn around and walk into his arms. Give him everything. Then I remembered what I was about to do. How much it would hurt him and his family. And not just in the obvious ways. Not just because we would steal from him, but because it would shake his faith in himself. In the goodness he thought lived in everyone because it was so absolute in him.

I didn't want to cross that line. Not yet.

I blinked back tears as I turned around. Logan was bent over the fireplace, placing a large log on top of a couple of smaller ones. He reached for a match, struck it on the stone, and lit the newspaper. The fire crackled to life.

He stood. "Did you find something?"

I couldn't speak. Could only stand there, looking at him.

"Grace? Are you okay?"

I closed the distance between us slowly, stopping when I was right in front of him. "I don't want to watch a movie," I said softly.

His eyes were locked with mine. "You don't?"

I shook my head, lifting my hands to his shoulders, letting them run down his chest, feeling the muscle under my palms. I moved my fingers to the top button of his shirt and undid it.

"Grace . . ." His voice was hoarse.

He kept his hands at his sides, like he was afraid to touch me, as I undid the buttons of his shirt. I leaned forward, pressing my lips to the warm skin of his chest.

"I want to be with you, Logan."

I heard the intake of his breath. "We don't have to . . . I'm happy just to hold you."

I wrapped my arms around his neck and looked up at him. "I want to."

"Are you sure?" His eyes burned into mine.

It would make saying good-bye harder. It would mean leaving a bigger part of myself in Playa Hermosa. But on the eve of my betrayal, I wanted to give him something that was real. Something that might make him doubt all the things he would hear about me in the weeks ahead. Something that might make him believe in me despite what I would do.

I didn't answer. Instead I took the blanket from the couch and laid it on the floor with some of the throw pillows. Then I took his hands and pulled him down next to me.

He held my face in his hands as his mouth found mine. And then his hands were in my hair, lifting my T-shirt over my head, burning into my skin like a brand. There was nothing but him: his lips on mine, his hands exploring my body in the flickering firelight. I was lost, and I shut out everything, made him the center of my universe, if only for a couple of hours.

Afterward, I lay in the crook of his arm, the lights from the Christmas tree playing across his face.

He kissed the top of my head. "I love you, Grace. I think I've loved you since you first looked into my eyes in the hallway, the day you dropped your schedule. Remember?"

I nodded. "I love you, too."

It was true. And it was all I had to give.

Fifty-Three

It was after eleven when I got up for water. I'd been careful not to drink too much of the wine, but I was feeling drowsy and a little sluggish, too comfortable in Logan's arms by the fireplace. I couldn't put off the job forever. I needed to get on with it.

I padded to the kitchen on bare feet and poured two glasses of water. Then I pulled the vial from the pocket of my jeans. I uncapped it, holding it over one of the glasses. This was it. Once I drugged Logan, there would be no going back.

But there was already no going back. Parker was at Allied, baiting the guard. My mom and dad were parked somewhere nearby, waiting for the signal that Logan was out. I couldn't leave them hanging. And even if there had been time to rehash everything, to tell them I'd changed my mind, then what?

One way or another, we were on a collision course with the Fairchild job. It was too late for me to develop a conscience. Or too late for me to do anything about it, anyway.

I tipped the vial into one of the glasses and pulled a spoon from one of the drawers, stirring until the powder dissolved. Then I picked up the glasses, careful to keep Logan's in my right hand.

I climbed the stairs with my heart in my throat.

Compartmentalize, I ordered myself. *Stop thinking about Logan and what this will do to him. To his family. Think about this moment. About the job.*

It was a tactic Cormac had taught Parker and me when we'd first started grifting. He told us it went all the way back to Buddhist teachings. They called it mindfulness, but it was the same thing: Focus only on what's in front of you. Block out everything else.

I entered the media room and handed Logan the water, taking a drink from my own glass as I sat down next to him on the floor. I had a fleeting hope that he wouldn't drink it, or at least not enough of it to put him out. I shouldn't have worried. He downed the whole thing in one long swallow and then set down the glass.

He reached out, pulling me back onto the floor with him. I lay against his chest, listening to the soft drumming of his heart, trying to memorize the rhythm of it, the feel of his bare skin under my cheek. I stayed there too long after his breathing had settled into the regular cadence of sleep, not wanting to set into motion the string of events that would solidify my betrayal.

Finally, I eased out of his arms and sat up. I leaned down and kissed his cheek, trying to imprint his sleeping face on my mind. Then I got up, grabbed my bag, and hurried downstairs.

When I got to the foyer I texted my dad. *All clear.*

His reply came a few seconds later. *Stand by.*

I sat on the bench near the Fairchilds' front door, pushing away the thought of Logan, upstairs in a drug-induced sleep. I wanted to go to him, pull the blankets over us both, and pretend the rest of the world didn't exist. Pretend I didn't exist.

The house was dark and eerily quiet. The soft ticking of an old-fashioned clock sounded from somewhere down the hall, the occasional gust of wind ringing the chimes Leslie had scattered throughout the property.

I checked my phone. It had been ten minutes since my dad's last message. I texted him again. *Everything okay?*

My phone lit up a second later. *No word. Stand by.*

I tapped my toes against the tile floor, trying not to read too much into the delay. I don't know if it was instinct or paranoia, but I was suddenly sure something was wrong, and a burst of energy forced me to my feet as adrenaline flooded my body. I paced the floor, forcing myself to take steady, even breaths.

I was getting ready to text my dad again when a muted buzzing sounded from my hand. I looked down, surprised to see that Parker was calling.

"What's going on?" I asked as soon as I picked up.

"Listen carefully, Grace." Everything seemed to slow down when I heard Parker's labored breathing, the sound of distant sirens in the background. "The guard didn't come out like he was supposed to. Someone called the cops instead, and they're on my tail. I'm—"

"Where are you?" I demanded. "I'll send Mom and Dad to pick you up."

"You have to listen!" he shouted, panting. I could picture him running, trying to put some distance between him and the police. "I'm going to ditch this phone in the water and hope for the best. I'll be back in touch with you later if I can."

"Parker . . ." I paced the floor, barely able to breathe. "We'll come get you. We'll come right now!"

"No, you won't." His voice was strangely calm, like he had known this would happen all along. I could hear the roar of the ocean on the other end of the phone. He was trying to lose the police at the cliffs. It was what I would have done. "Everything is in place. You have to move. Make sure Cormac and Renee save my share. And Grace?"

"Yeah?" I could barely get the word out.

"It's you and me. No matter what."

The call dropped, and I looked down at the screen, not wanting to believe it. I fought the urge to throw my phone, to scream, to run. Then I called Cormac.

"We're still waiting, Grace."

"Parker's on the run," I said. "The police came instead

of the guard. He's going to ditch the phone and try to lose them."

There was a moment of silence on the other end of the phone. "I'll call you back in one minute."

I dropped onto the bench in the Fairchilds' foyer. "Let him be okay," I whispered to the silent house. "Please let him be okay."

The phone buzzed in my hand. "We're heading to Allied," my dad said, his voice even. "We'll be back in half an hour. Sit tight."

"But I—" I didn't have time to finish. The phone was dead.

Fifty-Four

I spent the next hour and a half pacing the house, listening carefully for any sound, worried that Logan would wake up earlier than planned, that whatever had happened at Allied had alerted the guards to a potential problem at the Fairchild house.

By the time my phone buzzed, I was a nervous wreck. The text was from my dad.

Open gates. Proceed as planned.

I wanted to ask him about Parker, about what had happened at Allied. But this wasn't the time. They were outside, exposed as they waited for me to open the gate.

I went to the keypad and pressed the Gate Entry button. Then I walked to the big window in the living room, watching for the truck. A few seconds later, headlights bounced through the trees along the driveway. I hit the button to close the gate and disarmed the alarm before picking up my bag.

I headed into the kitchen, stopping at the terrace doors. The lawn was dark and quiet, no sign of the drama playing out elsewhere on the peninsula. Was it still okay to cross the lawn in full view of the cameras? Had my dad put them on a loop in Parker's absence? There was no way to know for sure, but he had said to proceed as planned. I reached into my bag and pulled out the mask he'd given me that morning.

Opening the terrace door, I stepped out into the cold night and hurried across the lawn. I couldn't see the carriage house, but a visual of the property was imprinted on my mind, and I made my way down the footpath and over to the driveway.

The truck was just a shadow in the darkness, the headlights off. The doors opened as I moved toward it. My dad emerged first, duffel bag in hand, and my mom stepped down from the passenger side a moment later. They wore masks identical to mine, and I felt a thrill of fear, like we were all unwitting participants in some kind of horror movie.

We didn't speak. Voices carried in unpredictable ways outside, bouncing off buildings, drifting on breezes. I was dying to know what had happened at Allied, if they'd heard anything about Parker, but I followed them silently to the carriage house and helped them ease open the doors as quietly as possible.

Cormac waited until we were inside to take off his mask and turn on one of the flashlights. Working with anything brighter would be too dangerous. Light, like sound, had a way of bouncing where you didn't want it to.

He dropped the duffel bag on the floor and unzipped it, rifling through its contents.

I shook my head. "What are we doing?" My voice rose in panic. "We have to find Parker!"

My mom grabbed ahold of my arm, her grip a little too tight. Her eyes were bright, her blond hair pulled back into a sleek ponytail. "Parker knows what he's doing. He's probably holed up in some cave at the cliffs, waiting for it all to blow over. We continue as planned and get Parker later. It's how he would want it."

I heard Parker's voice on the phone: *Everything is in place. You have to move. Make sure Cormac and Renee save my share.*

My mom was right. We had to finish the job.

"What can I do?" I asked.

"Pull back the mat," my dad said, standing with the bolt cutters in one hand.

My mom held the flashlight as I slid the gray mat off the bunker door. The light bounced around the room as she bent to help, and I caught sight of something on my dad's shirt. I squinted through the darkness, a large wine-colored stain coming into focus on his chest.

"What is . . ." I swallowed hard, my gaze riveted to his shirt. "Is that blood?"

His gaze turned cold. "Don't worry about it, Gracie. Just keep moving."

I took an involuntary step backward. "What did you do?"

"We did what had to be done," my mom said softly.

"Your safety depends on it. Parker's safety depends on it. We were in too deep to call it off. You'd already given Logan the Valium. The buyers are waiting. We won't have another chance, and without the gold, we can't make a run for it. We'd be stuck here, sitting ducks while the police put together everything that was in process. And that's doubly true if they pick up Parker. At least this way, we'll have the resources to help him."

I was flailing around in my mind, on overload as I weighed the merit of her argument. Something bad had happened at Allied, but my brain was shutting down, focusing on the fact that my dad had the bolt cutters out, wondering how long it would take us to load the gold so we could find Parker.

"We took care of the monitors at Allied," Cormac said, grunting a little as he snapped the first lock with the bolt cutter. "The cameras are looped. Parker knows how to handle himself. Everything's fine."

Everything wasn't fine. Even I knew that, despite the layer of cotton in my head, the void that was opening up between my panic and the reality of the situation. I was on autopilot by the time my dad snipped the last lock, and I bent down, heaving open one of the double doors with my mom's help while my dad grabbed the other one.

The doors weren't even open all the way when a wave of cold, damp air hit my face. It smelled like concrete and metal and, somewhere underneath it all, wet earth.

We folded the doors back against the carriage house

floor. My mom shone the flashlight into the hole in the ground, illuminating a staircase and rows of metal shelving far below us.

"Moment of truth." Cormac pulled a headlamp out of the bag and turned on the light. Then he looked at my mom and me. "You coming?"

I looked around. "Someone needs to cover."

"Come take a look first," he said. "You were a big part of this. You deserve to be there when we find the gold."

I hesitated.

"Go ahead, Grace," my mom said. "I'll keep watch. Your dad's right; this one's yours."

I started down the stairs, her words ringing in my ears.

This one's yours.

I didn't want it. Didn't want to acknowledge how big a part I'd played in this moment. But they were right. It wouldn't have been possible without all the snooping I'd done at Logan's, without my access to the Fairchild estate.

It was my fault. All of it.

The stairs were metal. They rang under our footsteps as we descended into the darkness below, Cormac's headlamp the only source of light. It was a lot farther down than I'd expected. I wondered how long it had taken Warren to complete the bunker. Had he hired someone to build it? Or was doing it himself part of his obsession? His paranoia?

Finally, my dad stepped onto the concrete floor. I looked up, trying to gauge how far down we were by the distant shine of my mom's flashlight at the bunker's entrance above us.

My dad whistled softly. "Jesus . . ."

I turned around. "What is it?"

"This is crazy." I walked over to where he stood. He lifted a thick length of metal tubing hanging from one of the cement walls. "Looks like Warren's planning some kind of ventilation system."

I looked around, shocked by the size of the place. It was huge. At least one hundred feet by one hundred feet. Way bigger than I'd imagined. My gaze came to rest on the rows of metal shelving. One entire wall was stacked with five-gallon bottles of water. Another was lined with packaged food, canned vegetables and beans, cases of energy bars, dried fruit, rice, cornmeal, flour, sugar, powdered milk. I could make out partitions at the far end of the room and, beyond them, a set of bunk beds.

"I can't believe this," I said. I had a sudden flash of Warren Fairchild, manning the grill with his Kiss the Cook apron, smiling and greeting his guests. And all the while, he was scared enough of some unknown future to have a massive bunker under his property.

Cormac was moving around on one side of the room. "Help me look, Grace."

I took the other wall, shifting and lifting, looking under the tarps that covered medicine and first-aid supplies, a shortwave radio, a rack of fishing poles. I was beginning to give up, beginning to think we were wrong, when I came to a large metal cabinet. A heavy padlock identical to the ones on the bunker doors was threaded through its two handles.

"There's something here," I called out. "I think it might be a gun cabinet."

Cormac appeared over my shoulder. "Let me see."

I stepped aside, and he studied it for a few seconds. "Go get the bolt cutters."

I took the stairs two at a time. My mom was still there, eyes on the carriage house doors. "Anything?" she asked.

"Not yet," I said, grabbing the bolt cutters off the duffel bag. "But we found a locked cabinet. Be right back."

I hurried down the stairs and handed my dad the bolt cutters. After positioning them just right, he snipped through the padlock in one try. It fell to the floor with a noisy clunk.

He tipped his head at the cabinet. "Go ahead, Grace."

It was suddenly hard to swallow. I'd told myself I didn't want the gold to be there. That not finding it was the only way to get out of Playa Hermosa without hurting Logan and his family. But now, with Parker on the run, maybe already in custody, I knew it was a lie. I needed the gold to be there. Otherwise it would all have been for nothing, and we'd have no way to help Parker. To make our escape.

I pulled on the handles. The doors swung open.

And there it was.

Fifty-Five

It didn't take up nearly as much room as I'd expected. In fact, it fit neatly inside the metal cabinet, the racks that had been meant for guns removed to make room for the bars of gold stacked in its interior.

I don't know why I thought it would be shiny. It wasn't. They were just dull, golden bars, stacked like bricks.

"Bingo," my dad said. "Well done, Grace."

"What now?" It was all I could manage with the emotions warring inside my heart and head.

"Go upstairs and relieve your mother. Send her down to help load."

I walked back to the staircase and made my way back into the carriage house.

"Well?" my mom said, peering over the ledge as I came closer to the top.

"Found it."

She exhaled her relief. "Thank God. Is it all there?"

"I have no idea," I said. "There's a cabinet full of it. I'm supposed to relieve you and send you down to load."

She nodded, reaching behind her. A second later she withdrew something from the waistband of her jeans. It took me a second to register that it was a small black pistol.

I looked at it in disbelief. "What are you doing with a gun?"

"It's a last resort," she said, holding it out toward me. "In case of an emergency."

I recoiled. No one ever got hurt in our cons. Most of the time we stole jewelry and semivaluable artwork from houses when our marks were out of town. Once, we'd gotten the pass codes to an investment account and transferred money offshore, moving it twice more before Cormac took a trip to withdraw the cash. After that it was deposited into our personal, untraceable offshore accounts. And that was that.

We didn't use guns. Then again, we'd never stood guard over twenty million dollars' worth of gold. But still.

"In case of an emergency? What kind of emergency would make us use a gun?"

"I don't know, Grace. But this job is bigger than any of the others. There's more at stake. Just take it." She thrust it into my hands.

I was still in shock, still making note of the cold weight of it, when she headed down the stairs into the bunker. It took me a minute to move, to resign myself to the fact that

I'd have to hold the gun until she came back. I held it away from my body, careful to keep my finger off the trigger, as I moved to the carriage house door.

It was dark outside, but the almost-full moon still threw a little light around, and I stood in the shadows offered by the eaves, scanning the driveway for movement. There was nothing, and I turned my attention to the house, barely visible through the trees. I thought of Logan, asleep in the media room where I'd left him. I hoped he wouldn't be sick from the Valium. That he'd feel okay in the morning in the moments before he realized what I'd done.

I looked down at the gun in my hands, wondering when everything had gone so wrong. When we had become the kind of people who carried guns and stole from someone like Warren Fairchild. Had all our marks been as human as Warren? Had they all had fears and weaknesses hidden beneath a veneer of money and power? And what did it say about me that I was only now asking that question?

A thump from inside the carriage house pulled me away from my thoughts, and I turned around just as my dad's head came into view at the top of the stairs.

"Give it a push, for fuck's sake," he growled, tugging on the ends of what looked like one of the tarps from the bunker.

The load seemed to lighten, and a moment later he stepped onto the carriage house floor and yanked on the tarp. The rest of it spilled out with a clatter. My mom appeared a second later, breathing heavily, her hair askew.

"Is that it?" I asked.

"Not all of it," he said. "It's going to take a while to get it all up, but this is the fastest method we could devise with what we have."

I looked at the tarp, its contents bulging from the gathered middle tied with rope. They'd loaded gold onto the tarp and tied it off, using the ends as a handle like a Santa's sack of toys. Clearly my dad had been the one to pull while my mom had pushed from the bottom.

"How much did you get in there?" I asked.

"Not enough," my mom said, still panting. "Only seven. They're heavier than they look."

I was trying to think of a way I could help, if only to get us out of there faster, to get to Parker faster, when sirens wailed in the distance. We froze, looking at one another with wide eyes as we listened.

They weren't close. Not at first. But a few seconds later I couldn't deny it. They were getting closer. Louder.

"What do we do?" I hissed.

"Shhh," my dad said, holding up a finger. "Wait."

We stood perfectly still, like that would somehow stop the cops from finding us, when the truth is, if they were on their way to the Fairchild estate, we were done. My heart was pounding, a roar in my ears, as I listened.

The sirens got louder, then louder still. Just when I was sure the police were going to come barreling down the driveway, lights blazing, guns drawn, they seemed to get a little farther away.

"Are they—"

"Quiet!" my dad ordered.

I swallowed hard, tuning back into the sound. But I was right: they were getting farther away now, fading into the distance. I only had a second to be relieved before I realized why they were there to begin with.

"Parker . . . ," I said softly. "They're still after Parker."

Cormac's eyes turned flinty. "It doesn't matter, Grace. Not right now. We proceed as planned and go back for Parker later."

I swallowed my dread and turned my attention back to the gold, still bundled in the tarp on the floor. If loading the gold was the only way to Parker, I wanted it done as soon as possible. "What can we do to move it up faster?"

He shook his head. "Nothing. They're heavy. We'll have to do the best we can with what we have."

My mom threw a bunch of canvas bags my way. "Why don't you unload them into the bags and put them in the truck while we bring them up?"

I nodded. Whatever it took.

My dad untied the rope on the tarp and hurriedly unloaded the bars. Then he and my mom disappeared into the bunker to get the next load.

I set the gun aside and went over to the gold, loading all seven bars in one bag. I couldn't lift it. My mom was right; they were heavier than they looked. I took two of the bars out and tried again. Still heavy, but at least now I could half drag, half carry it to the truck.

I took a quick look around outside to make sure we were in the clear, then returned to the carriage house. I'd just put the last two bars into a new bag when I heard the thud of footsteps on the stairs in the bunker. They were coming up with the next load.

It took me two hours to realize we wouldn't make it by sunrise. We had averaged six trips in that hour, with seven bars in each trip. That was only forty-two gold bars. With over seven hundred to load, it would take us fifteen more hours to get it all up the stairs.

And that was time we just didn't have.

After a quick conference and a few different ideas, we decided we'd each have to carry our own load. My mom and I wouldn't be able to carry as much as my dad, but we'd still average more bars per trip, which would translate into less time.

"Whatever's left at sunrise, we leave behind," I said, when we'd finally agreed on the strategy.

My mom shook her head. "We can't do that. The buyers are expecting seven hundred bars."

"They'll get zero bars if we get caught," I snapped.

She looked surprised, but my dad nodded. I thought I saw admiration in his eyes. "She's right, Renee. Let's get what we can and get out of here."

I followed them down the stairs. We were leaving ourselves unguarded up top, but it couldn't be helped. I grabbed a tarp and made my way to the metal cabinet, loading what I could carry. Then I started back up the stairs behind my dad.

Time seemed both to stand still and speed up. I lost count of the trips we made up and down the stairs, afraid if I kept track I'd just sit down and cry. It was the last place I wanted to be, the last thing I wanted to be doing. Parker was alone and in trouble, but this was my only way back to him. I kept moving.

There were fourteen bars left in the cabinet when I noticed the blue-gray light seeping into the carriage house. The sun was coming up.

"Two more trips," my dad said. "We can do it."

We made the last two trips and hurried to the truck, my mom organizing the bags in the back while my dad and I hurried down to the bunker. We closed the cabinet and replaced the broken padlock, leaving everything as close as possible to the way it was when we found it. If anyone really came searching, they'd see that the lock had been cut, but we might buy some time if everything looked the same from a distance.

We closed the big double doors at the top of the stairs and replaced the padlocks there, too. Then we dragged the mat over the top of the bunker and put our masks back on, just in case the camera outside the carriage house was back in operation.

I was heading for the truck when I noticed the gun, still on the floor where I'd left it. I picked it up and slipped it in my pocket. It gave me the creeps, but leaving it on the floor of the carriage house would be like handing evidence to the people who would eventually investigate our crime.

My mom, back in her mask, was lowering the rear door of the truck when I got outside. My dad got into the driver's seat and we slid in next to him. I took the passenger side door so I could get out, open the gate, and reset the Fairchilds' alarm on our way off the property.

Cormac started the truck and headed back down the driveway. The sky was turning a paler shade of indigo, the sea becoming visible again as the sun climbed out of sight in the east. I checked my phone. Six thirty in the morning.

Something thudded under the truck, and my mom braced herself against the dash. My dad put it in park and climbed down, circling the truck to the passenger side.

"Fuck!" he shouted, too loud.

"What is it?" my mom asked.

His sigh was muffled through his mask. "We have a flat."

Fifty-Six

I raced to the house to open the gates and rearm the alarm while my mom and dad changed the flat. We were already running late, pushing the boundaries of the darkness that had been our ally while loading the gold. With no idea what had happened to Parker or how much heat it had brought down on the peninsula, we needed to find him and get out of Playa Hermosa as quickly as possible.

I entered through the kitchen door and hurried to the keypad in the foyer. For one brief moment I hesitated, my finger hovering over the Gate Entry button. Then I pushed the button, rearmed the alarm, and walked out the door.

When I got to the truck, my dad was rolling out the spare while my mom paced nearby. The truck was jacked up, the front passenger side sporting an empty wheel well.

"Can I do anything?" I asked, my breath warm and moist inside my mask.

"Just keep watch," my dad said, positioning the tire.

"Everything okay in the house?" my mom asked.

Okay wasn't the word I'd use for the fact that Logan was drugged upstairs, oblivious to the fact that we'd just stolen twenty million dollars from his family. But what was the point in saying it?

"Everything's quiet. Gate's open. Alarm is back on."

She looked up at one of the cameras near the driveway. "I hope to God the cameras are still on a loop."

"If they weren't, we'd be done already," I said. It was weird talking to her through our masks. Without her face and smile, she was like a stranger.

Her nod was tight.

The breeze was frigid, a fine fog blowing in off the water. I stuffed my hands in my pockets and glanced up at the sky. It was more orange and pink than blue, and I wondered how long the Valium I'd given Logan would hold out. Getting caught with the gold wouldn't be the worst thing. It would be having to face Logan. Having to look in his eyes when he realized what I'd done would be the thing to break me.

I paced the driveway as my dad tightened the lug nuts on the tire. I felt exposed without the carriage house to shield us on one side, the dense strip of woods on the other. Now there was just the open expanse of lawn leading to the house, the cliffs beyond opening up to the sea, the rising sun casting more light by the second.

I thought of Parker, on the run from the police or maybe even already in custody, being questioned about his motive for baiting the guard at Allied. How long would it be before they realized the monitoring equipment had been tampered with? How long after that before they figured out it was only the Fairchilds' video feed? And why had the police been called to handle a simple vandal? Why tonight, after weeks of Parker baiting the guard?

I couldn't even think about the other thing. About the blood on my dad's shirt and the guard who must have been hurt—or worse—when Cormac had gone to Allied. There wasn't room in my already overcrowded head to consider the possibilities.

I tasted copper and realized I'd bitten my lip hard enough to make it bleed. I had to stop. I was running in circles. It wasn't doing us any good. Most important, it wasn't doing Parker any good. I needed to focus. Concentrate on getting off the Fairchild property. On finding Parker.

"How much longer?" I asked.

"Almost . . . there . . . ," Cormac said, steam puffing out around his mouth. He gave the wrench a couple more turns, tightening the lug nuts on the new tire. "Let's go."

He had the truck in gear before I'd even shut the passenger side door.

We continued down the driveway, past the house. Everything looked the same. Logan's BMW was still in front of the garage, as if nothing had changed since I'd arrived the night before. I took one last look as we entered the winding, tree-lined drive.

Cormac eased off the accelerator as he came to the open gates. Hitting the road at an excessive speed would only draw attention. If we were careful, anyone who happened to be watching would think we were one of what were probably many trucks that made deliveries to the Fairchild house.

He pulled out into the street and headed for the stop sign at the corner. We were halfway there when something wandered in front of the truck, a splash of blue-green against the asphalt, barely visible in the gray light of early morning.

"Stop!" I yelled.

Cormac accelerated. "We don't have time to stop."

A dull thud sounded under the truck as we hit the animal at full speed. Cormac kept going until we came to the stop sign. I pulled off my mask and opened my door.

"Grace!" he yelled after me. "Get back in the car, Grace!"

I ran back to the peacock lying in the middle of the road. It didn't look dead, but I knew it was. It was perfectly still, its magnificent blue and green feathers fanned out against the asphalt, one glassy brown eye staring unblinkingly into mine.

A wave of grief hit me like a battering ram, and I stumbled backward, stifling a sob.

"Grace!" Cormac was half out of the truck, his mask still on. "We have to go. Now."

"I'm sorry," I said softly, taking a step backward toward the truck. "I'm sorry."

Fifty-Seven

"Where are you going? We have to go back for Parker!"

My dad was making his way down the peninsula, careful to keep the truck under the speed limit on the winding roads.

"We can't do that," he said. "Not right now. We have no idea where he is, and he ditched his cell phone. We need to get off the peninsula. Then we'll figure out what to do about Parker. We'll keep our cell phones for a few more hours. See if he makes contact from a landline."

Panic welled up inside me until I was afraid I wouldn't be able to contain it. Afraid it would escape in a scream that might never stop.

"We can't just leave him!"

My mom pulled off her mask and turned to me. "Keep it together, Grace. What do you expect us to do? Wander around Playa Hermosa with a truck full of gold looking for Parker? The police may already have him in custody. If they do, we need to get somewhere safe so we can find a way to help him. If they don't, we have to wait until we know where to find him."

I clutched at the armrest, scrambling for a response that would allow us to go back for Parker now. But she was right. I don't know what I expected. Back at the Fairchild estate, all I'd been able to think about was loading the gold so we could get to Parker. I hadn't had time to think through the how of it.

I stared out the window, watching the ocean turn silver as the sunlight threw diamonds across its surface. Parker was farther away then ever, as unreachable to me as Logan and Selena and the sham of a life I'd built in Playa Hermosa.

"See anything?" my dad asked softly as we approached the turnoff for the road that would take us off the peninsula.

"Nothing," my mom said.

She was right. There were no cops. No checkpoints.

"They must not have him." I heard the note of hope in my own voice. "He's probably hiding out somewhere, waiting until it's safe to contact us."

My mom grabbed my hand and squeezed. "Maybe."

I had no idea where we were going as we wound our way through a series of backstreets to the freeway. Now it was all about following the plan for our escape, carefully laid out in advance by my mom and dad. It was a system that had served us well, and I sat back, trying to make my breathing even and calm, telling myself that we'd get Parker back, that everything would be okay.

We took the freeway into downtown Los Angeles and spent ten minutes navigating a clutch of one-way streets until my dad finally pulled next to the curb in front of a parking garage. He turned to my mom.

"You all set?"

She nodded. "I'll see you at the safe house. You and Grace get out of town if I'm not there by four. I'll contact you through the online portal if I get sidelined."

He touched his lips to hers in a quick kiss. "Take every precaution."

"Will do." She slid over to the driver's seat as my dad climbed out of the truck.

"Let's go, Gracie," he said.

I reached over and gave my mom a hug. "Be careful, Mom."

She hugged me tight, held on a little longer than usual. Then she pulled back, smoothing my hair, looking at me with tenderness. "I love you, Grace. You know that, don't you?"

I nodded. "I love you, too."

She smiled. "Go with your dad. I'll see you soon."

Cormac got out of the truck and zipped up his jacket to hide the blood on his shirt. I followed him into the parking garage as my mom pulled away from the curb.

We walked up to the window and he reached into his pocket, withdrawing a ticket. He slid it through a hole in the glass to the mustached man behind on the other side.

"One moment, sir."

He removed a set of keys from one of the hooks on the wall inside his little cubicle and stepped outside, disappearing into the shadows of the garage.

My dad put an arm around me, squeezed my shoulders. "You okay?"

I wasn't, but I knew he wasn't really asking. I nodded.

A couple of minutes later the attendant pulled up in a nondescript Ford Taurus. My dad tipped him and climbed into the driver's seat while I got in the other side.

It was Saturday morning, and traffic was light as we headed back to the freeway. A few minutes later we were heading north, leaving the skyscrapers and grit of the city behind, putting more miles between us and Parker. Between me and Logan.

"Where to now?" I asked, trying to distract myself.

Cormac didn't take his eyes off the road. "The Valley," he said, referring to the San Fernando Valley. "We have another switch to make."

I wasn't surprised. We usually only switched cars once when we needed to get out clean, but this wasn't just any job. With luck, the Fairchilds wouldn't know what had happened for a while. Logan would wake up wondering why he'd passed out. He'd try to call me, assuming I got a ride home from Parker. It would be hours before anyone knew something was wrong, before they realized we were gone or that the gold was missing.

If Parker hadn't been caught. If.

But once the loop was discovered on the Fairchild monitors at Allied, the police would lower the boom. They would ask Warren if he'd experienced any kind of intrusion or theft. Warren would check his stash, just to be sure. Everything would happen quickly after that. We needed to be as hard to find as possible—and as far away.

I lost track of time as we sped north. By the time we exited the freeway, I was starting to feel drowsy, lulled to sleep by the rhythm of the car, the heat blasting through the vents, the loss of adrenaline now that we were out of immediate danger. I sat up straighter, trying to pay attention. It was too soon to be tired. We weren't out of the woods yet, and Parker was still in danger.

We dropped the car at a seedy outdoor lot, and I followed my dad through the rows of parked cars to a gray Honda Civic. It was older, but clean, and we headed out of the Valley, back to the freeway.

We merged into traffic and headed south on the freeway. I looked at Cormac with surprise when we made the turnoff for Long Beach.

"Isn't that a little close to home?" I asked. Long Beach was only forty-five minutes from Playa Hermosa. We'd just spend two hours driving north to pick up the dummy car only to double back to within an hour of where we started.

"It is," he admitted. "But we've taken every precaution, and Long Beach has both an airport and a seaport."

I nodded, understanding. If we couldn't get out by air, we

had other options by sea, especially if there were cargo ships and cruise lines.

Almost three hours after we left Playa Hermosa we pulled into a derelict parking lot, a sign reading SEA VI_W MOTEL blinking forlornly over a faded one-story structure. Weeds pushed their way through cracks in the asphalt, and a swimming pool filled with a few feet of dirty sludge stood beyond a rusting chain-link fence.

Cormac stopped the car in front of an Office sign. "Be right back."

I listened to the soft tick of the engine, wondering how long it would be before we could sleep. More than the rest, I needed the darkness, the blankness that would come with it. My head was too full of worry—about Parker and my mom and Logan. I was approaching shutdown.

The driver's side door opened. "The exchange must have been easy," my dad said, starting up the car. "Your mom's already picked up her key."

I exhaled a breath I didn't know I'd been holding.

We parked in front of room 213. There were only two other cars in the parking lot, a beat-up old Impala and a Town Car that looked too nice for the Sea Vi_w Motel.

Cormac used the key to unlock the door, and we stepped inside. It smelled like every other motel room I'd ever been in—like moldy carpet and pine-scented cleaning product with an undercurrent of cigarette smoke. An AC unit rasped noisily in the window.

A light was on in the bathroom. My dad headed for it.

"Renee? That was quick," he said, moving through the room.

I looked around, taking in the full-size beds covered in tacky polyester bedspreads, the generic artwork on the walls, the old-model TV. My eye caught something on the table near the window, and I walked over to it and set down my bag. For a minute all I could do was stare, my mind drawing a blank, unwilling to comprehend what I was seeing.

A single gold bar sat on the table. Next to it was a key attached to a plastic tag marked 213. Against the bar of gold was a handwritten note.

I'm sorry.

Fifty-Eight

"This can't be right. There must be some kind of explanation."

I was sitting on the bed, still in shock. Cormac's face was white as he paced the room, muttering to himself and running his hands through his hair. He'd greeted the sight of the gold bar as I had—with shock that had quickly turned to denial. Now he doubled back toward the table, sweeping its contents onto the floor with a roar of anger.

I jumped as the gold bar fell onto the carpet with a thud. My bag landed between the table and the bed. "Dad . . ."

He stood up, straightening his jacket like that would somehow put things right. When he looked at me, his eyes were clear for the first time since we'd found my mom's note.

"It's exactly what it looks like, Grace," he said. "She's gone."

"She wouldn't . . . she wouldn't do that. She wouldn't leave us. Wouldn't leave me."

His laugh was bitter. "And yet that's precisely what she's done, isn't it?"

I stood, wanting to reason with him, to stem the tide of words eating away at the life I'd known—the life I'd sacrificed for—like waves eroding sand on a beach.

"She'll be back," I said. "I know she will. We just have to wait."

"Stop being so fucking naive!" Cormac shouted, his face red. "This isn't something you do at the last minute. She planned this all along." He sighed, trying to compose himself. "She's gone, Grace. And we can't sit around here waiting. We have to go."

I shook my head. "We can't leave. Parker—"

"Parker's fucking gone, too." He threw his phone onto the bed. "I got the local news alert on my phone twenty minutes ago."

I picked up his phone and clicked on the alert, still open on his screen.

LOCAL BOY ARRESTED IN POSSIBLE
PLAYA HERMOSA ROBBERY

An eighteen-year-old boy was arrested Friday night after vandalizing a local security company in the affluent community of Playa Hermosa. A spokesperson from Allied Security alleges the boy has engaged in a months-long campaign of vandalism against the company. A source inside the local police department told WBHC News that the FBI had been dispatched to investigate the possibility that the vandalism was a cover for a robbery that occurred last night on the peninsula. Stay tuned for updates as they become available.

I put the phone down and stared at the carpet. So they knew. Logan and his family knew they'd been robbed, and they knew we'd been responsible for it.

"We have to go." Cormac picked up my bag, gathering the other stuff in the room, including the gold bar.

"We can't leave Parker. Not now! He needs us!"

"What do you propose we do, Grace? Walk into the Playa Hermosa police department, past the FBI, and tell them it was all a misunderstanding?"

I scrambled to come up with an answer. "We can hire a lawyer, post bail . . ."

"He hasn't even been arraigned yet," Cormac said. "And it's not as easy as you make it sound. They know something happened at the Fairchild estate. Which means they probably know we were part of it. We can't do anything until we get out of here. Find some cover. Then we can hire an attorney to help Parker."

He was still moving around the room, wiping doorknobs and light switches, erasing his prints from anything he might have touched to give us a little more time if someone were to trace our steps.

My mind clamored for some kind of answer, something that would refute what he'd said, that would give us a way to help Parker without leaving him behind. But I had nothing. I was hollowed out, empty of all my usual reason.

I was only delaying the inevitable, avoiding the moment when I'd have to admit that he was right: We were no help to Parker if we were picked up, too. To help him, we had to escape and regroup.

"Where will we go?" I asked. Obviously our plan to flee the country was out. If the FBI was involved, we couldn't risk it. Our window of escape had closed faster than we'd expected because of Parker's arrest.

Cormac walked to the door, put his hand on the knob. "North, probably. I'm not sure. We just need to get in the car, keep moving."

"And we'll come back for Parker?" I asked.

"We'll help him however we can once we're safe."

"Promise?" The question sounded childish even to me. What good were promises when you couldn't count on the only woman who'd ever been a mother to you?

He sighed. "I promise. Now can we go? Before the police show up and we're thrown in jail?"

Resignation settled over me like a shroud as I stood and walked to the door. "Thank you," I said, taking my bag from Cormac's outstretched hand.

He nodded, holding open the door. A shaft of sunlight eclipsed him, and for a moment it was like he'd disappeared, like he'd never been there at all. Then, all at once, he was back, his face grim.

We hurried to the car, and Cormac backed up, heading out into traffic. I looked out the window, tears stinging my eyes. I couldn't even begin to process my mother's abandonment, but the loss of Parker thrummed through me like an instrument out of tune. I heard his voice in that final, frantic phone call.

It's you and me. No matter what.

Parker wouldn't leave me. I knew he wouldn't. But here I was, speeding away from Los Angeles like the coward I was. Would he forgive me when I came back for him? Would he understand? And what would I say to justify my defection? What could I say?

I saw him as he had looked that day in the early-morning fog, the day we'd stared out over the water, trying to find a way back to each other even as our loyalties in Playa Hermosa had ripped us apart. He'd been so sure we were someone else. Sure that we weren't liars and thieves and cowards. That we'd only become those things because of the way we were raised.

And even though I'd tried to deny it, there had been a tiny part of me that hoped he was right. That might have believed.

But I had been wrong, and so had Parker.

As Cormac got back on the freeway, I finally accepted the truth: it was too late for me. I was done looking for a better part of myself that didn't exist. Parker and I were family, partners. I would go back for him, but there would be no more delusions about who and what I was.

I leaned my forehead against the window, my breath fogging up the glass as the city passed by on the other side. It wasn't complicated. I was a thief. I was a con artist. I was a coward.

Believing anything else was just another lie.

Acknowledgments

Thanks always go first to my agent, Steven Malk, without whom I would not still be writing full-time. I don't know what I did to deserve such a tireless and insightful advocate, but I've lost track of the number of times your guidance and support have kept me going—in more ways than one. I hope you like me, because you're stuck with me for life!

Thank you to everyone else at Writers House, all of whom go above and beyond for their authors on a daily basis. Everything is a little easier knowing you have my back. You are the best of the best.

Heartfelt thanks go to Jennifer Klonsky, who believed in me when I was beginning to wonder if anyone still did. It's tough to articulate what that belief has meant—both personally and for my little family—but there aren't enough words in the world to thank you properly. That you are an extraordinarily talented editor and a joy to work with has been an added bonus. It is not an exaggeration to say that you have restored my faith in publishing.

Thank you to Catherine Wallace, Cara Petrus, Lillian Sun, Bethany Reis, and everyone at HarperTeen who has given my work a home and has worked so hard on this project. You are all incredibly talented and you make everything so easy for me. That is no small task.

Thanks to dear friends and colleagues M. J. Rose, Tonya Hurley, and Jennifer Draeger for being there.

Thank you to my mother, Claudia Baker, who always believes in me, and to my father, Mike St. James, for gifting me with words through our strange and mysterious writing DNA.

Lastly, I can never let an opportunity pass to thank Kenneth, Rebekah, Andrew, and Caroline. We're in this together. I wouldn't want to do any of it without you.

Grace's story continues in

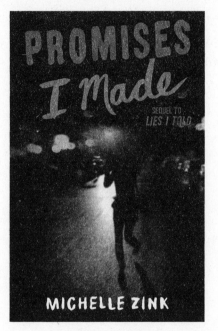

Coming in Fall 2015

When I think about what happened in Playa Hermosa, it's not the gold that gets me. Gold is like money. Something tangible that can be obtained, lost, regained.

But trust, faith, love . . . Well, those things are a lot more tricky. Where do you find trust once it's lost? How do you make someone believe in you when you've given them every reason not to? And how can someone love you when you've proved beyond a shadow of a doubt that doing so is dangerous to them and to everything and everyone they love?

Those are the kinds of things I thought about after Cormac and I arrived in Seattle. I was too numb to do much thinking before then, too focused on the growing distance between Parker and me, too busy imagining him in jail for a crime we'd all committed.

And then there was my mother. Renee. All the times

she'd called me Gracie. All the times she'd pushed the hair out of my eyes, called me her daughter. It had been a lie. I'd known Cormac and Renee weren't my biological parents. That Parker and I had been adopted by them to run cons with wealthy suburbanites as our victims. But somehow I'd believed that Renee loved me. That she was my mother in every sense of the word. I'd believed it even when Parker had called me out on my näivety, even when it set me against him, the one person who'd proved over and over again that he'd do anything for me.

Knowing that Renee had taken the gold, leaving us to clean up the mess, left me hollowed out, like all the little bits of love and security and hope I'd been accumulating had been sucked out of me all at once. I thought it would get better with time, that I'd adjust to the reality of the situation like I'd always done before. But this time was different. The emptiness was palpable, a black hole that seemed to gather more power with each passing day. Sometimes I thought I would disappear inside it completely.

We'd all sacrificed in the name of the Playa Hermosa con. Cormac was on the run, forced to be cautious even with the underground network of contacts we usually relied on. There was twenty million dollars in gold at stake; there had to be at least a few fellow grifters who would use information about our whereabouts as a get-out-of-jail-free card. In the meantime, that was where Parker was: in jail. I hadn't seen or talked to him since the night of the Fairchild con. I didn't even dare send him a letter, and the loss of him sat like a lead weight on my chest.

My sacrifices might seem insignificant in comparison, but they didn't feel that way. I'd come to love Selena, the only real friend I'd ever had. And I loved Logan Fairchild and his parents, too. Stealing from them—especially with the knowledge of Warren Fairchild's mental illness—had blown out the tiny light I'd kept burning in the darkest corners of my heart. The light that told me I was better than a life on the grift, that I was only doing it because I had to, because after a string of lousy foster homes and no contact with my real parents, Cormac, Renee, and Parker were the only family I had.

Parker had tried to show me the better parts of myself, to keep those parts alive, and I'd abandoned him in Los Angeles when I'd chosen to run with Cormac. Now I knew the truth about who I was, and I didn't waste any more time trying to fight it. I spent the time in Seattle settling into the role of Cormac's daughter as he worked to con a rich divorcée, hoping to get us flush enough to go after Renee and our share of the Playa Hermosa take. In the meantime, I waited for Cormac to follow through on his promise to get help for Parker, to go back for him or find him a lawyer, to do *something* to get him out of jail. I waited for five months, until I couldn't wait any longer. Until the thought of Parker locked up started to unravel me.

Then I used everything Cormac and Renee had taught me and I did it myself.